MW01596720

If Pain Could

Make Music

To Adriana,
You've always been there
which means a lot to
me.

ISBN: 9798389294462
Printed in the United States

Cover painting by Ron Morin
Back cover painting of Ron Morin by David Lowrey

If Pain Could Make Music

Ron Morin

For Lisa

"What matters in life is not whom or what one loves, it is the fact of loving."

—Marcel Proust

I

"Man is born free, and he is everywhere in chains."

—Jean-Jacques Rousseau

1

A new little American,
As darling as can be,
Has just become a member
Of our Happy Family

On this birth announcement was a picture of a newborn swaddled in the American flag, and under that a handwritten message.

> *Dear Tocard,*
>
> *Baby boy 7 pounds 12 oz born 29 Nov 1944, 802 AM mother fine Baby two big dimples. His name is Lemeilleur. What a joy.*
>
> *Your brother, Alcide*

Lemeilleur was not conceived on his parents' honeymoon, which was three days in *Montréal, Québec*, where on the first day his mother, Isabel, to ask for forgiveness for killing her sister, climbed the 99 wooden steps of *Oratoire St. Joseph* on her knees, which were so sore afterwards, Lemeilleur's father, Alcide, could not get between them for days.

Lemeilleur's conception can be traced back to two possible venues: Either in a cockroach-infested apartment in Drayton

Hall, Harvard Square, or on a spongy couch in Everett, MA at his maternal Uncle Blaise's after a riotous party. Alcide says Lemeilleur's conception occurred in Harvard Square where they said the rosary first. Isabel says it was on a couch where she was afraid of waking her older brother. Either way, the maculate union of an ambitious sperm and a dejected egg made, again according to Lemeilleur, a masterpiece, an obscure and unfinished masterpiece, alas.

That baby announcement was as close as an angel would get to chant a hymn of joy for Lemeilleur's birth. Ultimately, that would never matter to Lemeilleur: the air in hell is too thick for hymns. Still, Lemeilleur was born hopeful, and wanted to believe he was—at least for a little while—a pleasure to his father, Alcide, a man who was born in Canada, near Sorel.

Alcide was one of the Ducrottes that hailed from Niort, France, from where in the 1600s a certain Poitevin had come to set up a fur-trading company. Hundreds had come over. They became *coureurs de bois* (French-Canadian trappers) who caught the animals that became the pelts for the leather products that the Versailles crowd wore . . . and that is why Alcide's grandfather used to say, in front of the big stone fireplace in a cabin deep in the Canadian forest where he held forth after a gathering to whomever, "Marie Antoinette, when she lost her head, was wearing a Niort belt." Which, of course, made every one laugh. His ancestors, Lemeilleur had written in one of his notes, smelled of beaver dung and powdered cloves.

After the 1937 worker riots in Sorel, Alcide traveled to Nouvelle Bouville with nothing but a scuffed suitcase of clothes, a high school diploma, and a copy of *David Copperfield*. He was twenty and eager to start a new life in a country known for something he knew nothing about, political freedom. His brother, Tocard, a bricklayer, already here, had gotten a family-sponsored green card for Alcide. When Alcide hopped off the train in Nouvelle Bouville, he was near tears— in America he would get rich, and, no slacker, he immediately got a job at an A&P, in the produce department, where, over leeks, many months later, he met Isabel, his future wife.

2

After Alcide and Isabel had married, and Lemeilleur was born, Alcide abruptly made Isabel move back with her parents so he could enlist in the Navy, save some money, and eventually get an education in embalming with the GI Bill. He had vision. Alcide had seen his own father lose the family farm in Lanoraie through bankruptcy during the Great Depression— nothing drove Alcide more than the fear of poverty, and embalming, he'd heard, was recession-proof.

Isabel was so miserable those four years, she threw up almost every morning, which made her look like that prostrate woman in Fuseli's *Nightmare* with the dark demon sitting on her chest and a white horse hovering hauntingly above her. It would be years before Lemeilleur realized his mother's life was over before he was born.

When Isabel was five or six, her mother, Lemeilleur's grandmother, was changing the diaper of Isabel's little sister and cooking in the kitchen—which was about the size of a chicken coop—and, after changing the baby's diaper, the grandmother put the baby on the edge of the kitchen table and told Isabel to hold the baby while *Mémère* rushed to the stove to do something with the sputtering deep-fried beignets, *pets de nonne* (nun's farts). Isabel could barely reach up to the top of the table and she struggled to hold the wiggly child. Desperately Isabel squeezed her little fingers around the thighs of the baby, but the child fell, smashed its head, and died. Isabel passed out and couldn't remember what had happened. From then on, her parents called Isabel *la meutrière*. (The murderess)

Isabel and Lemeilleur were stuck there for four plus years before Alcide, who had saved $1,500, finally returned from Recife, Brazil.

3

One night, probably a year after Alcide had returned, and they had their own apartment in Nouvelle Bouville, Isabel, hearing the sound of clinks, rushed into Lemeilleur's bedroom, which was the living room in their attic apartment, and Lemeilleur, upon hearing her distress, went into a panic—flapping his French-Canadian firebird wings wildly—trying to get away from the menacing clinks, until—that is—he finally woke up.

Lemeilleur, already no stranger to nightmares, was always a bird trying to fly away from the ubiquitous inauspicious, but that was the least unusual part of that night. Awake now, he peeked out from under his blanket and through sleepy, five-year-old eyes saw, in the bleak light of the bare bulb hanging from the dropped ceiling, his mother crying. She was bent over—like a Millet peasant—picking something up from the floor next to the couch, his bed—PENNIES.

As Lemeilleur listened to his mother and father yell at each other, he realized those pennies—over a dollar's worth—had—APPARENTLY—been taken out of HIS piggy bank, which lay on his bureau OPEN, and those saved pennies had been placed around HIS blanket BEFORE falling, one by one, clink after clink, to the floor.

Isabel, hysterical now, warned Alcide that she was going to call the police. His father, who for some reason was in the kitchen, was adamantly against that. And as the disagreement blistered on, Lemeilleur went back to what should have been the dream of Rousseauian innocence—a dream he'd chase, with monomaniacal earnestness, for the rest of his life because those penny clinks would go on falling, clink after clink, for the next forty years before he figured out what mark—HOW DEEP A DENT—they'd made in the tender membrane of his soul—the imprint of a future fossil—trauma, the fuel of rage.

4

"Stay in the yard, if you know what's good for you," his mother grumbled as Lemeilleur descended the stairs of their attic apartment. Inured to his mother's moodiness, he shrugged off the emptiness of another boring day in Nouvelle Bouville penal colony.

It had been a year since his family moved into the attic apartment on Houghton Street, and he'd never met the landlord's daughter. But once out in the backyard today, Lemeilleur saw her. She was chasing a butterfly. His mother had told Lemeilleur the girl downstairs was a year younger—Lemeilleur was six years old—"and for God's sake, be nice to her: She's the landlord's daughter."

As he stood on the top step watching her frolic merrily, a fleeting curiosity to see what was between her legs flitted through his otherwise dull, despondent mind. That's stupid, he thought to himself. Then, moving out of the shadow of their sullen brown house, Lemeilleur stood in the sun-dusted, dry air of a hot morning wondering how he could play with her.

The world burst open when, suddenly, he was entranced by the girl's black hair—so iridescent in the sunlight—with luminous blues and greens swirling sumptuously. O to touch it—to feel the electric shimmers of that sheen with his fingers. He was brimming now with fear but daring thundered in his soul.

He had, however, no plan, and the girl had no idea what he wanted. She was Syrian and shy, and she didn't go to his school. His English was very spotty, and he didn't know if she spoke any English at all.

With gestures alone he managed to communicate, and she, taught to be dutiful, followed him, her eyes pinned to the ground before her, like a nun going to church, as they solemnly crossed the yard. Lemeilleur was jubilant, but where were they going? The scorching day forced him to improvise a shelter for his hastily devised plan.

"Come. Sit here."

Eagerly he pushed the pale lilac bush aside and she, mute as a swan, glided in under the heady pungency into the cool shade. His desire to touch her hair was as strong and shameless as the cloying lilac. He tried to get her to lift her face to his. She refused. He looked down at her bent head, but in the shade, his eyes blinking, her hair had lost its morpho blue luster. His mad, clumsy, shameless, agonizing desire evaporated.

"Hey, I talk English. Do you?"

But it was too late. Sadness deflated him. Lilacs only grow in a dead land.

"Hey, talk. Say something," Lemeilleur urged her.

She was silent, and he was on the verge of dismissing her when he saw that her dress had ridden up. Ah, he remembered his curiosity. Her underwear was decorated with red ducks. Red ducks. His courage plucked up; he had just begun to pull the red-duck panties down, when a man with raging black eyebrows reached in and grabbed him.

5

The landlord was enraged and evicted them. His father bought a house, a two-family house, several blocks away from the Syrians, with the money he had saved in the Navy—in a more uniformly French-Canadian neighborhood.

Lemeilleur knew his father never wanted him to see the landlord's daughter again. Life, however, is always constructing a skein of relations around us which we are ignorant of, and when Lemeilleur read, years later, *"Human life is but a series of footnotes to a vast obscure unfinished masterpiece." (Lolita)*, he knew that was what he wanted to believe: Life is a masterpiece, the plot of which he had just entered. This would mark the beginning of a lifelong development of a personality trait of Lemeilleur's—his chameleonic absorption into the life of whatever book he was reading.

6

One Sunday after church, a few weeks after they had moved into their attic apartment, Alcide, now a manager of an A&P, took Lemeilleur to his store. Why were they doing this? The place was spooky with no people around.

"I shook Jack Kennedy's hand here last week," his father said to him, as they walked up the bread aisle.

Jack Kennedy? Lemeilleur asked himself. Sounded familiar.

They walked behind the meat counter into a back room where a lot of boxes and canned food were stored. Then, as they went through another door, his father grabbed a sleepy, calico cat—probably with the same hand that shook Jack Kennedy's—and they all went into yet another room where there was a slop sink, buckets, mops, and a little door in one of the walls opened onto an alley behind the building. His father opened the door, threw the cat in, and slammed the door shut. The stiff stink of rat's urine stung Lemeilleur's nose.

Alcide looked at his son and said, "You are a big worry ta your fathar. Can you imagine how embarrassed I was? A Syrian! A Syrian knocked on **my** door because **my** son had dishonored HIS family by taking a Syrian girl under a lilac bush! Fathars have ta teach deir kids. Dat was a bad thing you done ta the landlord's daughtar. You never worry about what people think. Dignity—dat's what's important; dat's all what people want—dignity. Why can't you understand dat? 95% of your success is getting along with othar people. Nothing's more important. You will not get through dis life if you're not like othars. Look at Jack Kennedy. That's dignity."

Dignity! Lemeilleur wanted Meaning. Wasn't **that** what everyone wanted?

"When I was a little kid, we had a blind lamb, and she could never stay with da flock. Munching grass they'd just drift away. When da lamb figured out dere was no one around, the lamb started baaing. Baa, baa, baa. The others never baaed back. You know why? There's no social program in nature."

A loud screeching and thumping came from behind the door. It raised the hair on the back of Lemeilleur's head. But soon it was over. His father found a flashlight and opened the door.

Beyond the door, a few feet away, lying on whitish-chalky ground, red raw flesh bursts from a calico mat of fur, while deeper in the alley a dozen or more rats slinked and snarled.

"Dere's only one rule of nature, Lemeilleur: Survival. Dis is what happens ta people who don't fit in."

7

Lemeilleur flunked out of kindergarten when he went to public school because he didn't speak good English—though he could jump, dance, and didn't piss his pants. They also beat him in the schoolyard—"Fuckin' canuck."

Public school, to Alcide, was more American than Catholic school, especially a French-Canadian Catholic school. But, after three torn shirts and his mother's crying they couldn't afford any more shirts—very reluctantly, because Alcide wanted Lemeilleur to learn American and get Dignity— American Dignity—his father put him in a French-Canadian Catholic school.

When Lemeilleur entered St. Joseph's, he had to start kindergarten over, which made him a year or two older than anyone in his class, which had the delusional effect of making him feel smarter than most—and he often ended up punching above his I.Q.

At St. Joe's, classes were half a day in French-Canadian and half a day in French-Canadian English. It would be years before Lemeilleur learned American English, which, in his father's eyes, was a monumental disaster. But his father—ever ambitious—was working three jobs: A&P during the day, a liquor store on weekends, and selling *St. Jean Baptiste* life insurance nights to other French-Canadians—so he didn't have much time to hassle Lemeilleur about his fate.

8

Lemeilleur was not sure what was happening, but in fifth grade, while his class walked in line, two-by-two, down the main corridor of his school on their way to an eye test, he saw Loretta—a classmate who was nothing but a dull, snotty girl with piercing eyes—in a way he'd never seen anyone before. She was so . . . so . . . so. Unsure of what he was experiencing, he used a word from his father's *Reader's Digest* vocabulary section, words which his father insisted he memorize for his future Americanization, to describe this foreign feeling he was having: "rapture"!

The pain of this vision was so intense, he started to cry. He couldn't take in what he was feeling! Loretta had become as beautiful as a flame!

Utterly overwhelmed, he changed the word, "rapture" to "purity" because he really didn't understand the word, rapture. Purity he had some notion—the nuns were always talking about purity.

Sister Philomene, seeing his tears, rushed over to talk to him.

"Tu n'as pas à t'inquiéter, Lemeilleur, les tests oculaires ne font pas de mal."

(You don't have to worry, Lemeilleur, eye tests don't hurt.)

But Lemeilleur's heart pounded on. He was afraid he'd explode.

"Tu m'entends, Lemeilleur?" (Do you hear me?)

He waved her a quick okay and marched away. He thought he was floating. Had he made contact with beauty? How could he know? He was a fledgling. Just as his feathers hadn't caught on to flying, the meaning of his experience hadn't caught up with his growing soul.

That afternoon, when he got home, immortality beating wildly in his hellbent desire to contact beauty, he wrote a love letter—his first—to his muse. "Dear Loretta, I need you. You are beauty! Lemeilleur."

The letter mailed, expectant Lemeilleur, beauty gestating in his imagination, waited. He'd done it: flown unexpectedly into beauty's power. Or, as he would read much later—in a more precise formulation: "You are but a proud lie composed of nothing/ In the eyes of the solitary dazzled by faith."

◑

Three days later his father called to Lemeilleur as he walked into the kitchen, "Can you explain ta me what goes through dat head of yours?"

"What are you talking about?"

His father was holding a piece of paper. Lemeilleur pretended not to notice and got some milk for his cereal.

"Why do ya insist on not fitting in?"

"I'm late for class."

"Goddamn it! I'm the fatha here."

Lemeilleur was quiet; he hated these explosive moments with his father.

"Why do you do it?"

"What? What did I do this time?"

"You sent dis love letter ta Loretta!" And his father waved the piece of paper in the air.

"Oh damn!"

"Don't swear!"

"I'm not!"

"Do ya believe in God, Lemeilleur?"

"God can go to hell!"

◑

The following day Alcide took Lemeilleur to talk to Father Pointeur at St. Joe's rectory, where the good father was sitting on the veranda sipping French wine—a beautiful label Lemeilleur noticed: *Pommard*—with their family doctor, Dr. Plomber. Plomber? Plomber? ah! Lemeilleur remembered! He was the doctor who, when Lemeilleur was two years old to prevent him from sucking his thumb, had wrapped that thumb in a huge bandage. Lemeilleur, according to his notes, had been a breast-starved suckling: His mother's nipples had been too short to feed him.

"My son doesn't respect God," his father said shamefully to the handsome Father Pointeur.

"Is that true?" the curly-haired prelate-to-be leaned forward to ask.

"I guess so," Lemeilleur answered.

"You only guess so—good; there's still hope for you," Father Pointeur said as he poured more *Pommard* into Dr. Plomber's glass.

It was said Father Pointeur was the smartest priest they ever had at St. Joe's. He had a ton of degrees, and he spoke English, French, Latin, and Italian.

"Hmm . . . what do you think when you look up at the stars at night?"

Lemeilleur knew he was supposed to say how beautiful it was that God made the universe, instead he said: "I see the dead—they are trying to warn me—that's what all the twinkling is about."

"What do you mean?"

"Things down here are hard."

"That's why we have religion."

"I'm sorry, Father, but religion only makes things harder."

"How would you set the world up?" Dr. Plomber, his eyes rolling, chimed in.

Lemeilleur actually had not only thought about that but had talked to Mice, his best friend, about it.

"No sin, make injustice illegal, and give every child a tutor. Oh, and give everyone at least one chance at love."

The priest sat back, picked up his wine, sucked in its bouquet with his perfect nose, and said to Lemeilleur's father, "Your son is a romantic."

"I forbid ya to talk ta Loretta," his father exploded.

Lemeilleur was astounded. His father had misunderstood—Lemeilleur was only looking for beauty.

"No, no," Father Pointer scolded Alcide. "Your son has ideals."

"Ideals?"

The doctor averted his eyes as he choked on his wine. There was a cruel blaze in Father Pointeur's eyes as he slowly sipped his wine and watched Alcide founder.

His father was speechless and blank-eyed. Lemeilleur felt sorry for him. Father Pointeur continued with a yawn, "Don't worry; he'll outgrow it."

The priest stood up, bowed to Lemeilleur's father, and extended his hand for Lemeilleur to shake, which Lemeilleur did.

"Go in peace, Lemeilleur. I'm sure you will find what you are looking for."

Father Pointeur didn't shake his father's hand, which hung in the air, inanely submissive.

As they began to walk out, Lemeilleur heard the doctor, who was looking out the window, whisper to Father Pointeur, who was smiling into his wine glass, "Can't even get their name grammatically right." To which Father Pointeur nodded with a smile and, pouring another glass, said as he toasted, "You mean De La Crotte?"

9

Within desolate Nouvelle Bouville there is a desolate place— Crow Hill—where kids went to be alone. It was about as ugly as nature gets, which helped them face whatever it was that tore them apart. After you climb the hill and the neighborhood behind falls away, you walk to the other side which is massively eroded—as large as a football field either way, left or right, there is a rain-rutted, steep drop of about sixty or seventy feet to a flatland of five or six acres of mostly bushes and briars.

Eleven-year old Lemeilleur stood there at the top, sipping T-bird. He flapped his arms—he missed Mice, his best friend. He wanted the rapture back. He wanted to transform. To fly like a butterfly. But discouraged, he dropped his arms to his side as he realized he had to admit he hated his life—some song that was going to be. He had no idea what love was.

It was August; he was drunk, and deep in despair. Mice, the person he most admired in this Meaningless world, was gone. A judge had put Mice in the Shirley Department of Youth Services detention center for six months—only for stealing some S&H green stamps from a gas station—like a month before S&H went out of business. Why? Mice had told Lemeilleur he'd stolen enough to buy a small plane—twelve books worth. "What the hell do you want a plane for?" "I was going to sell it to pay for college." Maybe a judge would put Lemeilleur in Shirley with Mice if Lemeilleur did something bad.

10

That week Lemeilleur decided he had to get a job. He had to stop feeling bad about his life. With his father now full-time in embalming school, their finances were almost non-existent. Some days they ate cereal three times a day. His mother was miserable. Lemeilleur decided to become an altar boy. After he learned all the prayers, instead of being sent to St. Joe's, his parish, to serve Mass, he was exiled to St. Anthony's Home for the Elderly. He didn't know what was behind that decision, but he was okay with it because he would get fifty cents a Mass, which was more than his parish was paying. Mass, however, was at six am, which meant getting up at five.

Serving Mass Monday through Friday was two fifty a

week, and with his paper route, he was good for fifteen or twenty dollars a month, depending on tips. That was good money.

St. Anthony's Home was about a half a mile from his house. Though he was still far from owning a Jaguar, it was a beginning—he was a step closer to getting away from his father.

Even though the nuns at school took the students over to church to confess once a month, Lemeilleur couldn't tell the priest that he loved touching himself. No, he just couldn't confess his mortal sins, even to Father Pointeur, who got drunk regularly with their neighbor, Miss Morue. Lemeilleur was fairly sure Father Pointer was doing it with Miss Morue, but Lemeilleur couldn't know for sure; Miss Morue's windows were too high to see in.

Lemeilleur started to wonder again: Was Father Pointeur in love with Miss Morue, who was twenty-five, blonde, always wore a red head-scarf, worked at the bank at the bottom of the hill, and lived alone?

In retrospect, Lemeilleur should have confessed his mortal sins to Father Pointer because Lemeilleur's honeycomb obsession was giving him black depressions—and probably the good Father would have given Lemeilleur a light penance. Lemeilleur imagined his confession: "Bless me father, for I have sinned: I've seen Miss Morue's gold-tangerine honeycomb twenty-five times in my dreams."

11

When Mice got out of juvie, Lemeilleur wanted to dance! Mice calls Lemeilleur Speedoo. The Cadillacs were Mice's favorite group. Mice loves Doo Wop. Mice's real name is Ronan Petitesouris. And Mice and Lemeilleur were going to be part of the "rise of the meritocracy." That's why they read books together. Some poor people really understand the need to be smart because they know most people believe poor people are poor because they're not smart enough to be rich.

Mice and Lemeilleur were now reading *The Catcher in the Rye*, and they would underline sections they liked, and then read the underlinings back to each other.

Mice and Lemeilleur were looking for something—something bigger than themselves—something that would save them—a big concept that would lift them out of their loveless penal colony where they choked on injustice.

Lemeilleur loved hearing that Holden Caulfield was just as troubled as he was. Lemeilleur couldn't imagine somebody learning something from him, but if they could, it would be, as Holden said, POETRY.

The Catcher in the Rye was the origin of Mice's obsession with justice. It was like a mantra—his mystical formula of invocation or incantation: He wanted to save people.

"Hey, do you know what Salinger's I.Q. was?"

"Yeah, the Army assessed him: 110. That's what I want to be, Speedoo—a Catcher in the Rye."

That's when Lemeilleur fell in love with Holden Caulfield. He called it "love," but to be honest "love" was just a word he used—he had no idea what it meant.

Lemeilleur wanted to tell Mice that Lemeilleur had hopes of turning his life into a song, but all he managed to say was "why do birds sing, Mice?"

"They either want to get laid or they're warning someone to stay away. Why?"

"Is that what you think of love?"

"It's too hard to think about love."

12

One night that spring, Lemeilleur woke up and thought he was bleeding. He felt something hot and sticky on his belly. Jumping out of bed but trying to stay quiet—the last thing he wanted was Ma to see her sheets messed up with blood—it was bad enough he peed the bed once or twice a week—no blood—thank god. He got back into bed.

As he lay there trying to figure out what the hell had happened, his pecker started getting hard, which wasn't super unusual. So, he petted it like he usually did only this time it started to feel real good—a lot better than usual—a lot, lot better, and before he knew it his body was in spasm, and he was seeing stars and all this hot stuff was all over his hand.

A few months later, he realized he had to find a place to do this in a more organized way. So, looking around he found the perfect place—under his back porch, which was enclosed. There was actually a door—on hinges—that led into this dark, damp, probably four-foot by four-foot space. It was right under the landing of their back stairs.

⑪

About a week later his mother's best friend, Femme, as her bald-headed husband called her, came across the street to see Ma. It was summer now, and Femme, a big, voluptuous gel of flesh clambered up the stairs, and Lemeilleur—finally getting his erotic wish—luckily was able, as a breeze ballooned her dress, to peek up her clambering legs just before she got to the landing—SHE WASN'T WEARING UNDERWEAR. He saw IT—his first vagina—he was ecstatic—rapture—his favorite *Reader's Digest* word—was taking on Meaning.

As the soft days of summer passed, Lemeilleur became a priapic wonder. He was drunk on Circe's wine. He loved his fits of concupiscence—his seizures of sensuality.

An hour later, he saw his mother's—*The Origin of the World*—that weirded him out because he saw IT as a scar—a wound—where he had pushed himself through so many years ago. Now he knew he was going to hell—still he couldn't stop himself—he'd go to hell on the wings of a vagina. This was the music of his sphere—his song. Sweet, sweet vagina. His new avatar. A deity in another form—the impossible quest for the lost original. How can they call this sin? No matter. If this sin stained his soul, even indelibly—he was now more colorful: His soul was flocked in shabby chic vagina.

13

After Mice got back home from juvie, he found a letter from his brother Billy, whom Mice hadn't seen since Billy ran away from home. The letter was addressed to Mice's mother who swore she'd never open it.

Ever curious, Mice had learned from his brother's return address on the unopened letter that Billy lived in Boston, on Beacon Hill, which meant to Mice that his brother was fabulously wealthy, because Mice had read *The Late George Apley*.

Mice, only thirteen at the time, was convinced his brother Billy would pay for Mice to go to college; and Mice was hopping hot to get that promise in person.

The next day, skipping school, they took off for Beacon Hill. Lemeilleur had never met Billy or been to Boston, so he was excited, too. They walked to Route 9, which took an hour and a half, and started hitching.

Three hours later they were in Brookline, which, they were told, was near Boston. Nobody would pick them up, so after an hour or so they started to walk. Eventually they found a trolley car. They rode to Park Sq. By then it was 3 pm. Starved, they ate at Buzzy's Roast Beef and then headed out to find 85 Revere St. On the way, Lemeilleur asked questions about Billy.

"Why do you think Billy will pay for you? You never talk about him."

"What's to say? He used to pee the bed every night."

"You think he owes you?"

"We slept in the same bed, then. Now he's rich. Of course he'll pay for me. He pissed all over me."

Lemeilleur clammed up. Mice's icy tone meant he was in a foul mood.

They got to Billy's building close to 4 pm and rang the buzzer. A voice wanted to know who they were. Mice told him, and the voice said, "He's not here."

"Can we wait for him?"

"That is not a good idea. William won't be home till late."

"How late?"

"After midnight. Shouldn't you be in bed by then?"

"Why's that?"

"You're young boys."

"I mean, why so late?"

"He's a bartender at the Playland, young man."

"Where's the Playland?"

"In the Combat Zone."

"Where's the Combat Zone?"

"I really think you should go home. I'll tell William you called."

"We're going to wait here."

Two minutes later a short, chubby body attached to the voice opened the door. He had on a rich, red, brocaded bathrobe, leather slippers, and a hairnet over his head.

"Gentlemen, this will simply not do. Our landlord does not take kindly to loiterers, and, I'm afraid, he has a gross misperception of who we are. We can't add to that."

He started to wave his stubby fingers with large rings to shoo them away.

Mice yelled, "I want to go to college. Will you ask Billy to pay for me?"

"Shoo—go away."

⬭

They managed to catch several rides in the heavy flow of traffic out of town but were catching only short ones. By the time they got to Framingham, it was after 10 pm, and they were freezing. The temperature had dropped into the high forties. An hour later they were still freezing their asses off in Framingham—another definition of hell.

"Fuck this; I'm going to find a furniture store."

"Furniture store," Lemeilleur repeated.

"That's right—one with a bed so I can get some sleep."

The next thing Lemeilleur knew he was on his back on a *Serta Perfect Sleeper* with Mice next to him, only Mice couldn't sleep.

"My brother's a fucking faggot."

"You think that's why he ran away from home?"

"I used to think it was because my father beat him. Who the fuck cares? My brother's not going to pay for me to go to college."

His body curled fetally, and Mice whispered, "Will you hold me, Lem?"

That really threw Lemeilleur. Mice had taken Suzie right in the kitchen of Lemeilleur's house once—right in front of Lemeilleur, while his parents fought in the parlor.

"It's no big deal, Lemeilleur. It's just . . . I'm hurting. I'll never get to fucking college."

Lemeilleur thought about holding Mice. It meant Mice liked him, and that made Lemeilleur want to sing, but he was careful not to let Mice see **that** as he grabbed Mice around the shoulders.

"My brother hates me. We were too friendly as kids. We're not gonna make it out, Lem."

"Out of what?"

"Our class."

Mice was crying. Lemeilleur couldn't believe it—Mice cry.

Mice, between tears, whispered, "Jail was hard, Lem. Those kids were tough."

14

Lemeilleur was very affected by *Blackboard Jungle—Yeah, I've been beaten up, but I'm not beaten. I'm not beaten, and I'm not quittin'.* No, he hadn't given in to the hopelessness of his situation. He still had fight in him, but he misused it.

Everyone knew Tony was a bully, but Lemeilleur wanted

Tony to like him, but they had to go through a ridiculous play-acting thing—like two dogs, sniffing around, posturing, and trying to determine who had the bigger balls. Lemeilleur really didn't understand what was happening but played along nonetheless.

And one day poor Donald walked right in between them.

They were standing in line waiting their turn to get their *T&G* newspapers for delivery that day. Mac, the office manager, counted and handed out the papers, which they paid for at the end of the week. Tony was just ahead of Lemeilleur in line and about to get his papers, when Donald walks up—probably to pay his late bill.

Donald was a nice kid—a little slow, he had a hard time remembering the alphabet, and his face was covered with eczema—it looked like gray sandpaper—but nobody bothered with him.

Shamelessly Lemeilleur used Donald to show Tony how tough he was. Lemeilleur grabbed Donald by his shirt, just under his neck, and dragged him out to the street, where Lemeilleur tossed him to the ground.

"What are you doing, Lemeilleur?"

"Just play dead. I won't hurt you," Lemeilleur whispered as he leaned into Donald.

But, to Lemeilleur's surprise, Donald jumped up and started to fight.

Donald was banging on Lemeilleur's chest like some kind of crazed kangaroo. By then all the paper boys, including Tony were out on the sidewalk shouting, "Fight, fight."

Lemeilleur and Donald swapped punches, until Lemeilleur saw an opening and got Donald down on his back. He sat on Donald's belly, but Donald was still flailing away, kangaroo-style.

Lemeilleur was supposed to be showing Tony how tough he was, but he was barely in control. He doubled his efforts by leaning forward and getting between Donald's flailing arms, which allowed Lemeilleur to grab Donald by his ears and bang his head against the pavement.

"Blood," someone screamed.

Lemeilleur looked down and behind Donald's head blood trickled. Mac pulled Lemeilleur off and sat Donald up. Mac ran his hand over the back of Donald's head and found a little stone imbedded in Donald's scalp, which came out in Mac's hand with red blood. Donald was dazed. Mac asked him if he wanted to go to the hospital. Donald seemed confused by that question.

"Come on, Donald, I got a business to run. Do you want me to call an ambulance?"

Donald ignored Mac's question. Overwhelmed by the wantonness of Lemeilleur's aggression, he looked at Lemeilleur—his eyes awash in a hurt WHY. The pit of Lemeilleur's stomach fell out as Lemeilleur considered how many times this must have happened to Donald before. Donald had never said boo to anyone—he was Mr. Timid. Lemeilleur lost his bravado and forgot about Tony.

"If you want, Donald, I'll go to the hospital with you?"

"Oh, Christ," said Tony, "he's jus' a niggah," and walked away.

"Naw, it's okay, Lemeilleur; I want to pay my bill, get my papers, and do my route. It's okay."

When Donald left the office with his papers, Tony followed him and dragged him into an alley and beat Donald up. This time Mac called an ambulance. Lemeilleur watched them take Donald away. He was sick to his stomach. The police never came. But Lemeilleur eventually fought Tony—it was a bloody draw—and they became friends for a while. Lemeilleur had gotten what he wanted. Later Lemeilleur found out Tony had no family. He lived with a foster family that to punish him made him eat off the floor out of a dog's bowl. After that, whenever Lemeilleur wanted to piss Tony off, he'd say, Hey, doggie. Life was becoming less and less Meaningful. Why should he wonder about love? Lemeilleur felt like a dog that howls just before the dog dies. If ever he got a song, he carped, it would sound like a gang of boys castrating a dog.

15

Lemeilleur heard that St. Anthony had a job opening in the kitchen for a dishwasher—a dollar an hour. He applied and got the job. He would be, said the rosy-faced nun who hired him, paid in cash. Hours were from 4 pm to 7 pm every weekday, and from 5 am to 10 am Saturday and Sunday, and 4 pm to 7 pm also on weekends. He could also take time off— without pay—with one week's notice. Boy was he happy. His life was working out—after all. He would have money and could see that on Fridays he'd fly out of St. Anthony's on the golden wings of the dollar's eagle to go out to eat—by himself—fish and chips. Independence! It was as if this job gave Lemeilleur a new reason to live. He would save his money for prep school.

He got fifty dollars for his paper route and quit the altar boy gig. He would not miss Father Wocki who said Mass at St. Anthony. He had had a leg shot off during World War II in Poland, and Pope Pius XII had sent him to St. Anthony's and given him a dispensation: Since he couldn't genuflect with a wooden leg, he was allowed to bow before the crucifix during Mass. The nuns told Lemeilleur he was a living saint, but Lemeilleur had never seen his aura.

Father Wocki was a pain, always criticizing little details about the way Lemeilleur had served Mass—hold the cruets higher; don't walk so fast—one day after Mass he said to Lemeilleur, "Stop mumbling your prayers, you sound like a Jew."

Lemeilleur had not a scintilla of an idea what that meant, but he was glad he was moving to the kitchen. Now he'd make almost twenty-five dollars a week. And no wooden-legged priest was watching him like a haggard buzzard cruising for roadkill. No, he was happy, happy, and like Doris Day, he was on a "Que Sera, Sera" high. He was going to go to prep school.

Sister Claire, who only spoke French-Canadian, was in

charge of the kitchen, and she explained to Lemeilleur how the work was organized. Lemeilleur worked with two other people, Randy, who was a junior in high school, and Georges, who was getting a master's degree in French literature from a college that was started by a group of Augustinians who were suppressed in France for attacking Dreyfus as a traitor.

Randy was assistant cook and Georges was head dishwasher. Lemeilleur helped prepare meals and dried dishes.

"Just listen to me," Randy said, "and you won't get into trouble. The sisters here trust me. I'm a good Catholic, like John F. Kennedy. Have you read *Profiles in Courage?*"

"Ah, no. Not yet, but I read a lot."

"I don't, but I liked *Profiles in Courage.* Watch out for Georges. He thinks Sacco and Vanzetti were innocent!"

Randy was a bushy-tailed aficionado of all things culinary. He was 5'4", weighed 148 pounds, had short, curly hair, bent-over shoulders, and pale skin with a tendency to acne and considered himself a moderate Republican.

After the meals were distributed, they collected all the serving dishes, which piled up in a back room with two large, deep metal sinks and a long metal table. Georges washed and Lemeilleur dried. Georges was 6'3", weighed 198 pounds, a butch haircut, and had arms like the legs of a baby grand piano. Lemeilleur was intimidated. The only thing Lemeilleur knew about Sacco and Vanzetti was what Mice had once said to him—they were anarchists, which in Mice's mind was a good thing. But Lemeilleur couldn't think of a way to bring Sacco and Vanzetti up to Georges for conversation, and he had never looked up the word "anarchist."

"So what's your life like?" Georges said as he scrubbed pans.

"Me? I'm an intelligent hoodlum."

Georges stopped scrubbing and for the first time looked at Lemeilleur, who—he couldn't believe it—blushed.

◑

Randy had a car, lived with his mother, and met daily with the nuns who supervised and planned meals. Bushy-tailed Randy made sure everything got done in the kitchen, while lugubrious Georges made sure all the messes got taken care of. So Randy didn't bother with Georges.

Randy trained Lemeilleur, so he got friendlier with Randy first.

"Hey, why don't you come over tonight," Randy asked Lemeilleur.

What came about in this new friendship was Lemeilleur couldn't overcome his aversion to Randy's piano playing. Randy had studied piano for five years, and all he ever did on his time off was practice piano, *The Moonlight Sonata*. After several visits to Randy's house, Lemeilleur, having heard the first forty seconds of the piece at least 14,000 times, was on the verge of suicide. Aaaaaahhhhh.

To Lemeilleur's immoderate imagination Randy's piano notes sounded like a slow drizzle of semi-solid droppings crepitating from a treacle-filled, semi-constipated jelly donut. How could Randy make Beethoven's *adagio sostenuto* (slow and sustained) sound like a plodding dirge for a dead toy poodle? And to add to Lemeilleur's suffering, Randy loved Liberace, who, Randy told Lemeilleur, was a conservative, who fervently believed in capitalism and had a piano-shaped swimming pool in his backyard. Lemeilleur's father loved Liberace!

Randy was planning to study at the Culinary Institute of America near Yale University, which was like way over Lemeilleur's head.

Between Randy and Georges, Lemeilleur felt he had entered a new universe.

Lemeilleur never got into *Profiles*, but when he researched anarchist, *"a person who rebels against any authority, established order, or ruling power,"* he vowed to read all the books Georges read, and Georges was very agreeable, which really pleased Lemeilleur. In fact, rather than giving books to Lemeilleur, Georges read to him. The first book Georges read was *The Golden Ass*. Georges thought it was very funny. Lemeilleur wasn't sure he got it, but he didn't care. It was the only Roman novel in Latin, Georges told him, to survive in its entirety! It was full of short stories that Georges explained to Lemeilleur, especially the parts where Lucius has sex. Lemeilleur had never read a book with sex in it. After being bought and sold, used and abused, Lucius offers a prayer to the Queen of Heaven who appears in a vision and explains to him how he can become human again.

"That was a good story," Lemeilleur told Georges.

Within a few months, Lemeilleur had decided that Randy was too boring, and he could not take another note of *The Moonlight Sonata*. *"La propriété, c'est le vol,"* (property is theft) as Georges had read to him, that would become Lemeilleur's kind of music. He now knew what anarchism meant.

⏼

Many more months went by, and Lemeilleur was saving money, learning about the food business, and Georges was reading more books to Lemeilleur. Georges loved *Howl*. He also took Lemeilleur to see Kurosawa's *Throne of Blood* at the Fine Arts movie theatre. Lemeilleur was convinced that he would go to college—after all he was a budding intellectual. The big themes of life were now in his environment. He decided to spend his savings to go to prep school.

When Lemeilleur told Mice that Georges was an anarchist, Mice, who had just read *Fathers and Sons,* intoned, *"We sit in the mud, my friend, and reach for the stars."*

16

Now there was an influx of new students to St. Joe's. In another part of Nouvelle Bouville a parish was closed—St. Mary's. The city was undergoing urban renewal and had taken the school by eminent domain. All their students were sent to St. Joseph's school.

Boris and his family had emigrated from France. They were Polish, and Lemeilleur liked Boris because, in Lemeilleur's mind, Boris, blond and blue-eyed, was European: his perfect French, his accent, his attitudes—well it was all style to Lemeilleur, an elegant style he wanted to emulate. He loved the way Boris held his cigarette, at the end of his fingers, like a soup spoon.

One night Boris's house caught on fire and the Red Cross put his family into different neighborhood homes. Boris ended up with two old lumpy ladies who looked like they had escaped from the potato bin in Mice's cellar—ex-nuns.

The ex-nuns lived with Dolores, whose parents couldn't take care of her, in a dilapidated cottage, wedged, like an orphan itself, between two dominant three deckers, in the Polish section of the city. Dolores was two years older than Boris. In the city's pecking order French-Canadian was higher than Polish, Syrians were lower.

Well, according to Boris, on the night of the fire, Dolores had crawled into his bed, and they had done it. Lemeilleur didn't really believe Boris—everybody lied about stuff like that, and Lemeilleur told Boris he didn't believe him. Boris, bruised, walked away. A day later Boris, aggressively, informed Lemeilleur that Dolores wanted to sleep with him. Lemeilleur smiled and said he'd consider it.

That night, by himself, Lemeilleur, looking out his window, studied the rain anxiously. He was trying to imagine how he would be intimate with a stranger like Dolores. What words would he use? Exhausting as many possibilities as he could, Lemeilleur was left with a blunt response. He must rise to the occasion—wasn't he, like his father, a resumé-conscious French-Canadian?

It was decided. Dolores would meet Lemeilleur at Dizzy's house since both his parents worked. They'd have to skip school. And to seal the deal, Dizzy, the Gonad, as he was nicknamed, who was also from St. Mary's and was physically bigger than either Boris or Lemeilleur, hung out of his third-story bedroom window screaming, "Eat his ear, Lem!" to celebrate Lemeilleur's acceptance of the challenge from Boris. Dizzy's model of courage was Canadian-American wrestler, Killer Kowalski, who ripped off part of Yukon Eric's ear way back in 1952.

The day arrived and Lemeilleur was still nervous—incredibly nervous. This was worse than getting an interview to go to Harvard. It was one thing to admire vaginas from a distance, like an art connoisseur, but quite another to get inside one, like a deep-sea pearl diver. Plus, just to throw him over the edge, his father, the week before, had decided to "tell him the facts of life" to scare him from having sex *hors de mariage* (out of wedlock). Because, according to his father, girls had crossbones in the vagina that could close up on you while you're in there, and you'd have to go to a hospital to be surgically liberated.

Now Lemeilleur knew his father was an asshole, but he didn't think he had the imagination to make up this kind of story—in short, Lemeilleur was rattled. It was bad enough that Lemeilleur had been living in mortal sin for years—risking hell if he should die suddenly—but the whole neighborhood would know if he had to be removed from a clamped up vag.

And, as Lemeilleur fretted, he realized who would Dizzy tell? Maybe Lemeilleur would lose his job at St. Anthony's. Jesus, maybe they'd throw him out of school. They threw kids out of school for only wearing their hair in a duck's ass. Was he about to ruin his chances of going to college? Fuck.

Was he saving money and reading all that literature stuff for nothing? He was about to risk everything on a girl he never met. Now he knew why Father Pointer said he was a romantic. Hey, maybe he'd fall in love. Fuck—college was no guarantee.

Lemeilleur met with Boris and Dizzy one more time before the big event.

"What's Dolores like?" Lemeilleur asked Boris.

"She's a good kid."

"Why does she live with her aunt?"

"Her father's in jail for killing her mother."

"Really?"

"He chased her out of the house with a big carving knife, and she ran into the street and was hit by a car. The driver saw her husband with the knife."

"Are you getting cold feet, Lem?" Dizzy snickered.

"I'm just trying to understand what's going on."

"He wants to understand what's going on," Dizzy shouted mockingly.

"What's wrong with that?" Lemeilleur shot back.

"You're gonna get laid! That's what's going on!"

Boris and Lemeilleur just stared at Dizzy.

"I can tell you're mad at me. I think you're afraid," Dizzy shot back.

Lemeilleur shouted, "I'm not afraid!"

"Mice was afraid," Dizzy countered. "Yeah, your friend, Mice. Don't give me that look. Mice was afraid to be with Dolores."

"That's not true," Boris interjected. "I was there. Mice said Dolores was pathetic and had rotten teeth. He wasn't interested in her."

Dizzy looked away—angry that Boris had contradicted him—and screamed, "Mice is queer!"

"That's ridiculous," Boris expostulated, and then turned to Lemeilleur. "Dolores's lesbian aunt is driving Dolores crazy—wants her to go to church every day."

"Are you going to do it, Lem?" Dizzy challenged Lemeilleur.

17

Dolores as it turned out was very shy, Lemeilleur noted when they met on the appointed day. Still Dolores jumped awkwardly into Lemeilleur's lap. Without a word they kissed. Lemeilleur liked her taste—something like chocolate chip cookies. They kissed more. Lemeilleur eventually got a bad case of blue balls. Still, he was nervous because Boris and Dizzy were hopping around them like horny baboons. It was Dolores's idea to go into Dizzy's bedroom.

"Go get 'em, Killer," Dizzy yelled, rubbing himself.

Boris looked smug when he waved to Dolores as she and Lemeilleur entered the bedroom where Dolores took off her underwear, pulled up her dress, lay down on the bed, and put a pillow over her face. Lemeilleur was working on his case of nerves, but when she pulled the pillow over her face, his self-confidence plunged. After a moment of reflection, he decided to take this pillow thing in stride. Hell, it gave him an opportunity to examine her black, now public, pubic floss which glistened purplishly with . . . with a . . . gloomy glory. Lust, he would learn later, was never as sure of itself as it was in *Lolita*.

Looking above her floss, he was surprised by her honey-brown belly with a soft covering of apricot lanugo, another word he'd learned from reading *Lolita*, which, by the way, does not tell you how to do it. Her knees were a little knobby, a fact, he thought, that was cute and unscary. And getting more serious, he spread her legs so he could continue with his exam. Ah, he could see her labial lips. He pulled back to study it. It all looked so docile—not some vicious bear trap. It certainly didn't look strong enough to hold him, and there were no bulging muscles on either side of her pale, streak-of-mauve door to heaven. He beheld the riddle of life, love, and lust. It was a kind of sacred moment wherein all defiant libidinousness evaporated. So solitary, so solemn, he felt as pure as fresh air.

Then he remembered that night in his kitchen how easily Mice had slipped into Suzie, but she had put herself on him. Lemeilleur wasn't getting any help here, and he wasn't falling in love. His thoughts were like candles, lighting the way through a dark and treacherous forest.

Dizzy banged on the door and giggled wickedly, "Hey, Killer, are you doing it like Roark and Dominique?"

Lemeilleur could hear Dolores laughing under the pillow. Had she seen Dizzy's copy of *The Fountainhead* with all the sex parts underlined?

"Fuck off," Lemeilleur roared back. He had to be careful; he didn't want his thoughts to be snuffed out by distractions—keeping the darkness at bay was uppermost.

He took a deep breath and got a little closer to Dolores and moved his hand up her leg until his fingertips grazed her lavender labia. Her whole body tightened. He immediately pulled back. Her body relaxed. What he felt at that moment was uncertainty. He remembered thinking, This must be the love thing because I want to be nice to her.

"I'm not going to hurt you."

Calming down, he morphed into a little scientist. He touched different parts of her body to see how she would respond. She started to giggle. That upset him. He'd had enough—I'm done, he mumbled, and he gave up—with relief. She must have heard him because she spread her legs—very wide—making her vagina beckon to him like an open door in a fairy tale. But he wasn't excited the way he had been when he saw Femme's. That disappointed him. Where was his desire? He froze momentarily wondering what fate would befall him if he put his dong in that dark place, beyond the purple slit, and he had to admit: He was scared. In his version of Little Red Riding Hood, the wolf eats the kid.

He was deciding how to extricate himself from this situation, when he heard some sounds coming from under the pillow. He pulled the pillow from Dolores's face. She was crying. Her eyeliner ran.

"What's wrong?"

He noticed she was wearing something that made her lips glisten pale red, like dogwood bloom.

"You don't want me?"

Her bashful eyes were black and sparkled under her tears. Until now, he'd been some insect exploring a Venus Flytrap—her falsely innocent, unanimated merkin, another *Lolita* word. But now, in the narrow interval between two honor-driven beats of his fear-weakened heart, he saw a girl, a hurt girl. He'd never felt more tender. He wondered how this connected with love. He took a deep breath and looked down again at her yawning but blessed portal, the *pièce de résistance* of this awkward drama, and for a second he wasn't afraid. Just the opposite, he wanted to hold her, be strong for her, and conquer all the fear in this world.

The two baboons started banging on the door, and Dizzy yelled, "Are you doing it, Killer?"

Lemeilleur imagined Dizzy's eyes flashing with garish gonadal glows like the smoky blues and pinks of a Wurlitzer jammed with nickels. Whatever ardor Lemeilleur had managed to summon in his flesh vanished in that flash of Dizzy's frantic fuming eyes.

"Will you do me a favor, Dolores?" Lemeilleur asked, giving up any possibility of spelunking in her cave. "If Boris asks, just tell him I did it, please."

"He told me," she said putting the pillow to her side, "to say the same thing to you." And she winked at him.

Lemeilleur looked down at her honey-brown flesh where a crenulated imprint had been left by the elastic band of her underwear, a spot of flesh he should have adored and kissed in this magic moment so different and so new. This was the moment for a "*fancy embrace,*" (Humbert Humbert's euphemism for oral sex), but bedeviled, there was no fire in his loins?

"So you're not going to impale me?"

"Impale you?"

"I looked it up. Boris said you like big words," and as she wiggled into her underwear, she added. "Don't worry, we'll do it one of these days."

"How do you know?" Lemeilleur shot back bitterly.

"I like you."

18

In spite of all his rancor with his family, Lemeilleur was happy with his new job: Georges liked him. And as Lemeilleur dried dishes at the old folks' home that night, he, a hundred times more relaxed now, bragged about how cool he was with girls.

"I'm telling you, Georges, girls love me. They fall over themselves at record hops to dance with me. Paula thinks I'm cute, Leona says I have beautiful eyes, and Joyce says—"

"—Let me guess," Georges said, putting his sponge down and turning toward Lemeilleur, "You're adorable."

"How do you know that?" Lemeilleur laughed.

"Because you're just like that monk in Boccaccio's tales. Nothing quenches your life force."

"You really believe that?"

"You have the power of love—you can change fortune!"

"Get out of here!"

"Why don't you write stories?"

That was all Lemeilleur needed. His father always said his grandfather was a storyteller. Storytelling, it probably skipped a generation, Lemeilleur told himself, like baldness.

"Hey, keep drying those pots."

Lemeilleur was fairly sure Georges liked him, and that made him happy. Georges was the key to his interior life, which was moving Lemeilleur into a whole new dimension of existence—foreign movies at the Fine Arts movie theatre and famous old books, many of which were on the Catholic *Index Expurgatorius* by authors who sinned against the Holy Ghost—the only sin beyond God's mercy. Lemeilleur was made of stories. That night he dreamed he was standing in a forest of auburn leaves, sprinkled in lush yellow light:

O to be a story. Locked in a family
of words that loved you.

19

For as long as he could remember, whatever was going on, Lemeilleur had always confided in his friend, Mice. However, something was different now; he didn't tell Mice he was getting friendly with Georges. Lemeilleur's gut was steadfast; he told himself at some point he'd surprise Mice with his new-found erudition. Only Randy had any idea that Georges and Lemeilleur were becoming friends, and that made Randy think Lemeilleur was weird—fucking Republican—always ranking people. Well Randy did not fall close to Lemeilleur's ranking of what was important. Randy, for instance, only liked American movies—the dumb ones—like *Gidget*—the ones that make all the money. Of course, there were exceptions: Randy hated *Peyton Place*. Georges, on the other hand, knew about things that Lemeilleur hadn't dreamed existed. Like eratomania. But none of that really mattered to Lemeilleur: He had TWO new friends—a little different—who cared?

20

Now don't ask Lemeilleur how Mice got the nickname Mice. Nobody knows. Mice's father was Cajun and one eighth black by descent; that's why Mice lived in Lemeilleur's neighborhood, but his mother was Irish; that's why Mice belonged to the Irish parish and went to St. Stephen's High School. Some people called Mice a mongrel, some called him worse. But what was interesting about Mice is—well one of the things—he learned French on his own, with records, so he could hang around with Lemeilleur and his friends. Lemeilleur couldn't remember when he met Mice. He just came with the neighborhood. What Lemeilleur did remember was—right from the first time he met Mice—how much he wanted Mice to be his friend. It was completely different than

Tony. Lemeilleur wanted to share everything that was important with Mice.

Things now had changed. Lemeilleur knew he was drifting away from Mice, but he was too excited about learning new things to feel the sadness of losing a friend. All he could think about was the books Georges told him to read. Those books would save him, like an amulet, and in the end Mice would be proud of Lemeilleur.

After the rats-kill-the-cat crap his father had subjected him to, Lemeilleur had figured out that in life, he was out in the middle of an ocean—alone and could drown at any time. Back then Lemeilleur didn't give a shit about the moral or spiritual—survival was strictly brain development—even his understanding of Salinger. It would take awhile for Lemeilleur to catch on to the poetry of staying alive.

One of Lemeilleur's fondest memories of Mice was sitting with him at the counter of Husson's Soda Fountain and talking French. Joe Husson, who owned the Fountain, was Syrian and spoke Arabic to his friends. The Fountain was a friendly place to meet—a little, multilingual oasis in their desert-like neighborhood.

"I'll have a Moxie, Joe."

"Hey," laughed Mice, "*tu te protéges de l'adoucissement du cerveau?*" (you protecting yourself from softening of the brain?)

Lemeilleur laughed nervously not understanding what Mice was alluding to.

"Don't worry, Speedoo, Ted Williams drinks Moxie too. His brain isn't softening."

Mice was two years older than Lemeilleur—that was cool—and Mice read newspapers and talked politics, which was very boring, except when Mice talked about Senator McCarthy, who "confused and divided the American people to destroy democracy. Truman was right when he called McCarthy 'the best asset the Kremlin ever had.'"

"What about us?" Mice crowed. "Who's going to protect us from the next McCarthy? Hey, making any new friends at the old folks' home?"

Lemeilleur looked away from Mice and said, "Ah, not really."

21

Randy was dating Lily, a sweet little girl from a large, extremely poor family—she had like ten brothers. She was a sophomore at Holy Flame Catholic Central High School, in the non-college track. Elvis had been inducted into the US Army and Randy wanted a driver to chauffeur him and Lily around. Lemeilleur was about to turn thirteen so, as a birthday gift, Randy had taught Lemeilleur to drive his '49 *Mercury*. Lemeilleur was okay with the job of driving because whenever he would run away from home, Randy took him in. Randy's mother, an asthmatic, laconic, garlicky woman with a black mustache above a purple lip, who stitched together chasubles in a factory, didn't mind that Lemeilleur stayed there. All she ever did was watch them like a parrot, and periodically she'd squawk *"Sois sage. Sois sage."* (Behave yourself. Behave yourself.) Christ, even Randy's mother had a song.

One night Lemeilleur, the chauffeur on duty, outside a dance hall, waited for Randy and Lily. He was sipping T-bird and reading Rabelais in the moonlight—it was an exceptionally warm night for mid-November.

Lemeilleur, reading in French, had already gotten beyond the part that Georges had told him about: *"A boire. A boire. A boire."* ("Drink up. Drink up. Drink up." Georges had told Lemeilleur that he was an *A boire* kind of character.) Lemeilleur was now up to: « *O Dieux et Déesses Célestes, que heureux sera celuy à qui ferez ceste grâce de vous accoller et bayser, et de frotter son lard avecques vous.* » ("O heavenly gods and goddesses, how happy shall that man be to whom you grant this favour to embrace you, to kiss you, to rub his bacon with yours.")

Like Gargantua, Lemeilleur believed he was born thirsty. *A Boire*. And that all his life, *par sa soif* (by his thirst), Lemeilleur believed he would seek the source, the fount of Freedom, the soul's nourishment. And sitting there in that parking lot, Lemeilleur was never surer of his mission: To get free—to drink up life!

"Hey, Lemeilleur, let's go."

Randy and Lily were laughing and running toward the car.

"Let's go, Lemeilleur."

"Go? Where?"

"Anywhere. Just drive around."

They got in the back seat and started fooling around. Lemeilleur drove. He didn't think he was drunk. He could hear them kissing and rubbing and moaning, which was immensely distracting. Then he heard Lily say, "I don't want to do it now—got my period."

"Okay, okay," Randy said, trying to calm down, while Lemeilleur, with Rabelais's phrase, *frotter son lard* (rub his bacon), saliently in mind, thought: Randy's going to have to rub his own bacon tonight.

"I'll blow you, if you want?"

"Moon-fucking-light-Sonata." Randy exploded.

Lemeilleur would have invoked *Ode to Joy*.

Anyway, all the way up Providence Street Lemeilleur could hear her sucking, which made him turgid with blind desire, and when he got to the corner of Winthrop Street across from St. Vincent Hospital, he tried to make a hard right turn, but he was going a little too fast and his turn was a little too wide—TOO WIDE!

He smashed into a car on Winthrop that was stopped for the red light.

"Jesus Christ," Randy screamed, "she almost bit it off."

"Get in the front seat," Lemeilleur yelled to Randy; "I hear a police cruiser."

Lemeilleur slid over to the passenger side leaving room for Randy to jump into the driver's seat, while someone from the car he'd hit yelled, "They just switched places!"

Lemeilleur threw his bottle of T-bird across the street, into the grass in front of the YWCA.

In minutes the police were there. Lemeilleur was shaking, but Randy was calm. First the police talked to the car Lemeilleur had hit, and, to Lemeilleur's surprise, arrested the driver and his passenger. After they got those two into the back seat of their cruiser, they walked over to Randy and Lemeilleur. Fuck—they were next.

Randy showed one officer his license and registration while the other officer held a flashlight on Lemeilleur. The officer with his license walked away, did something in the front seat of his cruiser, and came back. He handed Randy his license and registration and asked if they were okay. Randy said he was fine, but his friend, Lemeilleur, was a little shaken up—but he'll be okay. One of the cops flashed a light on Lily.

"How about you, little lady; you okay?"

Lily nodded enthusiastically.

"Could a been a lot worse," the first officer said. "Those two are very drunk. I can see by how far their car is in your lane why they hit you. The tow truck will be here soon."

The police drove off.

"It's just like Mice said," Randy shouted.

"You know Mice?" Lemeilleur asked.

"He's in my English class at St. Stephen's. The kid's a brain."

"What did he say?"

"Mice told me you're an exceptional person. Now I get it. **You** hit that car, and **they** got arrested! Fucking unbelievable!"

All Lemeilleur could think was Mice talks about him. He wanted to shout.

22

One day after a grueling one-on-one basketball game, Mice invited Lemeilleur over to his house for lunch. Lemeilleur had never been to Mice's house before. It must have been a Saturday because Mice's father was there. He worked for the City in the sewer department.

"Make us something to eat."

Mice's order to his mother caught Lemeilleur's attention because Mice made it sound like his mother worked for him or he was some kind of Prince.

She was wearing a sheer yellow house dress with nothing under it, but she was so skinny, her bones stuck out through her milk-white skin and made her look unbelievably ugly—a *Mad* magazine hag, which was striking because Mice looked like a twenty-year-old Chet Baker, the Prince of Cool. Anyway, while Mice's mother rattled around making canned spaghetti, Mice went into his bedroom to find an article in *Playboy* that he wanted to show Lemeilleur. But it wasn't in his room. Mice got very mad, ran across the kitchen, and started banging on the bathroom door.

"Hey Mister Petitesouris, I want my *Playboy*, you dirty old man," Mice screamed.

"Don't you snigger at yarh fahthar that way, he's intrasted in culchar," his mother said, mangling her words.

"You smell like a Russian musk ox gonad."

"If," she continued, "yaw and yaw friend wants ta eat here, yaw watch your languith."

"You. You." Mice exploded. "You are a fucking whore."

"Tha's . . . naw way . . . ta tawk ta ya . . . mawthar."

She was so drunk, she slurred her pauses.

"If you fucked that sap more often, he wouldn't be in there banging his baguette with my *Playboy*."

As she slammed the plate of spaghetti down in front of Mice, one of her thin teats slipped through one of her short sleeves. It just hung there, brown and wrinkled, like a yam with a pimple. She tried to retrieve it. Mice blinked his milky-blue eyes rapidly—then convulsed.

"PUT YOUR FUCKING TEAT BACK. YOU FUCKING WHORE."

His father flushed the toilet, came out, gave Mice his

Playboy, and walked away. Mice's mother was still trying to get her teat back, while Mice screamed, "This is not a house for the living—it's a vault for the dead."

Mice's mother stood up straight, lowered her arms, her exposed breast still hung limply against her arm, and she, swaying, declaimed: "Dere's many like ya rit now readin' a book or doin' a drug or sniffin' away for a slut or makin' fun of 'is mawthar, while da 'earse is drawin' near, an' a voice he don't ear is mutterin' earth ta earth, ashes ta ashes, an' dus' ta dus'."

"You're one sick bogtrotter," Mice said, dismissing her and turning to Lemeilleur.

"I coulda bin a GREAAT actresss," his mother shouted.

"Forget her, Lem. She doesn't exist. Now listen to this." Mice picked up the *Playboy* and read: *". . . the only people for me are the mad ones, the ones who are mad to live, mad to talk, mad to be saved, desirous of everything at the same time . . ."* Mice lowered the magazine and said, "That's us, Lemeilleur. We are the mad ones. Kerouac is for changing life."

"Changing life?"

"Rimbaud said, *'Il faut changer la vie.'* 'We must change life.' Kerouac gets it. Lem, we have to be absolutely modern. Our experience opens us to a new way of seeing."

Change life? Kerouac gets it? Lemeilleur was still trying to understand Rimbaud's 'Drunken Boat.' Jeez. Kerouac. Who was Kerouac?

"Come on, Lem. In 'Drunken Boat' Rimbaud is dancing on the edge of Meaning. If he missteps, he'll fall into the abyss— that's where the beauty is! Eighty years later and he still hasn't fallen."

What was Mice talking about?

"It's people like us who get Rimbaud: We know the edge!" Lemeilleur vowed to himself that he would study Rimbaud—he had to understand.

"Rimbaud escaped from his day-to-day—into his rabbit hole of poetry to a safe environment!" Mice shouted, "Listen to this." Mice ran to his bedroom and came back with a book. He read slowly in French.

Comme je descendais des Fleuves impassibles,
Je ne me sentis plus guidé par les haleurs:
Des Peaux-Rouges criards les avaient pris pour cibles
Les ayant cloués nus aux poteaux de couleurs.

(As I floated down unconcerned Rivers
I no longer felt myself guided by haulers:
Screaming Redskins had taken them for targets
Nailing them naked to colored stakes.)

"Words are actions, Lem. Did you know 'Beat' is short for beatific? We're going to learn the secret to change life—as soon as we find our genius. We're going to be Neo-Beats. We're going to change life. Let your imagination run free. We are the opposite of slaves. We're going to write agitational prose. We don't get sick on the 'Drunken Boat' of life. We are artists. We transform. We are what we desire. We live on the edge!"

On the way home, Lemeilleur tried to understand what Mice was talking about—the secret of life and finding their genius—then Lemeilleur started to think that Mice must be thinking of them as characters in literature—and *that* made Lemeilleur feel better. Literary characters had fixed personalities and set goals. They lived in an unchangeable plot, a stable environment. He thought about all the characters he could be: Lolita, Pip, or Gregor Samsa—an insect—he liked that: Most insects were nicer than people.

23

August 15, 5 am, Sunday morning at St. Anthony's Home: Georges was making coffee and Lemeilleur, daisy-fresh from a good night's sleep, was taking the beans—they had cooked slowly all night long in a gargantuan metal cauldron—out of the Vulcan stove. The cauldron weighed about fifty pounds.

Randy had the morning off. And as the ninety pound Lemeilleur struggled with the cauldron, the side of the huge pot burned his thighs, and as the acrid smell rose from his melting polyester pants, he felt something wet on his neck. He dropped the pot, but the beans—God bless Lemeilleur—didn't spill. Georges, who was crying, had tried to kiss Lemeilleur—and now, still crying, Georges, on his knees, next to the pot of beans, confessed: he loved Lemeilleur.

Georges loved him!

The nuns were upstairs in chapel at Mass, and in two hours 345 elderly would be clamoring for their beans. The world was changing: Che Guevara was almost in Havana, and Lana Turner's daughter had fatally stabbed her mother's gangster boyfriend. And Sputnik 1 had fallen to earth and burned up. Not counting Mice, nobody had told Lemeilleur they loved him—ever. It was 6 am. Lemeilleur was wide awake. And as crazy as this sounds, Lemeilleur wanted someone to love him—passionately—the way it happened in books, like Emma Bovary.

By 9:15 pm, when they finished work, Lemeilleur had decided. He would take a chance on Georges—he wanted to be Georges's Lolita—he wanted to know how love felt.

Georges offered to drive Lemeilleur home. This is it, Lemeilleur thought as a splash of anguish scalded his tender hope for love. Still committed, he said, "Sure." Georges got into the Impala first, pushed the front seat all the way back, Lemeilleur sat down on the passenger side, and then Georges jammed his hulk into the footwell between Lemeilleur's scorched thighs and pulled the front door closed.

Lemeilleur looked up at the full moon, which, embarrassed by her nakedness, began to clothe herself in dark clouds. A few dull stars waited for the drowsy afterglow of satiated desire. As Georges got comfy, Lemeilleur thought of Einstein: "If you want your children to be strong, read them fairy tales."

The trembling shadows around the Impala held their breath, and under the moon's shy but prying eye, Georges's hand found what it sought.

Lemeilleur entered yet another world as a dreamy and eerie expression slid down over his childish, gingery-brown eyes, and his narrow thorax deflated a little, as he got, in a word he would learn in high school, head.

Lemeilleur's neck was bent in a soft, drooping position, almost woefully, as the solitary pleasure mounted, Lemeilleur's otherworldly pallor began to emit a Georges de La Tour radiance, and all of Lemeilleur's body parts and intellectual components, hitherto suspended in usual isolation, joyously sought to hold hands to celebrate the only true unity in this meaningless universe:

orgasm.

Georges's butched head bobbed in and out of a slash of silver that cut through the windshield like a scimitar. Silently, ineluctably, Lemeilleur crept toward that distant glowing tingle—that explosion of absolute security, confidence, and reliance—pure euphoria. He floated upward, toward that vestibule of sublimity with sibilant intakes of breath, his thorax expanding in short gasps until the fog of lust was blown into eternity.

Lemeilleur opened his cinnamon-colored eyes and his innocence fluoresced.

Georges, wiping his mouth, looked up; pleasure sparkled in his cocker spaniel eyes; and he smiled. His nacreous teeth glowed ghoulishly in the opalescent dark. The super-voluptuous flame cooled. The hot load was gone. A little demon of power danced. The spell was cast, the hunted enchanted, and the poison in the wound.

That night Lemeilleur consulted his *Lolita* to clear the way for him. *"I looked and looked at her, and I knew, as clearly as I know that I will die, that I loved her more than anything I had ever seen or imagined on earth."*

He put the book down and went to his window and looked up at the midnight-blue-velvet sky and he noticed the stars were arranged like notes in a musical score—the universe was telling him his song was still out there. Before falling asleep, coltish Lemeilleur, his little heart trotting excitedly around his imaginary paddock, wrote "12 years and 7 months old and someone loves me."

Exactly ten years after Humbert Humbert had begun his verbally elegant destruction of his half-drugged, shamelessly summer-camp-devirginized Lolita whom, as Humbert Humbert, pleading cravenly to the jury, claimed had seduced him, Lemeilleur slipped soothingly into sleep—not wondering at all about who Georges was. Instead, he smiled knowing he was safely ensconced in the never-changing plot of Lolitaland.

24

Lemeilleur was in the old coal bin in Mice's basement holding a flashlight so Mice could see what he was doing. The house was now heated by oil, so the landlord let Mice's family store potatoes in the coal bin for the winter—ten or twenty bushels, and it was Mice's job to go in there every month to break off all the new roots on the dry tubers. It took hours.

Mice and Georges had met, but Lemeilleur had not breathed a word to Mice about any of the details of their relationship. Now, Lemeilleur realized, he and Mice were drifting toward different destinies. Mice was the only person Lemeilleur ever loved. Sadness rose around his heart like rising flames coming from just-lit kindling around the foot of a stake. That made Lemeilleur think of Carl Dryer's movie that Georges had recently taken Lemeilleur to see: *The Passion of Joan of Arc*.

"What the fuck are you thinking?" Mice shouted. "Keep the flashlight on my hands. I can't see the potatoes."

Lemeilleur snapped out of it and realized—happily—he did have something to tell Mice. Last month, he had found the *Syntopicon* in the public library.

"What the hell is that?" Mice asked.

"It's a collection of all the great books. And if you bought a copy and wrote an essay on one of their topics, they'd give you a scholarship to college, if they liked your essay."

"Fuck these potatoes. I could write an essay on justice. I think about that all the time."

"Shit, man. I could write an essay on love. I think about THAT all the time."

"Love? Point that flashlight on my hands."

"Have you ever been in love, Mice?"

"Hmmm . . . I guess . . . but only with you."

"Me."

"I'm pulling your leg. Did you know there's no definition of justice that people agree on?"

"Well, everyone agrees on love. But I don't see it anywhere."

"Why you so stuck on love? Is Georges still reading to you from the *Treasury of Ribaldry*?"

"Just finished Boccaccio's Third Day, Tenth Story, "Put the Devil Back into Hell." You'd like that one. It reminded me of the time you tricked Suzie into doing it."

"When you read 'Clay,' the short story by James Joyce, listen to 'I Dreamt I Dwelt in Marble Halls.'"

"What's that?"

"It's a song that puts a halo around the head of a loveless heroine."

"Why you telling me that?"

"Whatever you do, Lem, you don't want to end up like her."

Lemeilleur made a mental note to look into this story by James Joyce, "Clay."

"What are you reading, Mice?"

"Augustine of Hippo."

"Why?"

"He's just like us—poor and brilliant—and he's looking for truth and justice. He said, and I quote: 'In my time, I have come, through my pursuit of literature, to live the life of a nobleman.' Don't forget to listen to 'I Dreamt I Dwelt in

Marble Halls.' Maria is the saddest character in all literature."

"I won't."

"Hey Lem, ya really think we'll get to college?"

"I don't know. Why?"

"I want to change life."

"I don't understand."

"There's a genius out there who knows the secret to change life—the way to bring justice into this world—and I want to find that genius. The pricks are keeping that secret from us. That's the basis of the class system."

"Say you find your genius, then what'll we do?"

"Shit. We'll start a magazine—JUSTICE—and we'll only publish ideas that 'change life.'"

Mice was shouting as Lemeilleur flashed the light on the warrior of justice as he waved a potato in the dark bin, and Mice shouted again, "A country that doesn't listen to its poor will never know what justice is. Lem, we're only mudsills."

"What's a mudsill?"

"The timber driven into the ground to support the elegant house above. Mark my words, Lem, inequality will create such an abyss, capitalism will be swallowed whole, followed by a big bouzawzy burp heard round the world."

That would be the way Lemeilleur would always remember Mice—waving a potato in a dark bin—holding forth on justice—and pretending he didn't love Lemeilleur. As they walked up the stairs from Mice's basement, a curious Mice called out from his ice floe.

"Hey, Lem, did you hear about that girl, Dolores?"

"What about her?" Lemeilleur asked cautiously.

"Killed herself—drank iodine. She was in that girls' school in Marlboro."

Why was Mice asking Lemeilleur about Dolores? What did Mice know about Dolores and Lemeilleur?

"What do you know about Dolores, Mice?"

Mice, however, had already drifted away.

25

Months later, Georges, to get a teacher's certification with his Ph.D. in French, had to study I.Q. tests. He had to give five tests to get credit. Lemeilleur volunteered himself and Mice. During Lemeilleur's test, Georges got upset when Lemeilleur gave the definition of homunculus as a queer cloud. Georges decided to blow Lemeilleur to help him do better. Afterwards, Lemeilleur thought he probably was the only kid in America who had gotten blown during an I.Q. test.

26

A week later, Georges tested Mice. Lemeilleur asked Georges what score Mice got. "142."

A very anxious Lemeilleur couldn't believe Georges blew Mice too. Now knowing his own score and feeling entirely alone, Lemeilleur feared he'd never understand 'Drunken Boat.' Might he not survive? The world was coming apart and he was still a long way from saving himself—never mind creating his song. Georges had scored Lemeilleur: "106."

27

As Lemeilleur's grammar school career ended, he realized he hadn't saved enough money to pay for prep school. One year costs $500—for a day student. He only had $350. He'd have to go to Holy Flame Central Catholic High School. He was upset. Things were worse than ever between him and his father, who was now becoming a big deal funereal success. As it transpired, his father, because he had a gift for murder restorations which through word-of-mouth became the rage of the neighborhood, was getting extraordinarily rich. You know, cop blows away your face away—Ducrotte will repair—go with dignity—no need for closed casket—let your friends see you the way you always looked as they say goodbye. Ducrotte's Funeral Home.

Since Lemeilleur was always fighting with his swell-headed father, Lemeilleur, to avoid this idiotic conflict, was spending more and more time at Randy's. He couldn't stay with Georges because Georges lived with his parents and six brothers, three of whom slept in the same bedroom as Georges. This arrangement with Randy made Georges insalubriously jealous. In fact, Georges, during meal prep at the old folks' home, had pulled a Henckels's carving knife on Randy only last week. They'd laughed it off.

⌾

Victoria was Randy's older sister. And, well, her husband—for reasons Lemeilleur knew nothing about—was put in a locked ward at the State Hospital. Lemeilleur could tell puffy, poodle-headed, short-legged, big-breasted Victoria had eyes for him.

In order to avoid a needless and potentially dangerous kerfuffle between Randy and Georges, now, when he ran away, Lemeilleur would go to Victoria's squalid hovel—no *Enchanted Hunters* there. This was another step in the disintegration of his limbic system. Lemeilleur had to shed his fear of women! He had to step out of the shadow of homosexuality!

On the first night, as Victoria obligingly bent over the breadbox in her tiny pantry, Lemeilleur—quite unceremoniously—entered her begrimed, poodle-groomed groin, an over eager beaver for the symbolism this specious act begot.

Afterwards, still unsettled by his beastliness, sitting over beers, Victoria, in a very timid, unsforzando tone, said,

"Thanks for coming by." Lemeilleur, almost blushing, raised his glass, but said nothing.

In bed later that night, Lemeilleur blew smoke rings up at Victoria's bedroom ceiling and thought: He was no longer a virgin. No more fear of crossbones. He'd entered the tabernacle and had come out unscathed. But had he? Was it manhood that now beckoned with a smile?

He becalmed his spirit—imaginatively—and celebrated—imaginatively—this transformative moment, letting nude chubby child figures, often frequently seen with wings in religious paintings, dance in his guilt-ridden blood to the fanciful trumpet music of the royal entrance of the 'Fanfare-Rondeau' of *Suite of Symphonies*, regally announcing his first heterosexual orgasm—YES, YES, YES—all the while a shadowy demon *à la Fuseli*, eyes alert, lurked behind the velvet cloak of rapture.

28

Was it Victoria, who had given him crabs, which he was treating with *Kwell,* that set Georges off? Lemeilleur wondered.

"There's somebody else," Georges raged in the driver's seat of his Impala.

What imaginary shadow of infidelity had fallen across Georges's paranoid path?

"What are you yelling about, Georges?"

"Mice!"

"Mice?"

"You think I'm stupid! I've seen you with Mice at Joe's Spa! I've watched you walk home with him!"

"Georges, nothing is happening between me and Mice!"

"You're a liar. I see it in your eyes when you're with him!"

"Georges, I'm telling you—it's totally straight with Mice! We never—ever—touched each other! Never! You're losing it. You thought I was sleeping with Randy, too."

"I need you, Lemeilleur, but I know you don't love me."

Lemeilleur became frightened. To help Georges get over his jealousy, Lemeilleur let Georges lick his ass, which was something Georges was always asking for. Lemeilleur felt vulnerable.

"That's better," Georges moaned.

But then Lemeilleur felt Georges's thing trying to wedge itself into the saliva-wet gluteal cleft.

Lemeilleur fought him off—that time. But physically Lemeilleur knew Georges could take him whenever he wanted. How long would Lemeilleur be able to hold him off? More scared now, Lemeilleur felt little bits of vomit just behind his teeth.

Georges started to scream, and this time he pushed himself into Lemeilleur. "You don't love me. You never loved me," he gushed as he took Lemeilleur. "All these years," he shrieked, "I've given you everything. Knives, dirty books, I even bought you those pants with a buckle on the back. But no—you want to play house with some slut. O. I adored you. OO. Together we saw *Knife in the Water*. OOO. I loved you. OOOO."

Georges ejaculated. Lemeilleur bit his tongue to hold back the ache in his spasming esophagus.

"You can't answer," Georges yelled as he cleaned the shit off his pesky pecker. "That doesn't surprise me. You don't care. You never cared. You never touched me. I answered all your questions about Rabelais. You're hard, Lemeilleur. I give you the world and you give me shit. You used me. I can't believe I did this to myself. Get the fuck out of my car. You're nothing but a selfish whore. Get out. You tramp. Go ahead. Leave. Go back to Mice."

Lemeilleur felt rotten. His hip hit the pavement and he threw up on the sidewalk. He tried to pull up his pants as he watched Georges drive away. His belt buckled, he tried to stand up, but he slipped in his vomit and fell back into the gutter. Georges, he thought, had been a lot nicer than Lemeilleur's parents. Was Georges gone? Would Lemeilleur no longer be "Lollipop," Georges's pet name for him? Lemeilleur pounded the hard tar of the street. Had Georges decamped now that he'd had his foretaste of heaven? Was he moving on to another pubescent paradise? Lemeilleur wanted Georges to come back, sobbing or not, contrite or not, and Lemeilleur, seeing someone running towards him, rose from his vomit. He brushed himself off and looked up at the clearing sky.

29

"...if a violin string could ache, i would be that string."
Vladimir Nabokov, *Lolita*

Days later Lemeilleur found a book in the library that encouraged him. *New York Times* reporter, Harrison Salisbury in his book, *The Shook-Up Generation*, said: *"One thing I'll tell you, I'm going to get out of this dump. And never come back."*

Mice, who heard Lemeilleur was feeling down, came to Lemeilleur's house to play some music.

"Listen to this, Speedoo. This guy gets pain."

> *"I went to the crossroad*
> *fell down on my knees"*
> *Asked the Lord above, "Have mercy, now,*
> *save poor Bob, if you please"*

With Mice's encouragement, Lemeilleur's little French-Canadian heart refilled itself slowly with blind hope and extravagant ambition. In his notebook that night he wrote less sanguinely: I have to stop sabotaging myself. I have a completely normal relationship with Mice.

30

By the end of that year, Lemeilleur had saved enough money to go to the prep school. Proudly he paid, up front, in cash, his tuition of $500, for his sophomore year. No more Holy Flame Central Catholic High School. Now, he said to himself, puffing out his little chest like a blue parrot, he was going to listen to *Kind of Blue* music and study seriously. He was, at last, in control.

During orientation, he promised himself he'd write his memoir, and the title would be: *The Spiritual Hunt* to honor Rimbaud's lost manuscript. The connection being: Rimbaud had been jilted by Verlaine as Lemeilleur had been by Georges—a similarity Lemeilleur could add to his plot line in his unfinished masterpiece. Lemeilleur anointed himself Son of Rimbaud.

⊕

Thus began prep school, the new awakening for Lemeilleur. His teachers liked him and sincerely wanted to help. It was a little like an old girlfriend telling you what to do so her parents will like you, only the remake was more comprehensive. Turns out Lemeilleur didn't know anything. He had to learn English grammar, French grammar, and Latin grammar. He had to study geometry and American history. And he had to learn how to write an English sentence. Would all this learning turn him into a song? Fucking illusion. He wasn't even American yet. Still, he plugged on—he lived for his dream.

He had quit kitchen work at St. Anthony's and changed all his friends, except for Mice, who was graduating that year from high school. While all this was going on, Georges, who hadn't talked to Lemeilleur since Georges threw him out of his car, contacted Lemeilleur to tell him he'd gotten drafted for a new war—somewhere in Asia. Georges didn't ask about the prep school, and Lemeilleur, who didn't write back, wrote in his notebook: "I was already a superannuated roué. Some Humbert Humbert Georges was." Lemeilleur felt like an adult now.

All the while as Lemeilleur struggled for his grades, his father could not stop bragging to his friends about his son in prep school—an **Upper Class Prep School**.

⬦

All Lemeilleur did that year was study and learn. He couldn't believe how far behind the others he was. His classmates were shocked he'd never seen or read *The Wizard of Oz,* and Lemeilleur was blown away nobody had ever **heard** of *Lolita*.

⬦

They read Dickens that year—*Great Expectations*. It was his kind of a love story which helped Lemeilleur keep up. Often he would dream about his favorite quote from the book.

"Suffering has been stronger than all other teaching, and has taught me to understand what your heart used to be. I have been bent and broken, but - I hope - into a better shape." Estella.

He was already dreaming about a woman who would, someday, talk to him this way.

⬦

One morning, after the class had finished reading *Great Expectations*, he woke up screaming, "I love you, Pip."

31

In second semester, Lemeilleur took a national test in geometry and got an honorable mention—without a blowjob. He was so excited he called Mice, and after he told Mice about his success, he went on.

"I have to ask you a question. Did Georges blow you during your I.Q. test?"

"Aw, Jesus, Lem. Don't ask me that."

"I heard he gets excited by I.Q. tests."

"Are you shitting me? You are. For god's sake. Lemeilleur. Don't jape with me about that. Did Georges blow me? Was Humbert Humbert a good father? Did you read 'Clay?'"

"Did you really know the word homunculus?"

"Yeah, from *Faust*. Get with it, Lem. Fuck the faggots. You're Speedoo!"

Lemeilleur was silent.

"No faggot jokes. Nothing can stop you. You're going to change life—don't ever forget that—soon as you find your genius. Remember what FDR said: 'We're going to make a country in which no one is left behind.' Look, Lem, you're a great guy. You're going to have an exciting life. You have magic in your imagination."

Lemeilleur was too focused on school to appreciate the accolade: Mice considered him an equal—a talented equal. They were men, now, in the war against injustice. One of Lemeilleur's dreams had come true—a profound partnership with Mice. For years Lemeilleur had clung to Mice as if to a spar on Rimbaud's 'Drunken Boat', buffeted by all the ill winds of his absurd life. But now that Lemeilleur was in prep school, the phantom vessel that leaked badly and had no bilge pump would soon be replaced by a new self-confident Lemeilleur, or so he believed.

32

Unfortunately, when the year was up and his $500 spent, he realized he had no money left for the next year.

"I need to pay for my junior year. Can you help me?" Lemeilleur quietly asked his father.

"I knew you'd screw it up."

"What are talking about? I didn't screw anything up!"

"You ran out of money."

"I thought you liked me going to a prep school?"

"It's just book-learning. What are you going to do in life?"

"It's too early to know."

"When I was your age I knew I was going to be a funeral director! You need vision, like David Copperfield!"

"Please. You have a lot of money now."

"I worked for that money—nobody gave it to me!"

"You're not going to help me, are you?"

"I'll pay for you to go to embalming school—Now."

Lemeilleur, walking out of his father's living room while his mother lingered in a depression in her bedroom, turned to his father at the door and screamed, "You never read *David Copperfield!*" He slammed the door behind him.

As Lemeilleur, his hands jammed into his pockets, walked up Wall Street, he dreaded going back to Holy Flame Central Catholic High School. Georges had sent him a boring letter from wherever he was in the Army—some language school in California. Lemeilleur anguished over asking him for money, deciding it was a bad idea. Georges hadn't loved him the way he'd imagined, like Humbert Humbert loved Lolita. Humbert Humbert had given Lolita $4,000 in 1952. Lemeilleur realized he would have to come to terms: He was no nymphet, and no *petit cadeau* (little gift) was coming, and Georges was not going to die if he never touched Lemeilleur again.

The 'Drunken Boat' was back and taking on water. No longer feeling like a blue parrot, he decided to tell his spiritual advisor what was happening.

"I guess this will be my last year, Father Paul."

"Why? What's going on? Your grades have improved remarkably."

"I don't have any more money."

The spiritual advisor put his hands behind his back, and they continued their peripatetic walk. Lemeilleur was going to miss this attention. Finally, the spiritual advisor stopped and turned to Lemeilleur. "We have a seminary in New York, and if you went, we would pay for your education, room and board—everything."

33

Lemeilleur's adjustment to the seminary was almost instantaneous, but one day in early December, his English teacher, Father Richard, told him he had to speak to the Headmaster, whose name was Father Raimond.

As Lemeilleur walked to the Headmaster's office, he smiled. He loved the seminary. He hadn't masturbated in a month. St. Lemeilleur. No more 'Drunken Boat.' This was a vacation with God. And the food was good—cooked by nuns from Mexico, the *Siete Dolores*, which reminded him to ask God to forgive him for hurting Dolores.

When he got to the Headmaster's office, Lemeilleur noticed his term paper on *The Tragical History of Doctor Faustus* on his desk. Lemeilleur had worked hard on the paper for English class, so he thought Father Raimond was going to congratulate him.

"Ah, Lemeilleur," the Headmaster said looking up.

Lemeilleur remembered when he was searching for a theme, how he had found a scrap of paper—he had them all over the place because of his habit of writing down anything that he liked on a piece of paper—with a couple of sentences from *The Courage To Be*, the content of which gave him the idea for his interpretation of Doctor Faustus.

"Hello, Father Raimond."

Father Raimond was tall, about 6'3", muscular, dark-skinned, had an incredibly masculine jaw, black plastic eyeglasses, and a butch haircut. Immediately, he picked up Lemeilleur's paper and started to read aloud.

"Faustus," Father Raimond intoned, "perceives his familiarity with multiple intellectual disciplines as something of a problem because they cannot satisfy his appetite for more Meaning, and Faustus's method of solving the problem is to conjure the devil."

Father Raimond's hands, which clenched Lemeilleur's term paper, trembled. Lemeilleur tried to hide his pride behind a neutral face.

"However," Father Raimond continued, "now you quote Tillich, '*he who is the bearer of the final revelation must surrender his finitude—not only his life but his finite power and knowledge and perfection.*' Then you quote Tillich again. '*The vitality that can stand the abyss of meaninglessness is aware of a hidden meaning within the destruction of meaning.*'

"And that, you go on, is faith, but, you reason correctly, Faustus has no faith. He is simply a Godless materialist who will do anything to acquire power. The world is crawling with people like that—the morally damaged, the politically ambitious. He's a great example of Original Sin—Luciferian Pride."

"Yes, I wrote that," Lemeilleur beamed.

"And what about you, Lemeilleur?"

"Me? I have faith."

"What about trust?"

"What do you mean?"

"Do you trust us?"

"Sure—why?"

"I think we have to test that. I want you to delete all reference to Tillich in this paper."

"Why?"

"He's Protestant."

"I have to think about that."

"In that case, you will stay in your room until your decision is made. We will bring you your meals."

"But . . . why?"

"I just told you."

"But my paper is not about religion. It's about literature. I'm not discussing *ex cathedra* matters. I'm talking about a character in a play. An egomaniac. He put Desire first. He sold his future for the present. Adam's shadow is all over him."

"We are footing the bill for your training, and we have rules around here. We never quote Protestant philosophers. Anyway, your father warned us about your reading."

"My father!"

"Go to your room and decide."

That night Lemeilleur wrote Mice to tell him what had happened—how his father—500 miles away—had blown his scene.

34

Sitting in his room day after day, looking at his scraps of paper with Tillich's sentences, Lemeilleur wondered what the hidden Meaning within the destruction of Meaning was that kept us out of the abyss of Meaninglessness. Of all the sentences he had written down when he read Tillich, why did he pick that one?

He thought and thought about it and decided. When he read that sentence, he thought God was the hidden Meaning within the destruction of Meaning. That's why he used the sentence. Fuck—this was a seminary.

Father Raimond had said this was a test. Maybe this was God's moment for him. Maybe he could become a saint. He could get very emotional when he prayed before the tabernacle. And so, sitting there in his room, he became convinced God was going to send him a sign, like St. Paul. He would have been happy to delete Tillich—he was happy at the seminary. He wanted to stay. He'd never felt better. He'd be a good priest. Please, God, save me.

But days passed and no sign. Hell, he realized, is the place where there's no escape—all realities have limits, and that's hell—that's why we have illusions. Damn, God wasn't going to save him. Lemeilleur sighed. His father was right: Lemeilleur was fucked, which infuriated Lemeilleur. He had to save himself—but shit—he didn't want to leave—he was happy here. His life was turning into his new song—he didn't want that song to be the song of ex-saint Lemeilleur.

That night Lemeilleur let the horses of the night run softly through his troubled soul—a decision was coming—and he believed a magic carpet awaited him. Was he "picking up" the vibes emanating from the "inspiration stump" of Lily Dale across the lake? Why did he think he was special? Did Mice write back to him? Were they keeping Mice's letter from him? Would they really throw him out?

One night, which turned out to be his last night at the seminary, he stumbled over a passage in the Bible: Job 13: 1-4, 12-21. *Your maxims are proverbs of ashes, your defenses are defenses of clay. Let me have silence, and I will speak, and let come on me what may. I will take my flesh in my teeth, and put my life in my hand.* That was his sign—he wasn't going to sell his soul for free room and board in this seminary. Lemeilleur continued to refuse to delete Tillich.

The next day, as he packed his bags, he received a letter from Mice. He stuffed it in his pocket to read on the long train ride home.

35

Brother John drove him to Fredonia that morning. A sonorous snow storm roared. It took hours. Fortunately he liked Brother John, who'd given him his haircuts.

"We're sorry to lose you. Father Raimond says you have a lot to offer."

"I liked it here—I really did, and believe me I don't want to leave either, but I'm not good at obedience. I have a problem with authority, as they say."

"Yeah, that's important here."

"Where'd you grow up, Brother John?"

"Me? Like you, Nouvelle Bouville."

"Go away. Are you kidding?"

"Nope—grew up on Grafton Street. My father was a shoe salesman, but he really wanted to be a boxer. My mother was a secretary for an insurance company. Her big dream was to have a garden before she died."

"Did she get it?"

"Naw, my father died of a heart attack when I was a kid. She had to take care of me."

"How did you become a brother?"

"It just happened."

Lemeilleur looked out at the snow storm. He hadn't realized how good a driver Brother John was. They were driving through a tunnel of crazed white flakes.

"What do you mean?" Lemeilleur asked.

"I wasn't exceptionally good in school. I was angry my father died. But I was a rather good athlete, so I started hanging around gyms. I got fairly good at boxing. My coach thought I was Golden Gloves material. I was in love with Cassius Clay. But my mother didn't like what I was doing. She thought I was throwing my life away. What life? Anyways, we were at each other's throat. I moved out and we stopped talking. I kept winning fights, but I never saw my mother again."

"What happened?"

"She died—of cancer."

"I'm sorry."

"Yeah, me too."

"Did you stop boxing after that?"

"What—you think I'm a genius?"

"So what happened?"

"I waited till I got beat up so bad, I ended up in a hospital."

"Is that when you decided to join the order?"

"You really think I'm a genius, don't you?"

Lemeilleur was starting to think Brother John was his sign from God—his genius. Maybe he'd return to the seminary with him? Maybe Brother John, who was unfazed by the blinding turbulence of the storm around them, understood the Meaning of life?

"Okay—then what?"

"Went to barber school—became a barber."

"When did you become a brother?"

"My mother left me her life insurance—a hundred K."

"That's a lot of money."

"Yeah, but I didn't feel like spending it. All I could think of was my mother and her garden. I got so sad, I couldn't leave my house."

"It got that bad?"

"Before my mother died I was doing a lot of dead-end jobs and drinking at bars every night and getting into fights. One night I hit a cop and threw him through the plate glass of a storefront window. When the cops got me to the station, they took turns flushing my head down the toilet. I started praying after that. I knew I was a failed human being. I did my ninety days in jail and when I got out, my mother was dead."

"That's when you became a brother."

"One day many months later, I woke up from my depression, and walked all the way to the college. I told them I wanted to make a donation and join the order."

"Just like that."

"It worked out for me. It stopped my depression. I feel good now."

"Tell me what you know—about life."

"Me? Life? I don't know much."

"What do you tell yourself when things get hard?"

"Well, we all live in anguish. Ah, humankind is a riddle. And life is like this snow storm: we just have to drive through it."

Maybe Brother John was Lemeilleur's genius. Lemeilleur,

if he had a good reason, was still ready to delete Tillich. Wasn't he looking for a miracle? Maybe Lemeilleur had misunderstood the proverbs of ashes. Visibility was less than ten feet, and Brother John cruised onward, sublimely indifferent.

"You know, Brother John, I have to tell you. I started thinking I was a saint at the seminary. I never thought about sex all the time I was there."

"We put saltpeter in the food."

Saltpeter was not part of any illusion Lemeilleur wanted for his future. He just couldn't go on believing he was turning into a saint after Father Raimond, who looked like Georges with his butch haircut and big arms, had so unspiritually tried to control his mind—no—his soul! Lemeilleur was no longer interested in their ancient blueprint of salvation.

Lemeilleur watched Brother John's car fishtail back into the storm of large weltering snowflakes and vanish. A cold shiver shuddered through his body—fear had stopped him for a second with the thought he was going back to Nouvelle Bouville.

⦿

As the train rattled back to Nouvelle Bouville, Lemeilleur took Mice's letter out and read it.

"Cher ami de combat,

Come home, Speedoo. I miss you. And take that *brume sur l'âme* (fog around your soul) away. This is your *dies Faustus*. (lucky day) Christianity is not your genius. Think about it, Lem. Two thousand years— what have they given to the world? Joan of Arc? Galileo? Nazi Pope Pius XII? Idiots. Don't forget your Rimbaud.

'Christ! Oh Christ, eternal thief of energies!'

Fuck your father. He gives 'one hour to God, the rest to the devil,' which gives him permanent 'indigestible agony of mind.' He's the fat angel-faggot of the walking dead pretending to live in bouzawzy paradise, trying to keelhaul you into average American; he's an asymptomatic carrier of Philistinism. To that cockerel strutting on a dunghill: *le doigt d'honneur* (the middle finger). Don't worry. Someday you'll expel your father the way your body expels waste. I'll help you find your genius, and it will be a she, and you will sleep with her under a bedspread of Russian ermine.

From *une nature d'élite* (a noble nature),
M"

That letter made Lemeilleur think: Behind that little gold door of the tabernacle was the spirit of a genius that Catholics thought they had captured. And every once in a while they trotted that spirit out in a symbolic play called the Mass. Poor Christ, locked in a box of gold, waiting for people with saltpeter in their blood to love him. As the train rattled on, Lemeilleur decided he was wrong about Faustus—he was a martyr of the Renaissance because he valued knowledge more than his identity—his I AM—to understand the hidden Meaning in the destruction of Meaning—that was his tragedy: Valuing knowledge as more important than believing in himself.

Lemeilleur was right about the proverb of ashes: The hidden Meaning in the destruction of Meaning can only be found in the assertion of one's identity—being true to one's Self is the only Meaning in a universe with no Meaning.

Getting off the train in Nouvelle Bouville, thoroughly disgusted with the Catholic Church, Lemeilleur wondered again about himself: Did he give up his soul to understand this world when he, Faustus-like, took what he got from Georges?

When Lemeilleur got home that night, his father was in a bad mood. He swore at the TV and said, "The vote! For chrissake we let them go to school."

When he saw Lemeilleur, he turned off TV. His father was disgusted. "Don't you ever forget, Lemeilleur, you're not French-Canadian—never were—you're American." Then Alcide started to walk away, but he stopped short and turned and said, "I knew you'd never become a priest. Look at all the money you wasted. You'll become an undertaker, mark my words."

That night Lemeilleur, who had played Macbeth in the drama club at the seminary, wrote in his journal: "Stars, light your fires, see my simple and deep desires," because, unlike Macbeth, Lemeilleur's ambition was not going to drive him to kill the King. Nor was he going to make the same mistake as Faustus. He was proud of his ambition—it would drive him to find the King within.

END OF PART ONE

II

"The gift is torment. Not alone the still
Torture, isolation; or torture of the flesh,
That may come also. But the accepting wish,
The whole and fertile spirit as guarantee
For every human freedom, suffering to be free,
Daring to live for the impossible."

—Muriel Rukeyser

1

Lemeilleur, back in Nouvelle Bouville, fell in love on his first day at Classical High School. He had quit the Church and resumed his education at a public school, which his father approved, and in keeping with his damaged character, he fell for a tall, big-boned, feminine Syrian—a very funny girl. Simran was delivering a report without notes on *The Vicar of Wakefield*, which Lemeilleur had never read. Immediately Lemeilleur noticed she had the kind of mind that can see the whole alphabet at once. It was a way of assessing intelligence that Georges had shown him in a book by Virginia Woolf. All parts of *The Vicar* were accessible to Simran simultaneously. So, as she rambled on, she took advantage of her omniscient perspective to juxtapose—with a kind of sublime irony—one incident after another to hilarious effect—and the class was roaring.

Finally, Miss Oslander shut her down with the quip, "I'm glad, Simran, I didn't assign his comedy, *She Stoops to Conquer*; I don't think we could have survived **that** report." And Simran, as she sat down, mumbled, *The beast retires to its shelter, and the bird flies to its nest; but the helpless man can only find refuge in his fellow creatures.*

With those words Lemeilleur, without hesitation, fearlessly entered a state of leporine (resembling a rabbit; a *Lolita* word) fascination. Simran loved books! The undaunted rabbit in him was mesmerized by the sleeping snake in her. In his borderline state of phantasm, he imagined this first meeting had been arranged by wiseass angels who wanted to goad him into a fatal move. He smiled. There was no such thing as telepathic communication. He chalked this rendezvous up to the crisp charm of chance. Love, after all, was fundamentally unexplainable. He knew his *Lolita*.

At last, her jade green, snake-still eyes fell on him, but Lemeilleur, still cozy in his fantasy, couldn't tell if she actually saw him. Was her indifference serene or indolent?

She looked away, and he was deeply disappointed. A streak of dread, he would write later in one of his hundreds of notes, runs through all bliss—that's life—there is no freedom without risk. His worldly sophistication was improving.

2

Months went by and there was nothing Lemeilleur could do to get her attention, at least within the normal realm of social intercourse, and he wasn't ready—yet—to go *mondo bizarro*. Hey, he was in all honors classes. Why blow his scene for what might be an unattainable fantasy? He wasn't crazy. He had all his marbles; he just couldn't control the game they were playing.

Simran seemed to be wrapped up in her own world, biding her time with established friends, like anxious Agnes, until, Lemeilleur calmly postulated, Simran got into some ivy-league school and skedaddled out of Nouvelle Bouville. Though reluctant to act, his fantasy did not abate. His leporine fascination only swelled. Simran, as chthonic (belonging to underworld—*Lolita* word) dream, was definitely caloric.

Lemeilleur asked around and found out Simran considered herself an existentialist. Always excited by a big word, Lemeilleur looked up existentialism and marched over to EPHRAIM's bookstore to steal a book of plays by Sartre.

Boris was in honors French as were Simran and Lemeilleur. Boris, who had been at Classical for three years, told Lemeilleur what Simran was like.

"She's the genius of Classical High. She gets 'A's like a dog gets fleas."

"What do you think her I.Q. is?"

"Gotta be 150 at least. I heard she wants to be a writer. By the way, she ain't no Dolores: Her friends call her 'The Virgin Genius'."

The Virgin Genius—Lemeilleur loved that. The BMI (body mass index) of his fascination now, unhealthily, approached obesity.

"Hey, Lem, did you ever see Dolores again?"

"No," Lemeilleur lied.

"You know she's dead?"

"Yeah, I heard—suicide."

"Her aunt put her in that convent in Marlboro."

"Yeah, Mice told me."

"Drank iodine."

"I know. I feel bad about that. Can we change the subject?"

"Don't worry. Simran's no Dolores."

℗

Months later, at the end of the last day of school, morbidly fattened on his fantasy and more smitten than ever, Lemeilleur tailed The Virgin Genius to her bus stop. From a doorway, as he spied on his underworld fascination, his bunny-nose twitched, but he couldn't bring himself to do what he had planned. Finally her bus came, and, as she was climbing aboard, he threw caution to the wind and hopped up to her.

"You want to write a play together?"

On the third step up, Simran turned, recognized him, and said, "What will the title be?"

"*No Exit*," Lemeilleur shouted, his ears pointed outward.

She smiled and said, "Nice title, but it's been done before."

His ears flattened, and the bus door slammed in Lemeilleur's face. *Huis Clos.* (No Exit)

3

Lemeilleur was walking home slowly from school and in his head he composed a long letter to Mice, who was now working for the *Telegram & Gazette* as a cub reporter for **Police Notes**. Mice had been accepted to every college he'd applied, but none had given him a scholarship. Since Mice didn't have enough money to go to UMASS, he decided to continue to save money and go there next year. Mice was terrified of going into debt. To Mice the black hole of capitalism—the weapon of choice for class oppression—was debt.

Lemeilleur was still upset that Simran had rejected him at the end of last school year at the bus stop. His letter's theme would be: Other people are hell. Mice would like that. They both had read *No Exit*, which takes place in hell. "Choice of action—our freedom—forget the anxiety—creates our existence," Mice had shouted at him. "You decide: Hell or Freedom!"

"Have you decided, Mice?"

"Of course! Hell."

For months Lemeilleur puzzled over Mice's response.

Lemeilleur, however, wasn't doing all that good in school—Bs and Cs with an A in French; still he was convinced he was special. He started writing stories again—anything that happened to him he wrote down and turned into a story. The rabbit in him was certain he'd write something that would—someday—get Simran's attention.

As Lemeilleur continued to walk in gloomy hopefulness, a car, its top down, pulled up to the curb next to him, a racing green MG. A perfectly round head that belonged to a chubby driver, who turned out to be the brother of someone Lemeilleur had known in grammar school, called out to him. Joe was getting his master's degree in Communications at Boston University. His father owned a small insurance company, and his mother was a drug addict—painkillers. Lemeilleur thought she'd know other people were hell.

"Hop in; I'll drive you back to French Hill."

Lemeilleur hopped in.

"My brother used to talk about you all the time."

"What kind of things did he talk about?"

"Well, he was impressed you read French books, that you had lots of girls, and told stories."

"Yeah, so?"

"It's a little unusual—I mean, you know, for this neighborhood—mostly illiterate psychopaths," he said, rolling his eyes in his round head. "Most of the families around here," he continued, "come from St. Hyacinthe."

Lemeilleur didn't say anything as they cruised up Grafton Street; he wasn't interested in French-Canadian genealogy. He was looking at the old Metropolitan Cleaners neon sign— some fucking Indian was shooting an arrow at something.

"Some friends of mine are going to have a party this weekend. I thought you might want to go—lots of liquor, marijuana, girls, and no working class slobs."

"Who's your friend?"

"Freddy. He teaches psychology at Clark. He's counter-cultural; listens to Jean Shepherd every night on the radio. Freddy loves Jean's rants about the 'silent majority,' you know, Jean's the guy who calls all those Nixon supporters 'slobsville.'"

"Sure, count me in. Where's the party?"

"On Pleasant Street, over the Fine Arts movie theater, where they're playing the new Andy Warhol movie, *Blow Job*. I'll give you a ride."

Then he looked at Lemeilleur and rolled his eyes again, which were beginning to make Lemeilleur dizzy.

"Hey, you know where hyacinth comes from?"

"No."

"Apollo fell in love with Hyacinth." He paused, and then breathlessly added, "You do **know** Apollo was gay."

Lemeilleur wondered why Georges had never told him that.

⊕

When Lemeilleur got home a cousin who had just gotten out of boot camp at Fort Dix was standing in the living room. He was wearing a brand new uniform and telling Lemeilleur's father how happy he was in the Army.

"They gave me a test—I think it was I.Q.—and I scored 85. I never did that good in school."

Lemeilleur's father looked at his son as if to say, Can you

do better? Then his father grabbed his cousin's hand and shook it, saying, "I'm proud of you, son."

That "son" was meant to hurt Lemeilleur. Fuck him. Lemeilleur went to his room to finish reading *Silent Spring.* He was against toxins in the environment.

The next day his father asked Lemeilleur if he remembered his friend Tony.

"Years ago—he delivered papers—used to live off Wall St.—why?"

"I'm receiving his body this afternoon. He was killed in Vietnam. There's no next of kin. He's the first one from this city. There'll be news reporters here for the funeral. The Mayor's coming. It'll be all over TV. That kid's gonna make me rich."

4

Lemeilleur hoped Freddy's party would rouse him from the torpor of his academic blues and Simran's rejection. His father was delighted Lemeilleur's grades were average. Behind his father's glee was the thought: You're not as smart as you think, Lemeilleur. You'll become an undertaker yet. Lemeilleur wished and dreamed Simran would be at Freddy's party. He had this irrational belief Simran could take away what he called his *mal du siècle* (evil of the century), though he wasn't sure what *le mot juste* (the right word) was for his *cafard* (apathy). He didn't know it then, but Simran was his rescuer-fantasy. All kids like him have one. Lemeilleur dreaded that he was ordinary—one of the slobs like his father—who keep this quasi-human world going—squish, squish through the muck—by burying people at high prices. No. He wanted to be an *Ubermensch,* the ideal superior man of the future who transcends established morals and prejudices in order to define his own purpose and values in life. Yup, good ole Georges had introduced him to Nietzsche. That would be the stuff of his song.

"Hey, Lemeilleur—nice name," Freddy said as he handed Lemeilleur a beer. "Here we are—all the glitterati of Nouvelle Bouville," Freddy laughed. "We're celebrating our doom. We're just as imperialist as Rome. And the same barbarians will take us down. Drink up. To the end of yet another civilization. To America!"

Lemeilleur met two people that night that he would see again—Michael, a twelve year old flirt of undeniable vitality, and Aaliyah, a lovely shy thing with a splendorous, Joan Baez smile.

"They told me you were a writer," Michael schmoozed.

"Who told you that?"

"Fat-headed Joey."

"That's not nice."

"I'm not nice—hey, you **are** perceptive!"

Lemeilleur got stoned with Michael and they kissed, and Lemeilleur thought that was perfectly normal. But Michael didn't stay around long—within minutes he was in Freddy's bedroom getting stoned with someone else.

"The Times They Are A-Changin'," Mice's favorite song at that time, was blaring and everybody was stoned and drunk and talking politics—racism and the war. For a moment Lemeilleur's memory fixated on Simran's fascinatingly untender gaze—would it, he complained to himself in one of his notes, toy despotically with him forever? How fucked was he?

Lemeilleur walked over to a pretty girl and when she looked at him, he said, "Don't say a word." Then he quoted Henry Miller, *Words are loneliness*. He knew it was corny, but Aaliyah responded, *And writing is the solitude of death*. Whew. And he said, "Who said that?"

"Kafka, I think."

She was attending Classical too, but she was in a different honors class, so they didn't know each other. She was going to study poetry at Brandeis in September, and she was into Rimbaud.

After the party, Lemeilleur told Aaliyah about Rimbaud's

life—which he knew better than his own—as he walked her home. She was appalled by Rimbaud's gun-running and slave-trading. She'd only read "Drunken Boat" and didn't know much about his biography. Could a great poet do evil was the energetic topic of their conversation. She thought so, but Lemeilleur said poets were holy. Not resolving that profound issue, their passion moved on to less complicated matters.

They kissed on Chamberlain Parkway. What a setting, Lemeilleur thought—a lovely, tree-lined street with big, fat houses. They were kissing near her home. An hour passed and they were both hot and bothered. Lemeilleur's fevered hands were all over her body. He'd heard Jewish girls didn't have the same feelings about sex as Catholic girls. He was dizzy with freedom as sensuality engulfed him.

She broke away and apologized.

"It won't work. It would break my mother's heart. You're not Jewish."

"I could convert."

"Don't make light of my mother's feelings. My father died four years ago. She's all I have."

"I'm not. I stopped being Catholic over a year ago."

"How did that happen?"

Once again he resorted to a Henry Miller quote. *I found God, but he was insufficient.*

"Damn you," she said, semi-sorry to be conquered, "meet me after school on Wednesday, on the Chatham Street side. There're fewer people there."

As Lemeilleur walked away, she shouted, "Hey, did you hear about Medgar Evers?"

5

Joe was wild that Lemeilleur had kissed Michael. But when Lemeilleur told Mice about the party, he mentioned only Aaliyah and her interests, not Michael, and Mice said: "She's into Rimbaud, huh? That's good. We're different, Lem. We know there's such a thing as Justice. We know some of us can rise above Desire—look at Gandhi. We know that Truth exists."

Lemeilleur could tell—Mice was warming up for some kind of declaration.

"What the hell are you high on?"

"Possibility."

"Possibility?"

"The times are a-changing. The class structure is breaking down, Blacks are moving up, and college kids are tired of their fathers' wars. Conservatives are freaking out. Maybe this Aaliyah can help you. In fact, I think she's going to be your genius. We must dwell in possibility. This song goes out to my love-starved friend, Speedoo!"

And Mice started to sing.

I have heard of an island
Where young lovers often go

Lemeilleur wanted to tell Mice there's a thing out there called reality, and it's doing things to us—things we don't want to happen. But he knew Mice wouldn't listen. Still, things were happening. Outside of us, that's how Tony died. But Mice kept on singing. There were things inside of us too: Fear, self-hatred, passions—we're not born free.

I wanna go (go, go)
I wanna go (go, go)

Lemeilleur gave up: he loved it when Mice got crazy hopeful. Lemeilleur joined Mice to finish the song.

I dream I hold you tight
On an island, yes an island of love

6

Michael easily found Lemeilleur's house—the **Ducrotte Funeral Home**—the sign had letters that were three feet high—where Lemeilleur was living in the attic. This was before Marie LaJoie moved in. Lemeilleur had a separate entrance and could come and go as he pleased. His parents were discouraged, and to some extent they blamed themselves for their son's irresponsible behavior. As for Lemeilleur, he only wanted to be independent—he was still nibbling gingerly on reality in this, his caterpillar stage of development.

When Lemeilleur opened the door, Michael—breathlessly—told Lemeilleur that he needed a place to crash because his mother had taken up with a junkie, and they were driving him crazy.

"I just can't stand their sex sounds—they're sooo straight—all that bang, bang shit."

Lemeilleur wasn't sure he believed him, but Lemeilleur let him stay.

Since they slept in the same bed, they had sex—a wonderful, uncomplicated romp that lasted two or three days. Then Michael disappeared as mysteriously as he had appeared. Lemeilleur had enjoyed himself immensely, and for the first time in his life he wondered if he was queer, which threw his identity up in the air.

7

With Lemeilleur flipping out about Michael, Lemeilleur invited Mice on his first date with Aaliyah, and to Lemeilleur's relief they liked each other. Nonetheless lingering doubt continued to molest Lemeilleur's fragile image of himself: What the fuck am I doing? Could Aaliyah love me? Could I love her? What was Michael? And why was

I dreaming about Simran? Why do I always have so many desires on my plate?

⟠

To Lemeilleur's relief, they all became friends, and one night Mice and Lemeilleur decided to go down to EPHRAIM's bookstore to steal. Mice wanted a copy of *The Beautiful and the Sublime* by Kant, and he asked Lemeilleur if Aaliyah wanted to go.

Lemeilleur was worried that Aaliyah might get upset if they stole books from a Jew, so he asked Aaliyah. It was alright. She was cool; she wanted a copy of *Gogol's Tales*, which turned out to be two volumes, and Lemeilleur still hadn't read *On the Road*.

Off they went, in Mice's car. On the way to EPHRAIM's, Mice, who was in one of his weird moods, Lemeilleur noticed, proposed they play a word game. Aaliyah was super excited. Lemeilleur, still jittery, was happy that Mice didn't tell her that she was going to be Lemeilleur's genius. Mice said he would say a word and they would have to come up with a synonym with the same Greek or Latin root within three seconds.

"Amative"

"Enamored," Lemeilleur screamed. And Aaliyah said, "Oh my God. Paramour."

"Hey, that's great, Aaliyah," Mice said.

Yeah, fucking great. What the fuck, Lemeilleur said to himself, is he coming on to her?

"Miscellaneous," Mice roared.

"Promiscuous," Aaliyah shouted.

"Miscegenation," Lemeilleur hung in.

Hey. This was getting serious.

"Carnivorous," Mice shouted.

"Carnage," Lemeilleur threw out as he struggled with his doubts about Mice.

"Carnation," Aaliyah screamed in glee.

"Carnation?" Lemeilleur questioned.

"Yeah," Mice said, "flesh-colored. You're good, Aaliyah."

"Hey, have you read Rimbaud, Mice?" Aaliyah asked.

Mice swerved to the side of the road, stopped the car, and opened his glove compartment, from which he pulled out *The Anchor Anthology of French Poetry from Nerval to Valery in English Translation* edited by Angel Flores. Lemeilleur had the same one at home. Mice opened to page 105 and started to read—very solemn:

O pale Ophelia. Fair as snow.
You died, child, yes, carried off by a river.
Because a wind, tearing your long hair,
Bore strange shouts to your dreaming spirit;
Because your heart listened to the strains of Nature
In the wails of the tree and the sighs of the night.

Because the voice of mad seas, immense rattle,
Bruised your child's heart, too sweet and too human;
Because on an April morning, a handsome pale courtier,
A sorry fool, sat mutely at your feet.

Heaven. Love. Freedom. What a dream, O foolish girl.
You melted toward him as snow near the flame:
Your words were strangled by your visions

—And the terrible Infinite frightened your blue eyes.

"Be careful, Aaliyah; this poem is a warning," Mice said as he put the book back. Then he looked directly at Aaliyah, "One day you will be on fire—you will have wrenched yourself from the emptiness of human existence—and you will soar. But never forget there is no 'forever.' You will return a pale ember of a smoldering passion—only suffering lasts."

Mice then hung his head like an exhausted priestess presiding over the Apollonian oracle at Cumae.

What the fuck was wrong with him, Lemeilleur said to himself, you're talking to my genius.

"Come on, Mice. Don't be a party pooper," Lemeilleur said.

"By hanging with us, you've entered the unknown, Aaliyah."

"Don't pay attention to him, Aaliyah. He's gloomy tonight."

Aaliyah looked at Mice, then Lemeilleur, and with gleaming eyes said, "Let's go steal books."

⫘

Driving back from EPHRAIM's, The Sheppards came on the radio, and they all sang *Island of Love* together.

I wanna go (go, go)
I wanna go (go, go)

They were all so goofy and happy then.

When they got home—after they dropped Aaliyah off—Lemeilleur started to freak out. He was thinking about Michael again, and Lemeilleur asked Mice:

"Do you like me?"

"Cut that gay shit out, Lem. You're fucking Speedoo. You can't forget that. Stay with Aaliyah."

"What's the gay shit? I just wanted—"

"—I'll tell you what I think, Lemeilleur. A caterpillar that sets out to know itself would NEVER become a butterfly."

8

As soon as Joe heard the news, he rushed over to tell Lemeilleur.

Michael was dead.

After a long night dancing at *The Punch Bowl*, Michael was

found in the Fens, shot in the head.

Joe P. was hysterical. Lemeilleur was sitting in Joe's MG, which was parked in the funeral home parking lot.

"He was only 13," Joe cried.

Lemeilleur couldn't bring himself to tears, but he was astounded by Michael's death. He could never fathom the sudden disappearance of life. He was in awe of death. It was one of the reasons he hated living at the funeral home. DEATH. It pushes your face hard against the window of life and makes you see how little there is to existence.

"Jesus, he was a beautiful boy," Joe moaned.

Love and death were the two things in life Lemeilleur could not abide. He was sorry Joe had brought this news to him. He just wanted Joe to go away. He had enough on his plate with Aaliyah and Mice.

As Lemeilleur put his hand on the door handle to leave, Joe got more upset and threw himself at Lemeilleur and kissed him on the lips. Just at that moment Lemeilleur's father drove into the lot and his father's car lights flashed on them as his car swung into the driveway.

HIS FATHER SAW JOE KISS LEMEILLEUR.

9

The next morning, two guys in tan overcoats knocked on Lemeilleur's door. They knew Lemeilleur's name and showed him their badges—CID from the Army. Whatever the hell that was.

"You're going to have to go with us."

"What's this about?"

"We'll tell you down at the station."

"The police station?"

Walking through the station, Lemeilleur saw Mice, who was still doing **Police Notes**. Lemeilleur stiffened and acted as if he didn't know Mice. Lemeilleur was quite sure the CID guys didn't notice.

A minute later they were seated and asking Lemeilleur questions about his identity—name, address, does your father own a funeral home, did you ever work at St. Anthony's? A local cop came in to say he knew Lemeilleur because his father had called in several times over the years when Lemeilleur had run away from home.

"Do you know a Georges des Rosiers?"

"Yyyeaaah," Lemeilleur said tentatively.

"You were . . . ah friendly with him, weren't you?"

"I haven't seen Georges in three years."

"Ya, we know."

"What's going on?"

"Did Georges own a black, two-door Chevy Impala?"

"Yyyeaaah."

"Were you ever in that car?"

"Yeah."

"Did he have sex with you before he drove you home?"

"Am I under arrest?"

"No."

"Will I be in trouble if I say yes?"

"No. All we want you to do is sign an affidavit in which you state Georges had sex with you."

"Do you have that affidavit?"

"It's right here."

"May I see it?"

"Sure."

It was a couple of pages long, had a lot of information about Georges, who was a private in the Army learning Vietnamese. There was little about Lemeilleur. On the second page it just said Georges had had sex with Lemeilleur many times over a two year period.

"Why do you need this?"

"We want to get Georges out of the Army."

"Are you going to put him in jail?"

"Not our call—just get him out of the Army."

"I have to think about that."

"Well, don't think too long, we're busy."

"I always like to take a minute before I wreck somebody's life."

"What about your life?"

"What are you talking about?"

"You never minded doing filthy things together; never behaving like ordinary people?"

"I learned a lot from Georges."

"Usually kids get upset with their abusers."

"I'm not upset with Georges."

If anything marked Lemeilleur as feral, it was his not feeling what happened between him and Georges was not normal.

"Look, asshole, Georges told us you seduced him. That you were having sex with boys and girls long before him. You're fucked, kid."

Lemeilleur signed the affidavit, and they looked at each other, laughed, and one of them said, "Don't you ever try to join the service."

10

When Lemeilleur got home his father told him they were going to his father's brother's bar. His father was feeling bad. "They' got the vote." And now his father needed a drink.

"We're going ta Tocard's bar."

A slow, not-much-happening Friday night and, so, while Tocard and his father drank at the bar, Lemeilleur, who was in a booth and sipped the beer his father had bought him, surreptitiously read Mice's copy of *Observations on the Feeling of the Beautiful and Sublime*. Between sentences, Lemeilleur dreamed how nice it would have been if he could have talked to Simran about Kant's book.

His father, after having a short but intense conversation with Tocard, came over and told Lemeilleur, who had slipped Mice's book under the table, he was going home. It was so abrupt Lemeilleur barely had time to hide Mice's book. Usually Lemeilleur's father stayed in a bar until he could barely walk, especially if someone else was paying for the drinks. Lemeilleur really didn't know Tocard. He thought his father was ashamed of Tocard. Lemeilleur couldn't remember a family visit with Tocard. Didn't matter, Lemeilleur was too anxious and confused; he didn't care what had happened between his father and Tocard: Those CID people had rattled him, and he was worried about what he would tell Mice about why he was at the police station. Fortunately Kant's book took his heavy heart away by promising he would—someday— understand beauty. Excitedly he read what Mice had underlined: *Whereas the beautiful is limited, the sublime is limitless, so that the mind in the presence of the sublime, attempting to imagine what it cannot, has pain in the failure but pleasure in contemplating the immensity of the attempt.*

The immensity of the attempt, Lemeilleur dreamed, as he felt a real communion with Mice.

"I'll take care of him," Tocard roared, and slapped Lemeilleur's father on the back to say goodbye. Lemeilleur's father gone, Tocard poured Lemeilleur a glass of scotch— Oban. Said it was the best drink in all of Scotland. Lemeilleur loved it and drank it down quickly. Tocard told the bartender, Emma, a woman of probably forty years or so, to cash out the register. In the meanwhile, Tocard shooed away the two or three remaining barflies. There was some grumbling, but they left. Lemeilleur's head began to spin, and Kant's words flew away, like frightened pigeons, with his ethereal contact with Mice.

"Give him another, Emma."

Sitting in a booth, Lemeilleur watched Emma put another Oban before him. He could see how shapely her body was and how short her skirt and how comely her bosom. But he knew he was drunk now. And the only thing he was clear about was how attracted he was to her. This was clearly the beautiful and not the sublime, he mused. He took another little sip and Emma just stood there, tantalizingly sexy as her body parts swirled in his head. Lemeilleur wanted to say something, just to let her know he thought she was attractive, but he was afraid he'd slur his words.

"Okay Emma," Tocard said after he had locked all the doors and stood next to Lemeilleur, "come over here."

⬤⬤

Later that night Tocard drove Lemeilleur home.

When Lemeilleur woke up in the morning, one of his eyes was inflamed. He went to the emergency room so his parents wouldn't know something had happened to his eye. After a little wait, a doctor pulled a pubic hair out of his eye. He then put some ointment into Lemeilleur's eye and told Lemeilleur he would be fine. Standing back, the doctor, man-to-man, gave Lemeilleur a Nabokovian wink.

⬤⬤

When Lemeilleur got home, his father, looking out the window, saw him coming, and ran downstairs to greet him.

"Hey, Lemeilleur. Welcome home. I hear you're real good with girls. I'm proud of you."

Lemeilleur lunged at him and pinned him against the wall in the hallway. His father was shocked. Lemeilleur couldn't stop. He put his arm around his father's neck and started to squeeze—with everything he had. His father started to choke. "I can't breathe." His father's arms were flailing. He was drooling. He fell to his knees. Lemeilleur was killing him.

I WAS KILLING HIM.

Lemeilleur let go. His father fell to the floor. Lemeilleur walked away, discouraged: He couldn't kill his father. What good was he if he couldn't kill his enemies? He wasn't as hard as he had to be. Maybe he **was** queer.

Later, in a calmer mood, he reasoned with himself. In the

eyes of the world, his father was a nice man, an upright, small Republican businessman, an ambitious member of the Chamber of Commerce, an honoree of Nouvelle Bouville's Harmony and Calumet Clubs, as well as a member of the State Funeral Directors Association, Nouvelle Bouville's Board of Public Welfare, French Hill Post American Legion, and Pope John XXIII Knights of Columbus where he was 4th degree. Killing his father would only have put Lemeilleur away permanently—he had no credentials of justice.

11

Believe it or not Lemeilleur went to summer school after he graduated from high school. He finally took that creative writing class with Mr. Wells that Classical High School offered every summer. He'd renewed his commitment to become a writer. He thought he had found his story, and Miss Oslander said Mr. Wells was the best teacher for creative writing.

Ever since his father had left him alone at Tocard's a year ago, Lemeilleur had been working on his story, and now that he'd written it, he couldn't wait to show Mr. Wells. Lemeilleur was convinced that what causes writers the greatest pain creates their greatest Meaning, and that became the center of what it means to be alive—Humbert Humbert was still Lemeilleur's hero.

Baseball

What's a young poet to think? I'd just finished *Crime and Punishment* and was extra alert to the moral shallowness of people. Take my birthday, which up to now, had never been celebrated: My mother was always depressed, and my father said he celebrated my birthday every day by working hard for me.

I saw very clearly my father's not so subtle expectations were meant to shape my sordid instar identity and force me to assimilate, become like everyone else because my father suspected my secret. I was going to be the next Raskolnikov. I would prove that sin had no dominion. That Man is Free. How could I tell my father I only felt safe when I was between the pages of a good book? My best friend is fiction!

With the ceaseless misgivings of a controlling authority, my father kept a vigilant eye on me, and practicing baseball would lead me, his baseball shagging, soul-shamming son, to normalcy. He'd be damned if I were permitted to deviate from the future of becoming an undertaker—the last one, as he joked, to let you down.

Under such sublunar circumstances Tocard, my father's brother, had offered to celebrate my birthday. My father had had little truck with Tocard since he had not repaid my father the five thousand dollars he'd borrowed to buy his bar five years ago. I should have been suspicious.

Jacqueline, my father's godchild, and Tocard's blind daughter, had sung the *Star Spangled Banner* to open a Red Sox game recently and had met all the players. Surely this wondrous event which, when I had heard all the details, would lure the chary, charading me into the higher calling of undertaking—the next best thing to being a baseball player.

"And when Jacqueline calls," my father yelled to my mother, "tell her how many candles to put on the cake."

"He's just a boy," my mother called out.

"And he's going to stay that way," my father shouted back.

She looked so vulnerable standing in front of his gray funeral home, her rough hands in her paisley apron, her thin shoulders hunched against the deforming distress in her soul: she had no say in the activities of her husband. All the Miltown she had taken over the years had worn her down, like her old apron, ragged.

"You know, son," my father said as he eased into the

traffic, "life is difficult. We are considered the Chinese of the Eastern States."

That was straight out of the *Twelfth Annual Report of the Massachusetts Bureau of Statistics of Labor,* written by Commissioner Carroll D. Wright: "With some exceptions the Canadian French are the Chinese of the Eastern States." My father was obsessed with identity, self-image, and ethnic pride. That was probably the hundredth time he'd said that to me—boring.

"Why would anybody want to work in a factory if he could play baseball?"

My father was a member of the Calumet Club, founded in 1922, which was a leading civic and social organization; its membership was resolutely restricted: no one engaged in an *occupation salissante* (work likely to dirty hands or clothes).

"Look at Louis, your mother's father; was he happy with his life? He worked like a dog and what did he have to show for it when he died? Nothing. Your mother did not inherit one red cent. Baseball will free you of all that. Look at me; I have the funeral business. There are no recessions with death." My father handled 85% of the murders in the city.

"I'm not looking for a job."

"You will be. I know you're sneaking around reading trash."

"I'm reading great literature."

"Henry Miller! He's obscene. Why can't you read *Anne of Green Gables?*"

"Never heard of it. *One's destination is never a place but rather a new way of looking at things.* Henry Miller said that."

"Oh yeah, I saw you reading his cancer book. What a joke. Look, I'm your father. I'm trying to help ya. Books destroy things. Books are like heroin: they get you hooked and ruin your life. Communism was started by a book. Look at what happened to France. Voltaire was queer. You have to find a woman and settle down and get married."

It was not that I didn't take my father seriously. I knew how much he had suffered, how he had scraped by, trying to save enough to buy the funeral home. But I was tired of his obsession with security. It was endless. In fact, ever since he started making money in the funeral business he had packed the freezer with steaks. Security! I was a different person. He has his destiny and I have mine. My friend Mice tells me Thomas Aquinas said, *If the highest aim of a Captain were to preserve his ship, he would keep in port forever.*

If my father ever sniffed out my plan, it would have brought a farouche froth to his delicate lips: I was going to become a writer. I had to bring down the system. Somebody should know about my life. I want someone to learn something from my life. Salinger called that poetry.

"Lemeilleur, have you thought of studying embalming? Don't say anything. You're . . . at your age . . . well, it's time to think about these things. It's an awfully hard course. Just like medicine, only it don't take so long. You're out there practicing in two years. Baseball is baseball. But this is real. Think about it, son. We could work together. You could have the funeral home eventually, and a wife. Now I said it. Don't say a word. Think. What are funerals buying, Lem? Dignity. You'd be helping others bring a little dignity inta somebody's sad life—dat's da beauty of capitalism—you can sell emotion. You know your father's father had a story he used to tell that I never told you. You know he was a great man, smart as a whip, a natural storyteller, you would have liked him. I want you to understand that. He was a great man. Don't you ever forget it. You hear? A good man."

Everybody knew what my father's father was like. He had broken my father's nose as a child. He had broken Tocard's arm when Tocard was my age.

"What's the story?"

"One day, my father, he must have been your age, ah,

about seventeen," (I was sixteen) "he went rabbit hunting. The old-timers they ate a lot of rabbit. We loved rabbit. My father's father made a living selling rabbit pelts. Well, my father was roving around in the forest—you never saw the forests in *Québec*; they are . . . how can I say it? . . . virginal . . . remind me to tell you about *la voix du pays* (a mystical concept in Québec—the voice of the country) . . . yes—and my father came upon—this was in October, which is a difficult month because everything freezes suddenly, then unfreezes just as suddenly. In one month *les Habitants* go from fickle fall to wicked winter—and he came across a gaggle of geese. During the night, the lake had formed a layer of ice. There must have been two hundred geese whose legs were frozen in the ice, trapping them. Your grandfather, seeing this terrible tragedy, went to the water's edge. He wanted to help these helpless creatures of God. After a moment he knew what he had to do. He took his gun down and started to shoot. Then he saw one goose. It seemed to frown at him. Your grandfather decided to get closer, and it hissed at him. Your grandfather raised his rifle and the goose honked so high—a wild, frightened honking—that he lowered his rifle. But the goose continued to honk, flapping his wings wildly. He raised his rifle to put an end to the poor bird's fear. But, as he aimed, the bird got loose. It began to rise majestically into the air. Your grandfather put his gun down and said a prayer, and he wasn't deeply religious, you know. But he thought that bird was a sign. Behind, in the ice, were the bird's legs.

"You know what the lesson is? Even if you survive, life takes something from you—something especially important."

"That's a good story."

"French-Canadians are good storytellers. You get it from your grandfather."

That was the nicest thing my father ever said to me. Now I knew I had to become a writer.

"You know, Lemeilleur, you're getting to be that age. I told your mother I'd tell you about sex."

I couldn't believe he'd trapped me in his hearse to tell me about sex.

"It's beautiful; the most beautiful thing God ever made. I can't explain that to you; it's a beautiful feeling. When it happens it's as if God put his glowing hand on your thigh. But only between married people—a man and a woman— that's important—that's how God made the world: between a man and a woman—that's why they call them WO man. It's short for womb. Your mother and me got something beautiful. We've felt God's hand hundreds—maybe thousands of times. Now one of these days you're gonna get a feeling."

"You mean love?"

"Ah, not exactly. But you're gonna want to do something about that feeling. Don't. It's a mortal sin and it drains your brains." Then he threw his head back like a satisfied bull moose after a vigorous rutting season.

"It turns people into idiots," he started to rant. "I seen it with my own eyes. It's a beautiful feeling—for married people—a man and a woman. I never touched no woman but your mother. I coulda had Femme, you know. I mean, look at her husband—no teeth. No, your father has more dignity than that. I always kept sex in the right place. I was a late bloomer, like yourself. When I was about twenty years old I was out in a boat with this girl. All I wanted was to talk about baseball. It's all I thought about then. She sees this island and says, 'let's go there.' 'What for?' 'To pick blueberries,' she giggles. 'But it's too dark,' I say. 'I know,' she agreed, 'but we'll have fun.' Fun? That's when I started telling her about Leo, the lip. When we finally got back to the boat landing, she jumped out of the boat, right into the water, and ran away. I was too dense to understand what she wanted. You get my drift?"

⊕

We arrived at *The Sportsman* around 7 pm. As I walked into the windowless bar, I felt dangerous insobrieties lurking in the shadows, and I was overwhelmed by a stout stink, and my eyes were forced to adjust to a room of gloom, dimly lit in red-garnet. My family was a book; my life a novel! This was a room Dostoevsky's Liza could have lived in. Once I got this down, on paper, the world-as-is would be blown away by the explosion of truth.

Over the bar a garishly colored sign of Marines raising a flag over Iwo Jima bellowed: "A vote for Tocard is a vote for responsebility. Vote Republican." The walls were covered with metal framed pictures of baseball players -- all signed.

"You see that?" My father bumped me with his arm.

"Ha. Alcide. Welcome to my palace of pleasures. Hahaha."

"Where's Jacqueline?"

"She's in the kitchen where she belongs. What's wrong with you? Here, have a drink. Emma," shouted Tocard, "a beer and a shot for my brother. Emma, a Moosehead and a jigger of CC." To my father, Tocard winked, "She does anything I tell her. Stop worrying."

"I just found out Cauchemerd's son is coming into the funeral business."

Cauchemerd owned the other funeral home on French Hill. My father's fear of Cauchemerd was profound and irrational, and it didn't help that Cauchemerd's son was gay.

"So?"

"For chrissake, he's college educated."

"What's a college kid know about death? You got years of experience on him."

The two of them seemed ill-assorted, like unmatched clothes after a washing. My father was about ten years younger than his brother, was lean, not thin, but tightly knit like a handmade scarf from *La Belle Province*. Whereas Tocard was pot-bellied and seedy, more like an unraveling sweater formerly for the Big Cold.

I glanced up from time to time and caught the changes of attitudes of the two of them the way one flicks through a series of drawings that become, upon flicking, animated. Stiff and standoffish changed to loosening up and the clicking of beer mugs to downright laughing and back slapping. They were agreeing about something and clicked their meer bugs.

Tocard was wearing a huge cross around his neck, which, he told my father, had been given him by the local parish, St. Innocent, for his good work, especially with the boy scouts.

"I'm practically a saint, Alcide. You can trust me," Tocard brayed, his big bull's eyes blinking madly while his head slumped down as if he were about to charge, and his lumpy shoulders pulled his moth-eaten sweater taut.

The drunk and relaxed brothers finally started to look at each other's faces, and then they began to laugh over God knows what. Maybe Tocard offered to pay my father back. The men talked about their respective businesses: "We drug 'em; you slab 'em."

My father reveled in the fact that he had gone from twenty-one funerals to sixty-nine in three months. Similarly Oncle swore his business was booming, though I couldn't see it from where I was sitting. Since I'd been there only a postman and a cop ("Good luck with the election") and a guy Tocard called "Duper" had come in for drinks.

I was cloistered in a wooden booth, reading with monk-like diligence. I had prepared a bag of books to keep me company, books I kept out of sight, of course. I didn't want an argument, or worse.

"So," laughed Tocard, "I'll take care of it? See, it's settled."

My father bit his lips.

"Come on, for God's sake, are we not Ducrottes?" shouted

Tocard. "I'll take care of things. I know what to do."

"So where's Jacqueline?" my father asked again, this time much more casually, as if he'd decided and was agreeing to something.

"Emma, see if Jacqueline's ready," Tocard shouted in a sharp, staccato brio, like a drill sergeant whose commands were unchallengeable.

My father was staring into his beer—intently—as if it could tell him something, like a crystal ball, and just then, I saw Jacqueline, my father's *filleule* (godchild), come through the back door, which led to Tocard's apartment. Happiness and discomfort struggled for my mien, because, as I said, my birthdays were never celebrated, and I didn't know how to act.

She walked unerringly toward me through the gloom. I squirmed. Jacqueline carried a cake with sixteen candles ablaze. Her simple face, illumined by the blaze, like a saint's, was the languorous lambency of a foreshadowing: *lambendo lingua genitalia?* O Caravaggio. I could see your painting of David holding what was supposed to be slain Goliath's head—but it was your head. The head you offered in your picture for a pardon, so you could be free of your crime. And now like David holding your head, I was offering my head for a pardon. I wanted to be free of all my crimes. Jacqueline put my birthday cake on the table next to the poem, "The Secret Heart", I was reading. Like all blind people, her pupilless eyes sought focus but her hands knew all the locations of the bar and she placed the cake exactly in front of me.

She then broke into song, the sound of a golden woodland nymph, I mulled immured by drink.

Her voice was strong, rich, and melodic. What God has taken from her eyes was given to her larynx. At the age of eight she had already sung at many public gatherings. Tocard was happy with her popularity at the bar. My father said she brought in all the business. Finishing "Happy

Birthday," she sat down opposite me.

"Are you really going to become an undertaker?"

She had a warm smile and small white teeth, her large ears cocked for the sound of my voice in order to focus her colorless eyes and aim her earnest face at me.

"What makes you ask that question?"

"I overheard my father talking to your father on the telephone."

"What did you hear?"

"Your father told my father that you were going to study undertaking and marry a girl."

"Did he say anything about baseball?"

"I don't think so."

"Does your father have a girl lined up for me?"

Jacqueline froze up and looked away. Finally she whispered.

"I can't tell you anything. My father would kill me."

Jacqueline's mother died at Jacqueline's birth. Her mother had had syphilis.

We ate cake and I wondered about my enigmatic cousin. She had spirit, intelligence, and warmth. My father called over to offer her a beer, which she declined politely. She whispered to me how she hated beer, but then she laughed, spreading her hands across the table.

"What is this?" She ran her small fingers over my books.

"'The Secret Heart', a poem. Can I read it to you?"

"I never had a poem read to me."

"It's by Robert Tristram Coffin."

Lemeilleur read the poem.

"That sounds," Jacqueline said, "like the son sees his father's love for him. I never heard of a thing like that."

"I don't believe this poem. I think it's claptrap."

"Yeah. Heart-shaped hands. A bunch of bunk."

I liked her a lot, but I thought I was too drunk to say anything remotely intelligent. I wished I hadn't been so drunk because I wanted to talk to her about my father.

Instead, though I didn't want to, I asked: "Did you really meet the Red Sox?"

"Yup. They gave me a signed baseball."

I changed the subject: "And you really sang the *Star Spangled Banner* in front of all those people?"

"Yup. They gave us a tape of it."

"And who signed your ball?"

"All the players. Pa got it for me. Do you want to see—"

"—Hey, Jacqueline, how about a piece of cake; it's the kid's birthday." Tocard barked.

If there were a hell, it would be like this: a dark and gloomy place on the edge of civilization.

"Did you finish the laundry?" Tocard barked again.

An ominous threat lurked cagily in the cadence of his question.

"No," her eyes fluttering like quaking aspens before a storm.

"Well, what are you waiting for?"

She slid slowly from the booth and said, "Goodbye, Lemeilleur," her kind face focused directly on mine, "and be careful." And I watched her disappear, engulfed by the cold shadows behind the bar.

The three of us stayed in the caliginous bar for the better part of an hour. I liked drinking beer—the analgesic buzz, the annulling of nervousness: it made my thoughts more pleasurable. I was reading *The Uninhibited Byron.* Neither Tocard nor my father knew what uninhibited was and neither knew who Byron was. I had decided again there was no God—only great artists. The points of view of artists are highly desirable for those of us who realize they are lost. On page seventy-nine I found a word I wrote in my vocabulary book: irrumation. I couldn't wait to look it up.

"Leave him here. Emma and me will take care of him."

Emma was expressionless as she washed glasses behind the bar. She, like Tocard, was in her forties. She had caffè oscuro eyes, ferruginous hair, pageboy style, premature white roots, a strong, wide mouth like a baby hippopotamus with flavid dentures, and a stocky sausage-like body balanced oddly, if not precariously, on two grallatorial legs. She wore a white dress like nurses do, and she rarely spoke. She had had cancer of the larynx Jacqueline had told me when I had asked her what was wrong with Emma's voice. It was in remission now, but her voice, when it made raspy sounds, conjured a Malagasy cutthroat living in the alleys of Paris—or so I thought in my ambrosially tipsy reverie.

"We'll give him supper and take him to a movie."

My father hesitated; he was looking at his bottle of Moosehead.

My father dropped his bottle. He didn't appear to know what to say. Tocard reached over to pick the bottle up. I was dreaming of inspiring glendoveers and soothing fomas over a foamy beer in a dark bar, alone, alone, alone.

"Just leave him here; I'll bring him home tomorrow. I'll take care of everything."

"Tocard, talk to him about burning his books. Someday he'll have to earn a living and provide for a family. Tell him about baseball. Ha. Ha. Make him a man."

As soon as my father left, Tocard chased the few remaining drinkers out and locked the doors.

"Emma, get over here. It's time to do what I told you. Take out your teeth."

The next morning Jacqueline had made breakfast when I entered the kitchen. She served me coffee. I was morose and ate little. How she maintained her brightness was a mystery I had to admire. Still, I could tell, by the way she looked at me, she knew I was hurting.

After breakfast Tocard, who was puttering around anxiously, went out to put some liquor in the trunk of his car. He told Emma, who was going back to the bar, to sprinkle carbolic on the floor; a couple of regulars were already waiting at the door. Jacqueline told me her father was in a bad mood: his ulcers were acting up.

When I rose to leave, Jacqueline was doing the dishes quietly. I wanted to say something to her, but I didn't know what. Did she know what had happened last night? Her father tooted the horn. I looked at her. I turned the door handle; looked back at her. I pulled the door open, and Jacqueline turned from the sink and said: "You wanna see my baseball?" And she pulled her ball out of her apron pocket and lobbed it in my direction. The ball I caught was grass-stained with no signatures. It looked and smelled like a bruised green tomato.

12

Mr. Wells asked Lemeilleur to talk after class.

"Come in. Sit down. I read 'Baseball'."

"I sent it to a contest at the *Columbia School of Journalism*," said Lemeilleur, "and they wrote back, 'Sorry we can't use this, but we hope you get the help you need.'"

"Hmm . . . they assumed your story was true, not fiction. I don't think that's fair. The You that writes is not the same as the You that lives. Don't they read Proust down at Columbia?"

Lemeilleur didn't say a thing because he hadn't read Proust—though mentally he just put the poor man on an ever-growing list of books to read.

"You know there's a novel in most of us, but few will take the time to develop the technical and moral skills to let it out. Having an interesting life can help a writer, but it will never make you a writer. Look, I liked it. It has power, but it's not publishable—not yet.

"You have to relax when you write, Lemeilleur, and you have to believe in yourself—not just your experience, and never doubt your intelligence. You don't need to impress anyone with your knowledge, vocabulary, or subtlety."

Lemeilleur smiled: Mr. Wells liked it.

"And if your main character is angry with his father, the author doesn't have to be angry with him. In fact, if you can't separate yourself from the story, it will never end. Stories may come from your heart, but they end with your brain—objectively, for reasons inherent in the story.

"Good writing is sincere—skip any urge to show off. Don't be afraid to tell the truth. Beating around the bush is a turn-off for readers. Understand your content, know you are going somewhere, then go to it—whatever it is—honestly—with all your heart. All the reader wants is to feel what the characters feel. You might become a good writer, but you have a raging content to control. With practice and determination you will do it. I wish you the best."

Mr. Wells looked long at Lemeilleur. Mr. Wells wasn't finished, but he was trying to figure out if he should go on.

"What is it, Mr. Wells?"

"There's something missing in your story. What's driving the father? Why's he taking the main character to Tocard's? Your story hints that this get together is pre-arranged. Why? You know, Lemeilleur, there are a lot of nice things about this story—the relationship between the father and the son is heartbreaking, but why?"

Mr. Wells uncrossed his arms and leaned forward.

"You, the author, appear to be fearless, but you're holding back, not telling the whole truth. You drop two big hints: "*lambendo lingua genitalia*, which I looked up: licking genitalia with tongue. And at the end of the story the main character wonders if Jacqueline knows what happened last night."

He leaned back in his chair.

"Something sexual happened, and I'm sure it's hard to get at emotionally, but if you don't get there, your story suffers. Think about it and find the courage to tell it. The hardest thing is to write about yourself because yourself is the thing you are most vulnerable about. Remember, a poem is just a group of words passing through a soul. The words don't stay there forever."

Mr. Wells. He never judged Lemeilleur. Never asked what happened that night. He also made Lemeilleur understand that becoming a writer was a lot harder than Lemeilleur realized. How would he ever tell the world this . . . black secret?

13

To Lemeilleur's surprise, Nouvelle Bouville Community College accepted him unconditionally. Aaliyah was thrilled because she had threatened to leave Lemeilleur if he didn't go to college. His father, on the other hand, was pissy—wanted to know who was going to pay for it. Lemeilleur told him he'd get a job, which Lemeilleur did, at a Cain's Potato Chip warehouse close to the college. Tuition was $125/semester and Lemeilleur was making $60/week, loading orders onto trucks, and he could write his stories on the back of Cain's Potato Chip order forms. What could Lemeilleur say—he lived in a perfect world. Life is a masterpiece.

14

That afternoon Lemeilleur got his first letter from Aaliyah who was now a student at Brandeis.

Dear Lemeilleur,

I'm in the sunroom, and the reality of your absence rankles in my soul like clattering chains that remind me of our status. Even with light streaming in between the flowers, I feel a cold shudder, an unearthly cold. I wish I could turn and tell my mother, who's reading The Fire Next Time. But I have to hide you from her.

Jewish people can be so narrow. I'm sure she'd like you. Her parents grew up in your neighborhood, you know.

You looked great yesterday. I'm sorry we couldn't see each other longer. Remember Esther, my sister? She just asked me how long we'd been seeing each other, and I answered five months. She was surprised it's lasted that long. It seems like only yesterday you showed me your copy of Madame Bovary and your switchblade from Paris that guy gave you.

I forgot to ask you: who's Dolores? You dreamed about her all that night—sounded like she died. We ate Chinese food, which you had never tasted before. We read Crime and Punishment all day long. I agree with you, Dostoevsky was more into the crime than the punishment. I love the way you think. I wish I were in my senior year of college. Then we could get married. I want to get married to you to see your features and expressions on our children's faces. Maybe this sounds too Doll-Housish for you. I don't deserve you. I'm so lucky.

—Love, Aaliyah

PS. Can't wait for your next visit. Please send me the phone number of the hotel you're living in. I'd rather talk to you than write letters.

15

On the first day of college, Lemeilleur met McVeigh—a 6'4" cherub-faced alcoholic, who, though he grew up in New London, Connecticut, was nothing like his crewneck sweater and Weejuns penny loafers.

McVeigh had transferred from St. Nominis Umbra College in Oklahoma and loved bar hopping on Fire Island, where he once got arrested by the Coast Guard for trying to swim to Connecticut.

Out of a room of thirty or forty kids, the second Lemeilleur walked in for orientation, he'd picked McVeigh to sit next to.

"Hi," Lemeilleur said.

McVeigh, off to himself, had a sour expression on his face that said, "What the fuck am I doing here," and he looked hung over. Why was Lemeilleur making friends with him? The world is organized around principles invisible to those of shallow self-knowledge, Lemeilleur wrote on the back of a Cains Potato Chip order form that night.

McVeigh barely moved his head and said, "What the fuck do you want?"

"I'll be thirsty when this is over. Want to get a brew after class?"

"Why wait. Let's go now."

"It's 10 am."

"Okies is open."

Well, getting liquored up before class certainly made college more palatable, but it had its drawbacks too. Like the time they had to do a demonstration speech in which Lemeilleur pretended to be a can of tomatoes in a variety store on a shelf across from the rack of dirty magazines.

Drunk, Lemeilleur stood in front of the class describing various people who stole looks into the magazines—you know, the timid, the perverted, the curious, and all the other slobs crippled by desires they couldn't satisfy.

Lemeilleur's professor, who sat in the back of the class, thought there was something wrong with Lemeilleur and asked Lemeilleur to sit down.

Without much ado, Lemeilleur unsteadily made his way back to his desk to relax. Public speaking made him super anxious—his nerves were running around like a business of ferrets.

McVeigh was up next, and he pretended to be a tennis instructor demonstrating how to serve a ball. Each time he threw the imaginary ball up into the air and brought his imaginary racket down to hit the imaginary ball, a tall redhead in the first row would pop his lips to indicate the ball was hit. For some reason, this irritated McVeigh.

McVeigh leaned over, and sotto voce, so the professor wouldn't hear, told the redhead to "cut the shit."

McVeigh then stepped back and threw the imaginary ball in the air and as the imaginary racket came down—POP.

McVeigh dropped the imaginary racket and leaned over and punched the non-imaginary redhead in the face. The redhead tried to get up, but McVeigh—quite drunk—swung at him again, missed, and hit another kid, who jumped up and hit McVeigh, which forced Lemeilleur into the fray.

⬤

That night there was a party, and McVeigh and Lemeilleur were treated like war heroes. Agnes, Simran's high school friend, was there, and she and Lemeilleur talked for a while. She was a business major at Babson now, but to save money, lived at home.

Around 1 am the party was running out of liquor. McVeigh told everyone not to worry. To Lemeilleur he said, "Let's go."

They walked a mile or so to a lone, closed package store. McVeigh took off his overcoat, rolled it around his arm, and smashed the front window.

"Jesus Christ," Lemeilleur yelled. McVeigh's arm was bleeding.

"Go the fuck in and get some beer. I'll take these whiskies."

Lemeilleur jumped in through the broken glass, got a case of cold beer, and they got out of there.

⬤

Back at the party they were greeted as war heroes again. McVeigh's arm needed stitches, but he refused to go to a hospital. Agnes did some butterfly thing with Band-Aids and the party went on.

Lemeilleur asked Agnes how Simran was doing at Wellesley.

"They're trying to turn her into a girl. They have compulsory tea to teach you how to be a diplomat's wife. And her roommate is boy-crazy. Her taste in men—straight out of *The Heart of Darkness*: the horror, the horror. Simran hates the place."

"Why doesn't she just leave?"

"Are you kidding me? Do you know how important this is to her father? He'd kill her."

"I got into college to spite my father."

"Wellesley's the only school that gave her a full scholarship—she lives for her father. They're Syrian—immigrants—no one's ever gone to college before. All their hopes—her father works two jobs—everything is invested in Simran. That's why they came to this country. Simran's the fucking American Dream. They live in a shoebox on Houghton Street."

"I used to live on that street."

"Never been there—they rent their attic—it's illegal I think—one exit or something."

"What number Houghton Street?"

"I don't know. Look, there's going to be a rally in Harvard Square next weekend. Tom Hayden is speaking, do you want to go?"

"Is Simran going?"

"Yes."

"I'll be there."

"Hey, I heard you write short stories. Will you read one to me?"

"Read her 'The Triumph of Tohu Bohu'," McVeigh yelled from across the room.

Lemeilleur knew the story by heart; still he took out a sheet of Cains Potato Chip order form and read.

The Triumph of Tohu Bohu

Flora Dross, my first muddle class girlfriend, stopped me, after two hours of lush titting, to ask me, after all these months, where I got my cars. Umm? An uncracked pair of lover's nuts, I moaned, amazed. I released the two mammoth mammalias—damn. Christ. I liked her. And anyways, it was in the AIR—the times were a changing. Fuck it. I tell her— I steal them. Wham. If the pox ain't on me. She turned harder, colder, and greener than the fucking Statue of Liberty. And, pulling down her Lord and Taylor turtleneck over those massive *mamelles de Tirésias*, (my pet was in a pet) she says, the same year fucking Chou En-lai calls for the abolition of "booboisie" ideology, "If you don't stop stealing cars, I'm going to break up with you."

Ha. And Lou Christie is doing "Rhapsody in the Rain" on the radio. Fuck this. I don't do boobsy deals. Freedom— that's it. Rockefeller free equals Lemeilleur free. Foreplay finito. I seek the fruit, not the peel, the kernel, not the husk. I've had the BODY. It's the SOUL I'm after. I've seen too many dead bodies.

Get this, Thralls—from the allodial mind of Tohu Bohu: Crime in America is the meek inheriting the dearth. DaDa, America. The wild boy of Aveyron is back. Hide your boobies. Only freedom matters.

With a brain blanker than a child's, I ran, watching the world suffer a triumphant Toho Bohu. This storm blessed me with oceanic awareness. I danced on the breakers—the endless rolls of victims. I watched without regret through the stains of vomitings, fused in my memory with the white milk of stars, as I coiled through the depths rapt and sad.

I sang the song of bitter rednesses of love's ferment. I saw all the versions of Vision.

I is another. If the brass wakes the trumpet, it's not its

fault. That's obvious to me: I witness the unfolding of my own thought: I watch it, I hear it: I make a stroke with the bow: the symphony begins in the depths, or springs with a bound onto the stage.

But my bubbled, comic-book thought is purfled in dreary determinism: LIFE IS A DRUNKEN BOAT. Fuck Nixon. Fuck Nixon. Fuck Nixon. We will not rest until Alpha kisses Omega.

"Fucking power to the people," McVeigh yelled, and the room broke out into a chant:

TOHU BOHU—TOHU BOHU—TOHU BOHU.

Next day, the president of the college—with local police— expelled Lemeilleur and McVeigh.

16

"Of course, I'd stick by you if you quit school," Aaliyah whispered into the phone from her dorm, "but I'd rather you didn't. You're too intelligent not to get a degree."

"My father found all the books I stole. He wants me to return them and make a public apology. Says I'm hurting his business."

"It only figures he'd want you to do it that way. Doesn't he realize you're his son?"

"I want to come to Brandeis with Mice next weekend."

"What's Mice really like?"

"He's a genius. He knows everything about injustice."

"I'm sorry last weekend didn't turn out as we planned. I know it is difficult for you to get rides. Next weekend is good. I hope you liked the book I sent you for your birthday. I want every Dominion of Angel to hear you. Keep writing; don't quit college. Lemeilleur, something occurred to me about your lying. I think you don't like to separate reality from your imagination. What do you think? Lem, are you still there?"

"I'm fine with reality—it's just hard to become what you are."

"That's very true. I can't wait until New Year's. I want to forget the world and all its trivialities and sickening grotesqueries. You are, for the brief moments we are together, my freedom. Then, after you're gone, the dull, hopeless thud of the prison door closes."

"Fuck reality, Aaliyah!"

"It robs us of our dreams. How can this be? What a strange life. Why is it this way? Tell me, Lemeilleur. I know you know. My poetry professor says, 'We are deprived through words of authentic intimacy with what we are, or with what the Other is.' What do you think?"

"Believe me—I get it!"

"I have to tell you. It upset me after I spoke to you on Friday. Please don't skip school this week. Also don't go to that psychiatrist unless you really want to and are really willing to tell him everything, because unless you're willing to trust him, he won't be able to help you. I know that on your side of the city anyone who goes to a psychiatrist is considered nuts, but I don't feel that way."

"Why are you so nice to me?"

"You simply have some problems which you are unable, even with all your reading, to solve yourself. Forgive the lecture. I do it because I love you and want you to be happy. But I'm afraid, Lemeilleur."

"Aw, don't be afraid. I've been in tighter spots. Everything will be okay. I promise."

"I see your deep dimples in your face. I love the warm brown of your eyes and your unique, unholy laugh. I love your back, your shoulders, so hard and strong. I just found out: no history exam. I could have made time for you last week. Damn it. I wanted to see you, but I felt I should study. Goddamn it all. The last time I saw you I was so sad to see you drive off all alone in that big Cadillac. You cut a very aristocratic figure. Your friends sure have an assortment of cars. *Je t'aime avec tout. Jusqu'a Noel.*" (I love you with all my heart. Until Christmas.)

"Take care, Aaliyah."

"Wait. Before you go. After reading Ronsard, I had a dream about you. It was like a poem. You and Ronsard make me very horny. It went something like this. Your kisses, soft and delicious, made red my thighs tremble with desire. I heard you moan: *O fente vermeillette. Je te salue. Je sens ta force en moi. Rens ma vie heureusement. Remplis mon petit trou, mignard et velu. O Lemeilleur, rens ma vie heureusement. A beau genous venir m'adorer, tenans au poin flambantes chandelles. J'attends.*" (O scarlet slit. I salute you. I feel your force in me. Make my life happy. Fill my little hole, cute and hairy. O Lemeilleur, make my life happy. On bent knees come adore me, holding in your hand flaming candles. I await you.)

"I can't wait either, Aaliyah. I've never been in love like this before—with a girl who reads."

"You! I haven't been in my comfort zone since I met you!"

17

Lemeilleur had been living over the Warner Theater in a downtown hotel, a dollar a night, since he throttled his father. The hotel owner's daughter—about Lemeilleur's age, brown eyes, fake blond hair, hairy brown armpits, and she smoked cigars—wanted to sleep with him, which Lemeilleur didn't discourage though he did wonder why he was so easy.

Adding alcohol to his confusion didn't help anything. McVeigh and Lemeilleur were making a nuisance of themselves by fighting and stealing, especially cars, on a regular basis. And Lemeilleur couldn't tell Aaliyah—anything—he just wanted her to love him.

Liza—that's the girl at the hotel—really wanted to get out of her current life—who didn't? She hated the fleabag hotel business, which she ran with her drunken mother. We don't know anything about her father except that Liza said he was an asshole.

Lemeilleur liked Liza. She was inquisitive, friendly, tough, and sexy. She wore cutoffs and little halters over her firm but tiny breasts. Her teeth were small and uneven. She also had a cobra tattoo that curled around her belly button.

"Hey," Liza said as she put her bra on, "I want to tell you something."

"Sure. What's on your mind?"

"You're really nice . . . and . . . tender. You don't mind me saying that, do you?"

"I've had worse said about me."

"I got raped here, a couple of times. I never told no one."

Lemeilleur believed her.

"I'm not crazy about men, but I ain't a lesbian neither. I've thought about it. I can't imagine licking a vag."

"Yeah, well, that's the acid test."

"I'm scared, Lemeilleur. Look what happened to my mother. I'm sure she's been raped too. Now she's just a lonely alcoholic—with nothing."

"Shit. I get that," Lemeilleur said as he put on his shoes. "I'm afraid of the same thing. You know what my biggest, baddest nightmare is?"

"Dying in a hotel like this?"

"I'm dragging a bag of garbage out to the trash cans, and I have a heart attack. I die on some dark stairs, and rats eat my lips for a week."

"Jessus, that's bad."

"You seem anxious today. What's going on?"

"It's my mother. She introduced me to one of her drinking buddies."

"That's weird."

"She wants me to date the gal's son—a fucking biker!"

"Have you met him?"

"I don't want to end up with a biker, Lemeilleur. Jesuschriss, I got girlfriends who dated bikers—they all ended up 'pulling the train'."

"What the fuck is 'pulling the train'?"

"You fuck the whole gang. Look at me: I don't fucking do drugs. I don't even steal, and I don't wanta live on the road with a bunch of junkies. I wanta house. Fuck, I'd even do a family."

She banged her fists on Lemeilleur's wall.

"Fuck, I wanta feel good—you know safe and secure—no fucking crazy shit—a fucking boring life—that's what I want. I wanta be June Fucking Cleaver. And I want the bastard to love me."

"And you think I'm your man?"

"Hey, they ain't exactly falling out of the trees around here."

Yeah, he could understand that, but he wasn't willing to sacrifice himself to save her, even if he could save her, which he couldn't. Of course, this kind of moral dilemma raised havoc with his sexual problem—yes that's what he was calling it now. When Liza tried to get his wienie into her bun, his fear of what? stopped him cold, and that, to Liza, was a death sentence.

Come on, how could Lemeilleur save her—he couldn't save himself. He really liked Liza, and he wanted to help her—but save her. He was not going back to the funeral business. He tried to tell her she was barking up the wrong tree, but she was too desperate to hear him. She kept pulling on his wienie, but it out-stubborned her and never rose to the occasion. How he missed Mice—but he could never tell Mice what was happening.

18

"I love the way you smile," Aaliyah whispered into the phone, "your laugh, the way you walk, like nothing in the world bothers you. Cheer up, honey. Things could be worse. I'm so happy my mother didn't find out about our plan, I wouldn't have been able to see you when I was home."

Lemeilleur just listened. He was afraid if he talked he'd cry.

"I'm glad about your appointment with the psychiatrist. I've begun to read the third of the four books you gave me, *Manon Lescault*. The hero's extremely naive. Lem, I know how sad you are. I can feel it through the phone. It's snowing outside, and inside the dorm where I should feel cozy and warm, I feel restless and cold. I had a dream last night, a trial of sorts. You were accused of not adhering to your identity. The prosecution alleged you played the role of Smerdyakov. From *Brothers K*, remember? As I defended you, you kept winking and making gestures as if you were hanging by the neck. And then the dream narrowed to your face, which fell forward, as the noose broke your neck—only you were smiling at me. My scream woke me and my roommate."

Lemeilleur pushed a tear away from his eye.

"What did it mean, Lemeilleur?"

"I wish," he sniffled, "I could tell you."

"Let's look on the bright side. I can hardly wait till Saturday. I want to give you *mon chapeau de paille* (my virginity). My *chatte* (pussy) is purringly calm. Don't be afraid. If I'm not, why are you? Nothing bad will happen because we both won't let that happen. I want to give myself— all of me—to you. If I said anything or did anything Sunday night that upset you, I'm sorry. I'm glad Mice wasn't there. Are our plans for Saturday still on?—even with the snow? Don't use snow as an excuse for us not to go to your friend's cabin. MEOW!"

Lemeilleur was full-out crying. Aaliyah was touched. She'd never been in a situation like this. Everything that crushed their love made her feelings stronger.

"Lem? I have a question for you. How do you know Dostoevsky deleted a chapter on child sexual abuse in *The Possessed*? You never told me why that was so important to you."

19

One day Lemeilleur bumped into Agnes who was shopping on Main Street in Nouvelle Bouville and asked her if Simran was still unhappy at Wellesley.

"Yeah, nothing's changed, unfortunately."

"What's she majoring in?"

"Philosophy—she has this crazy idea that she's going to figure out why this world behaves as it does. She thinks philosophy will save her."

"Is she reading Nietzsche?"

"Why do you ask that?"

"I used to have a friend named Georges who read *The Genealogy of Morals* to me. I thought it was cool—the whole priests-are-evil thing. I mean that morality itself is the cause of man's—as a species—failure to reach the peak of magnificence of which he is capable."

"I'm a business major; I don't read stuff like that."

"My friend, Mice, says the way the whole system is set up makes changing life almost impossible. The terms of justice are set by the powers that be. Fairness is a fantasy."

"You sound like a political ad."

"All the geniuses are always trying to figure out why things are so fucked up. I'll tell you: Things are fucked up because people are fucked up. Nothing changes. People don't change. '*The love of power is the demon of men.*' If we measured morality the way we measure time, nobody would need a watch. That's the Eternal Return. Institutions are nothing but people."

"Yeah, I got a professor who feels that way about the New Deal. Hey, what have you been up to since they threw you out of school?"

"You heard?"

"Everybody in the city heard."

"I kept my job—ah, did Simran hear too?"

"Yup."

"Well, I'm reading and writing stories."

"Can I read one? I liked the vibe of "Tohu Bohu". By the way, I asked Simran what number Houghton Street she lived at—46."

Amazing—Ducks—that was Simran.

Maybe Nabokov was right—life is a masterpiece—how exciting was that? Lemeilleur still remembered those duck-decorated panties. Her ducks were red. Amazing. And the scent of lilac—it all came back to him—vividly. He was having a Proustian madeleine—this was so much better than Miss Havisham's wedding cake!

Yes, he wanted to see Simran again. He was convinced now that he and Simran were in the plot of the same novel. He'd forgotten how much he thought he was in love with her. He wanted to understand why he did that? What was it about her shiny black hair, her unmoving green eyes? And now fate was going to put them together again. He was completely confident. They were footnotes in a masterpiece—the one he was writing on his scraps of paper. She was going to be in his story!

That's how he decided to give Agnes "Baseball": He was sure she'd show it to Simran. This was his Hail Mary pass to Simran. What a story this was going to be!

He walked home singing, "Know I love you, baby, but you don't even know my name." Songs exalted Lemeilleur; they were his first revelation of art. In music he blended with infinity, and he asked himself, Am I in contact with the hereafter?

☯

It was around that time that he started thinking that love was the biggest illusion of them all, but this news about Simran's address made him want to go home and write a letter to Nabokov.

Dear Mr. Nabokov,

I don't know if life is a masterpiece, but this new footnote is very encouraging. When Simran reads my story, things are going to change. Is that how you attracted Vera? Words move people. I still find that amazing. I remember pooh-poohing my father when he gave his eulogies, but my father knew—way down deep—that words have power—he's making serious money. You would have found my father a worthy character for a novel—he's fatally disturbed. A future writer, Lemeilleur—To words!

20

"Oh, Lem! I'm so happy you called. I'm so sorry we didn't get to your friend's cabin on Lake Lashaway, but what I got to give will keep—it's been intact nineteen years. Ha. Ha. You're so tender. I'm so lucky to have you as my first—and maybe my last lover! What did I do to deserve you?"

The conversation was annoying Lemeilleur, but he didn't know how to change it. He'd called to break up with Aaliyah.

"I really hope you get transferred here, to Brandeis. Since my father died in that plane crash, I haven't felt whole. It's been almost five years since he left me. I can't tell you how important you are to me."

Lemeilleur muttered "thanks" and decided to suffer through this call. He'd break up with her next week.

"By the way, my sister thinks I'm weird. She really doesn't understand our relationship, but she's not as trusting as I am. She thinks life is a game of *Cache-Cache*—people hiding from one another, while waiting for the game to end. She asked me if I could imagine a stable future with you. I still can't imagine being married to you except in a vague, wonderful, general, and romantic way, but that is better than imagining nothing. All futures are built on hope."

Lemeilleur muttered a "that's true."

"I know you're very upset. I hope you let a little of your emotions, I mean true emotions, out with the psychiatrist. I love you with *un amour sans fin mais non sans désespoir.*" (a love without end but not without despair)

"I gotta go."

"Don't give up, Lemeilleur."

"I'm sorry, Aaliyah. I gotta go."

21

Lemeilleur's father knew the hotel where Lemeilleur lived, and every once in a while he'd bring Lemeilleur his mail. Mice was on a training ship somewhere in the Great Lakes. He sent Lemeilleur long passages from an essay—*What is Justice?*— he was writing, a massive compendium of views on justice— from *The Fellowship of the Ring*, which Mice loved, to Mahatma Gandhi. It was a stupendous effort that had been ignited by what had happened to the Anion Family. However—and this was alarming—the essay didn't hang together. Everything was mixed up, horrifyingly incoherent. Lemeilleur staggered away from the letter wondering if he wrote a book about love—would it, too, be incoherent?

22

We have to back up here. The Anions had lived next door to Mice all his life, and Mice, though not palsy-walsy, knew and liked Rafael, the oldest. Frank, the next brother, was one year younger than Rafael, and the sister, Claudia, was two years younger than Frank.

About a year ago Frank hung himself in a closet, which, to everyone concerned, was an enormous and painful mystery. Mother, father, brother and sister, friends—no one had a clue why such an intelligent and handsome boy of eighteen would have done that. The incident faded away, but, apparently, it bothered Mice so much it launched his great essay on justice.

Lemeilleur's father handled Frank's funeral, at cost. Hundreds of people came.

23

A few months later, while Mice was home on leave, a murder was committed at the Anions. As the facts came out, we learned that Rafael had beaten his father to death with a hammer. Mice was all over this story. And when it went to trial, Mice went Absent Without Official Leave to follow it. What came out was this: According to Rafael, the father had made both Rafael and Frank have sex with Claudia. The father would watch. According to the mother and Claudia, who had returned for the trial, Rafael was lying. They said Rafael killed the father because he wouldn't give Rafael money to buy a car.

⏘

The trial meandered on another two or three weeks until all parties had their say. There was no conclusive proof of either story. The jury took two days and sided with the mother and Claudia. Rafael would go to jail for the rest of his life. Mice was shocked—not a shred of doubt? Outraged! He couldn't believe it. His whole world seemed to unravel. For Mice the question was never **Who** committed the crime, but **Why** was the crime committed. Shore patrol arrested Mice and took him back to his ship for a disciplinary hearing. Mice was furious.

24

One day, without hint or clue, Mice's rambling letters stopped coming. It was so abrupt, Lemeilleur thought maybe Mice had

had a heart attack, his ship had sunk, or more realistically he was in the brig without pen and paper.

25

Months after Rafael was imprisoned, Mice knocked on Lemeilleur's door.

"Mice, what are you doing here?"

"The Navy discharged me, and you know why."

"What are you talking about?"

"My commanding officer tried to fuck with me. I pushed him away. Then he tried to get me to swab a deck. I refused. That's when the sonavabitch called me a fag. I hit him."

He was strangely calm, and his milky-blue eyes weren't blinking.

"I have the discharge papers right here. You want to see? Your fingerprints are all over it. They threw me out because of you."

"What are you talking about?"

Indifferently he handed his papers over to Lemeilleur who started to read . . . blah . . . blah . . . then Lemeilleur saw the sentence. "After psychiatric examination subject was diagnosed with Adult Oppositional Defiant Disorder."

That sent a chill down Lemeilleur's spine—he'd never noticed anything unusual about Mice.

Lemeilleur put the paper down. How could he have missed something like **that**? He was dumbfounded.

Mice's eyes started to blink and his whole body started to convulse, like the time his mother's teat fell through her sleeve.

"Why," asked Lemeilleur, "do you think they threw you out because of me?"

"They knew about Georges."

He tore his discharge paper from Lemeilleur's hand, looked up at him, and beyond furious, he shouted, "You're no Speedoo. You couldn't change a diaper."

Lemeilleur could not believe his ears—was this Mice? "You're going to go with the rich—I can see you drinking our blood. Stop looking at my feet. You're a Salinger character: You had banana fever with Georges."

26

"Hey Lemeilleur," Liza all but screamed, "my mother says a girl keeps calling you here, and she don't leave her name. Says you should call her at Brandeis. What's Brandeis?"

Lemeilleur saw the hurt in Liza's eye. He wanted to get out of this mess, but he didn't want to hurt Liza.

"It's a job—I'm looking for work."

"I see," she said, her eyes glistening with doubt.

Lemeilleur never called Aaliyah back. Undeterred, Aaliyah wrote to Lemeilleur.

I took this pen in hand to thank you for one of the nicest and loveliest New Year's Eve I will probably ever have. The house was great. Too bad we had to break the window. Did you ever find the key? I hope your friend doesn't mind too much. I really had a wonderful time and though I was angry earlier in the evening, I am not angry now. I'm glad we didn't do it.

Don't get upset, but I don't know if what I feel for you is love. You can be so tender. It was so wonderful: before the fireplace, looking out the picture window at a moon hanging, huge and silver, over a frozen, crystalline Lake Lashaway. Thank your friend for me.

Esther is coming up today to talk to me. This is just not the time. O, well, I'll just have to grin and bear it. I called you last night after I got your letter, but you didn't answer. My sister is against our relationship. Hey, is Mice no longer in the Navy?

I accept your quitting school. Did the psychiatrist really say your problem was you thought you were

Dostoevsky? I don't love your new story: "The Triumph of Tohu Bohu." O, Lemeilleur, don't ever abuse me.

A.

27

Liza left a letter under Lemeilleur's door last night. He didn't see it until this morning.

Dear Lemayeur,

I need you. I know youre having a hard time. I know youre not crazy about me. But I would be good to you. I'll even learn to cook. You know a girl like me doesn't always get a chance to meet a guy like you. Youre smart, you read, youre gonna be something. You see I believe in you. We'll work it out. I promise. I'll do whatever you want me to: I'll wear wigs, tipless bras, watch dirty movies—whatever.

Please. Lemayeur, you can't do this to me, and leave me to my fucked-up life. I don't want to be hooked up to a biker for the rest of my life. Do you understand how much I need you? Do you understand how I can love you? Please Lemayeur, youre the only way out I can see.

Liza

He put Liza's letter down. The TV was on and Lemeilleur and three other million Americans watched Julia Child as she said, "Remember you're all alone in the kitchen and no one can see you"—at which point she retrieved a potato pancake that had dropped to the floor and tossed it back into the frying pan.

Julia, I know what you mean.

28

Dear Lemeilleur,

Have you finished your story, "Julia and the Pancake?" I can't wait till after mid-terms. I'll try to get you a room. Is Mice coming up that weekend with you, because if he is, I'll get him a bed too.

I don't know what upset you. If I have been thoughtless, I promise I'll try to be better. I want you to have a good time with Liza Saturday night, but not too good. I'm a little jealous of her. You're too nice and wonderful for only me to be in love with you. Is Mice going with you? Please return my calls.

A.

Lemeilleur decided he had to stop feeling bad for himself. He was at least as sexually healthy as Hans Christian Andersen, and he erroneously took refuge in the quote: *It doesn't matter, if you're born in a duck yard, as long as you are hatched from a swan's egg.* Erroneous because Lemeilleur didn't have a swan in his life.

29

Dear Lemeilleur,

You refuse to answer my phone calls. I did not enjoy your last letter. I'm sorry you think I've tried to change you. I have no real right. I only attempted to change you because I thought I would like you better. I don't know why you think I'm a masochist. I have known for some time you're considering Liza. My sister thinks it's

a class thing.
You say you want a girl who makes as few demands
as possible, who needs little to sustain happiness.
Well, a person usually receives what he gives. I give a
lot, I want a lot. My gifts to you measure my need.
What about your demands of me?
    Look, I realize that it is painful for you to give up
your independence. I am not trying to take away your
individuality. Don't you feel it was rather thoughtless
to send me this letter when I was studying for
midterms? You hurt me. Did Mice like his Valentine?
Thanks for Mice's address.

A.

30

Lemeilleur, dreaming that *un mec ordinaire comme moi* (an ordinary guy like me) was, in the middle of a hurricane, on the ocean's edge, shouting into the maelstrom's rage: "CLASS MUST BE DESTROYED," when he was awakened with a bang on his door. It was Liza and a mountain of a man with tattoos darkly running up both arms, all the way up his bulging neck, all the way to his meager hairline.

"Lemayeur, a girl dropped this off for you," Liza said.

"Hey, what's that?" the mountain roared, and he took the letter away from Liza and read it.

"For chrissake, Tiny, that's Lemayeur's."

"I thought you was sneaking him a note. Here, it's yours."

Lemeilleur took it from the huge paw and looked at it quickly. It was from Agnes, Simran's business school friend. What the fuck did she want?

"Look, ah, Lemayeur. You're gonna have ta move out of here," Tiny said to him. "Me and Liza here are gonna get hitched, and I don't want you to fuck that up. Got it."

"Got it."

Liza was crying. "I'm sorry, Lemayeur."

They left and Lemeilleur packed up his clothes and books. But where would he go? He found a telephone booth and called Mice.

"I'm schorry, Lem, Mice doschen't want to talk to ya," Mother's mother, drunk, said.

Lemeilleur hung up and started to walk. He could feel the key to the attic above the funeral home in his pocket. He really didn't want to go home. He was so angry. He threw Agnes's letter away.

31

Lemeilleur walked for a long time. He started to cry—not sobbing—just tears dripping down his face. He needed a rest. He decided to go to the attic. His books were getting very heavy. On the way to the funeral home, he had stopped thinking he was fucked beyond repair. After all, Hans Christian Andersen was a success. He stopped under a streetlight to read the last letter Aaliyah had sent to him.

Dear Lemeilleur,

Entrammeled in the net of the law? What's happening? Please don't tell Mice that I wanted to make out with him. Mice wrote me "truth and justice are molecularly entwined—the farther you are from truth, the deeper you are in injustice. Perversion is an artifact of the kind of capitalism practiced in this country."

I called him and asked what he meant. He said, "Injustice causes character defects." How? I asked. His answer: "You can't preserve one's faith, one's heart, one's most intimate being, without hope. Hope is the lynchpin of democracy."

I told him justice is what love looks like in public.

He screamed "Love! Inequality creates corruption—
even the FBI knows that." He hung up on me.

A.

Lemeilleur continued to freak out: Mice was crazy, and Aaliyah was slipping away. How could that happen? What was wrong with him? Why didn't he stop this from happening? It was almost midnight. He'd been walking for hours toward the funeral home.

When he got there, he threw his books through a window he'd opened and climbed into the garage. He knew where his father kept an extra set of keys to the hearse in case someone needed to pick up a dead body when his father was away.

With the keys in his pocket, he slipped open the garage door, and without starting up the hearse, pushed it out. Once in the parking lot, he started the motor and sped off. He'd done this a thousand times before—drive around at night and bring the hearse back before dawn. He had to calm down.

It must have been around 3 am. He was driving down Wall Street toward Grafton Street, about a block from the funeral home, when the car in front of him stopped and threw a body out.

Lemeilleur pulled over, got out, and found a girl heaving in the gutter. She was about 5'3", brown hair, purple eyeshadow, and purple lipstick. Her teeth were crooked. He asked her if she was okay. She muttered, "Stupid fuck. I'm sorry."

She was wearing a short brown suede skirt, a tan rayon blouse with buttons missing in the front, a purple bra, and brown loafers. She kept falling in her vomit, so Lemeilleur moved her to the sidewalk.

"You're a fucking asshole," she muttered again; "I'm sorry I heaved my heart in your car."

Lemeilleur noticed a sweater on the ground next to her and picked it up to clean her off. She let him. Then he asked her if she wanted a ride. She nodded yes.

He put her in the front seat of the hearse, and he got into the driver's seat, and they headed out. She fell over and put her head on his lap. Before Lemeilleur knew it, she was massaging his balls. He tried to talk to her, but she acted like she was asleep. He got very horny.

"Hey, will you stop that."

"Come on, Johnny; let's do it. I know you want me."

Johnny? Fuck it. Once desire set, it was like concrete—unbudgeable—did away with all the agony of decision. All conflict dissolved: body and soul were in harmony. He headed for the A.J. Club. It was a couple of blocks away. Desire, a determined silkworm devouring Lemeilleur's mulberry soul, had obliterated all consciousness other than the monolithic possibility of

orgasm,

the only antidote to misery.

Behind the dirty brick building there was an urban thicket of bushes, poison ivy, and nettles. Lemeilleur backed down a small car path and stopped. He saw through the rearview mirror a pile of oatmeal-like offal, which smelled haddocky. He carried the drunk woman to the back of the hearse, where, with one hand, he opened the door and the other laid her down where the casket usually went. Lemeilleur leaned in and pulled up her skirt. Her panties were gone. He pulled down his pants, climbed over the bumper, got between her legs, and pushed himself in.

She felt like marshmallow.

He pumped away and she said, "Are you fucking me?"

"Hang on—almost done."

"Go for it, Johnny; I'm too fucked up to be there too."

Who the fuck was Johnny?

"Are you gonna marry me, huh? I wanna get married."

She was fucking up Lemeilleur's climax.

"I know you won't, Johnny."

He came, got off, and pulled up his pants.

"It's okay, Johnny. You love me?"

"Where's your car? I'll drive you over."

"My car? You picked me up at my sister's."

She opened her eyes a little and said, "Hey, you're not Johnny."

"Do you want a ride or not?"

"You just fucked me."

Lemeilleur wanted to say welcome to real life, instead he pulled her out of the back of the hearse and sat her down near the thorn bushes that waved in a dull breeze with their hideous bits of tissue paper posing as pale flowers amid the prickles. Everything around Lemeilleur was soiled and torn. Death rose in his nostrils.

"Come on," he reached over to her. "I'll give you a ride. Where do you want to go?"

"You'll do that? Hey, I bet you're nice," she said as she struggled to stand up.

Lemeilleur, who helped her, shrugged.

"Hey, let's talk," she said sitting next to Lemeilleur. "How did you find me?"

"Someone threw you on the road."

"Johnny's a fucker. What's your name?"

Lemeilleur was silent. He wasn't going to let this Nameless One know who he was.

"What the fuck—is this a hearse?"

"I'll take you back to Wall St."

"I bet you wouldn't throw me out of a car. I can tell. You're really a nice guy."

"Me. You have no idea how fucked up I am."

"I don't believe it. I **know** fucked up and you ain't it. I'll get off right over there. Hey, can I see you again?"

"Look, I fuck up everything I touch."

"Me too—please."

"I don't think so. Take care of yourself. Get a new boyfriend."

"Thanks. Good idea."

The Nameless One left and Lemeilleur drove back to the

funeral home. He was worried his father might find out he took the hearse. As night merged into day, he pulled into the garage. Aside from the wenchy odor he couldn't keep out of his nose, he would put the memory of the weedy waste land behind him—in his already overcrowded and vulnerable hippocampus, which receives input directly from the olfactory bulb.

It must have been about six in the morning when he put his key into the lock of the door of the attic of the funeral home, promising himself that as soon as he got some money, he'd run away to Paris and become a sex slave to some rich dirty old man. But before he could turn the key, the door opened, and an incredibly old woman looked up. She was standing in front of an old oak kitchen table and stared him in the eye. She looked like a short-eared owl with large yellow, nictating (*Lolita* word) eyes, big head, and short neck. Her nose was short, strong, and hooked, her skin mottled tawny.

32

"Who are you?" a female voice with a strong French accent crowed.

What a question. Lemeilleur's mouth opened, and tears shot out of his eyes. He could smell his secret tomato plant.

"I'm sorry," the voice whispered. "When I heard the key, I thought it might be you. Your father told me you used to live here. All I have to eat is some pea soup?"

Lemeilleur nodded yes but continued to cry. He noticed her movements were floppy, moth-like.

"I'm glad you've come back. Your father was very worried about you. He told me you want to be a writer," she said as she ladled soup into a bowl.

"He did?" Lemeilleur managed to ask.

"Here. Sit down. I'm a writer. We have a lot to talk about, and I don't have much time left."

While he'd been away, Lemeilleur's father had had the

attic renovated to accommodate Mrs. Marie LaJoie. She was ninety-two years old, and because of her and her husband's book, *The Evolution of French Canada*, she was semi-famous among French-Canadians. Lemeilleur's father, who was an odd combination of generosity and business sense, likely hoped he would bury Mrs. LaJoie.

"You want some coffee?"

"That sounds good."

Every French-Canadian for miles would come to her funeral. You can't buy better advertising. But to be honest, his father probably was happy he could help her too.

When she returned with coffee, she told Lemeilleur he could sleep on the pullout sofa in the living room, and she would make sure the arrangement was okay with his father. She had energy to burn.

33

The next day Lemeilleur asked her how she managed to do so much.

"When you grow up on a farm, like I did in Contrecoeur, Québec, you are used to hard work. You know when we French came to Canada, it was regarded as a mission. We were not like the Spanish who crushed the Indians, nor were we like the *maudit* (cursed) English who scorned them—we embraced the Indians. I have Abenaki blood."

She threw up her eyebrows as if she'd seen a vole in the grass.

"Canada," she continued, "was lost to England by the corruption of Versailles. Old France didn't want New France to be anything but a trading post—they didn't want competition for their existing economy. The aristocracy by then were all inbred pea brains, and Louis the Fourteenth was a sex maniac."

Lemeilleur found her stories of Canada soothing. Every morning she'd make him breakfast and tell him about Canada. One morning, pacing before a copy of the engraving of *The*

Death of General Wolfe hanging in her kitchen, she shouted, "It all started there, on the Plains of Abraham."

She had stopped moving; finally pointing at the picture, she said, "Look at that myth-making painting. Only one of those soldiers was there when Wolfe died. And there was no Indian. And Wolfe was dead before the British won. But no, Benjamin West goes on to deify Wolfe. You know what galls me the most? West said, 'The same truth that guides the pen of the historian should govern the paintbrush of the artist.' What a hypocrite. After Wolfe, French-Canadians were systematically cut off from the rest of the world—compelled to trade—at a great disadvantage—with only their conquerors. When you write your book, tell the truth."

Marie would stop to look at him through the tender furry slits around her eyes. Then she'd say, "I want you to understand this because this is the culture that shaped your father." Then she fluttered off again—a fireball of energy—to do something and come back.

"Impoverished, French-Canadians were compelled to entrust their legal interests," and she picked up the book she wrote to read, 'to men unacquainted with their language and Customs and who, to the greatest ignorance, added the greatest rapacity.' Can you imagine living like that," she asked Lemeilleur. "This went on for a hundred years."

"How does this relate to my father?"

"French-Canadians clung to their identity even though they had been completely abandoned by la France. To evils beyond their control they submitted with resignation. Self-reliance became more important than achievement. Doing things on your own was more important than doing things well. All we thought about was how to survive."

She sipped her coffee.

"We saw what the English were doing to the indigenous people of Canada. You know what the policy was? 'Kill the Indian to save the child.' *Je me souviens*—what do they remember? Old France was gone—*une loi, un roi, une foi* (one law, one king, one faith)—it was all gone. We were a little campfire in a big English forest. Sacrifice became the highest value. When I was growing up, a son had to be ashamed to think he could do better than his father."

"You're kidding me?"

"The peasants of Millet—a hundred years later, when they found out about the revolution in la France—were appalled. What were Liberty, Egalité, and Fraternity to these people living in forest surrounded by darkness and English hostility?"

Lemeilleur just stared at her, overwhelmed by her erudition.

"Books, they decided, caused that revolution. Books threatened everything they believed in. They had very few books in Canada. The English wanted to deFrench us. French-Canadian life was reduced to one word—*Survivance*. That word became their philosophy."

"What's *la survivance*?"

"It's an expression that denotes the survival of francophone culture in the face of Canadian anglophone or Anglo-American hegemony. We were trying to get our power back! We used this expression in Quebec, especially before the Quiet Revolution of the 1960s, but it was also found among the culturally dispossessed francophone mill workers of northern New England."

"How do you know all this?"

"Does your father read *Le Travailleur*?"

"Yeah."

Marie stood up and searched her apartment until she found a copy of the newspaper.

"Here is an article printed in *Le Travailleur* (The Worker), a Franco-American newspaper, on February 16, 1950. I used it for one of the books I wrote. This excerpt appeared on the front page and was written in French. I translated it. 'Edmond de Nevers, historian and sociologist, maintained that faith and pride, faith in religion of their fathers, faith in the future of their race and pride of their French name, could only save Franco-Americans.' Now think about this, Lemeilleur: What if Racine had been stolen away and shipped to Canada, and reared as a *coureur-de-bois* in the depths of the *Québécoise* forest, do you think the world would have had *Phèdre*? But he still would have been Racine. At night, around their watch-fire he would have chanted wild songs of rapine and murder, till the dark faces around him were moved and trembled."

34

The next morning his father, who was happy Lemeilleur was not living in a flophouse with alcoholics and poor people, brought up two letters that had come for Lemeilleur.

Dear Lemayeur,

Just want ya ta know that Tiny is gonna settle down with me—no pulling the train—so ya don't have ta worry. Won't be a house with a white picket fence but fuck it. Miss ya. You're a good guy. Good luck. Let me know when youre famous. I'll watch for your book in the grocery store.

Liza

Second letter.

Dear Smerdyakov,

You incredibly evil bastard—you planned your escape months ago. From the day your mother started beating you to all the other unnatural things that "happened" to you, you've had a love/hate relationship with innocence. You've projected all your self-hatred on the world around you. You turned me into a hideous, faithless wench. You told Mice I wanted to kiss him. I finally understand your relationship with Mice. He was right: I'm your Ophelia, and you're a cheap imitation of Hamlet—paralyzed by your problems. You sent Mice to punish me! Why?

Well, dearest, your fucked up desire has come to pass: He can do it! You/we are undone. My sister says the handwriting's been on the wall for a long time. So, this was love. Mice told me you got him thrown out of the Navy. He said you don't care about justice. He was crazy; he blamed me; said I should have saved you. I cried for our love as he brutalized me. He hurt me— enough to go to a hospital—but nobody will ever hurt me as much as you.

Hell, Lemeilleur, is "the suffering of being unable to love." You do remember your Zossima? Are you still stuck in Humbert-Humbert-land—proud and selfish and fake—or are you just foundering in a literary hell à la Rimbaud?

Hang yourself you Smerdyakov.

35

"Goddamn it." Lemeilleur screamed. He had fucking gotten into college for her and when he was thrown out, he was even more dependent on her, though he did everything he could have to distance himself from Aaliyah. What the fuck was going on? Was he crazy? Now Aaliyah was blaming him for Mice. Lemeilleur didn't force her into Mice's arms.

He needed Aaliyah!

What could he do now? He was expelled from college— was lying to her about who he was—he'd never get into Brandeis—her sister was right about him—he never deserved Aaliyah. He was stuck in that space of nowhere below the classes—silent majority space where only resentment grows—waiting to be exploited by the miserable circumstances of life or a lying politician.

He tried to call Aaliyah—several times. She never answered the phone. He knew he was a liar, a fake, a fool—but he still wanted her. What did he want? All he could think of was Aaliyah's favorite Odilon Redon painting: *Eyes Closed*, a poster which she'd given him. Now he wondered if the unknowability of another person that the painting expressed was why she gave it to him?

36

Lemeilleur decided to confront Mice. He wasn't sure what he'd say, but he rushed over to Mice's house before his courage abated. He was jealous Mice had slept with Aaliyah and he was profoundly hurt—by both of them. He couldn't take betrayal. He knew he'd get over Aaliyah—but Mice!

Mice opened the door and his milky-blue eyes blinked rapidly.

"What the fuck are you doing here?"

"Why'd you do that to Aaliyah?"

"You never made love to her."

"What are you talking about?"

"You never did it. She wanted you. She told me."

"We were working on it—she wanted it to be perfect."

"Admit it—you were afraid—you're queer."

"I was confused."

"Because you were with Georges."

"Where did you hear that?"

"At the police station, I saw you, and I heard why you were there. Your father was upset too. He saw you kissing Joe P."

"How do you know that?"

"Your father goes to the Legion every night and cries about you—the whole neighborhood knows. He says you're queerer than a two dollar bill. How could I have been so stupid? You broke your father's heart with your secret life!"

"You can't be serious, Mice?"

"You were my friend. I thought we were going to change the world."

"We still can."

"She was crazy to trust you."

"We can still change the world."

"You're so slow, Lemeilleur—Why do you think I joined the Navy? SO YOU COULD HAVE HER. What's wrong with you? Get out of here. I knew there was something wrong with you the night you took me on your first date with her. I sacrificed for you. And in the end you fucked me—THE NAVY KNEW ABOUT YOU. That's why they call me oppositional. I'm over the edge—I'll never see the ancient ramparts of Europe! You ruined everything. We were going to change the world!"

Lemeilleur walked up Cohasset Street stunned.

37

Agnes called the funeral home because Lemeilleur hadn't answered her letter. She couldn't find him at the hotel, and his father, who was happy a girl called, gave her Marie LaJoie's phone number, where Lemeilleur had been living for the last four weeks.

He was crushed by Mice—BETRAYED. Sure, he FUCKED UP WITH AALIYAH—fine. He kinda always knew Aaliyah was a middle-class Love-Dream—Oh, one that he wanted, but he knew—way down deep—he could never have—working-class ILLUSION.

Aaliyah let Mice fuck her to hurt Lemeilleur, but why did Mice go along? Was he really that angry? Did the Navy really know about Georges?

⊕

Marie, in her own way, tried to nurse him back to health. But a thick concrete of contradictory thoughts, desires, and fears entombed him—like some fucking stone sarcophagus of a former hero in the middle of a new, irrelevant revolution. He needed life—people—something that would lighten the weight of the anger that crushed his heart. He'd lost Aaliyah—and MICE TOO! Why? What was going on with Mice? In Lemeilleur's world without Meaning, Mice had been the beacon! Life, Lemeilleur's shocked soul realized, was terror without Mice.

⊕

Agnes, undaunted by Lemeilleur's refusal to respond, called again at Marie LaJoie's to tell him, in her business-like way, Simran wanted to get together with him. Lemeilleur had a momentary flurry of hope when he heard that, but he knew better: he hung up on her. He couldn't handle another Mice—NOT NOW! It had been over two years since he'd followed Simran to that bus. A lot had changed. Why did he need people—so desperately—in his life?

At first he tried not to give in to despair—not be crushed by the momentum of his fucked-up history—but he knew he was sliding down Crow Hill's steep, rain-rutted cliffside. How could he stop himself?

He decided he didn't believe his grandfather's story about the Canadian goose's legs—it was just a cynical folktale: geese's wings are not strong enough to separate their bodies from their legs—survival does not mean you are maimed for life. If birds die in the ice when freezing occurs, the key is to get out before the freeze. Maybe hell wasn't other people?

"Trust," Lemeilleur wrote in a diary, "is the most fragile of all the human emotions."

38

A week or two later his father, huffing and puffing, ran up the back stairs to Marie LaJoie's apartment.

"Is Marie here?"

"No, she's out shopping."

"A real pretty," he caught his breath, "girl came by today. She asked about you."

"Me?"

"She's been looking for you for over a month, she said."

"Me?"

"She said she had relations with you—don't worry—I liked her. I'm happy for you! I talked with her for a while. She's a real dish, and smart too. She likes to read. I'm happy for you. She said you saved her life. I knew you'd settle down some day. I think she wants to marry you."

How the fuck did **she** find him?

"I think she thinks you own the funeral home. I got her number. You can tell her I'm going to give you the funeral home when I die."

"Give me the number. Did you tell her I live here?"

Lemeilleur took the number from his smiling father.

"I figured you could tell her yourself when you call her. She's a real dish. She reads poetry. How'd you save her life?"

Lemeilleur stared at the number.

"You marry her, and I'll pay for the wedding—you know, just family—a nice wedding, and I'll hire Dino's Italian Restaurant to cater—this will be great. Pepperoni pizza with sausage—Uncle Tocard—we'll have a blast. I'm so happy for you."

39

The next morning Marie said to Lemeilleur, "Why don't you

write? It always made my husband feel better."

Lemeilleur jumped up from the old oak table she and her husband had brought from Canada, ran into his bedroom (her living room), and brought back a book he'd been reading the night before.

"Listen to this," he shouted: "'*The strange mysterious perhaps dangerous perhaps saving comfort there is in writing; it is a leap out of murderers' row; it is a seeing of what is really taking place.*' Kafka."

"Yes," she said excitedly, "see what's really taking place. Writers see things that other people only look at."

For a moment, thinking he was a writer, he let himself believe he was happy. But how long could he live with a ninety-two-year-old woman over his father's funeral home with the Nameless One breathing down his neck? He knew he'd have to move soon. He wasn't ready for more complication. He was out of energy for a new relationship—especially this one.

"Look, Marie, if anyone comes here looking for me, please don't let on that I live here, okay?"

"I know you are in trouble. I see it in your eyes. I will protect you."

40

A few days later Lemeilleur was feeling stronger. His father came running up the stairs again calling for Lemeilleur.

"Fuck—she found me," Lemeilleur mumbled to himself.

"Mice's mother just called. You better go over there. She was drunk and crazy."

Ten minutes later Lemeilleur approached Mice's house. A swarm of police cars in full apoplexy flashed, blinked, and tingled the air with a dizzying array of colors. They were in front of Mice's three-decker. No one knew what was happening. The police wouldn't let Lemeilleur cross the line.

All of a sudden the front door blew open and Mice's

mother, in yellow housecoat, transparently naked, flew down the stairs screaming, "He's dead. He's dead."

The police grabbed her and put her in a cruiser. The line of onlookers was pushed back. A space was made for an arriving ambulance. A body was taken away. The crowd broke up. Mice's mother, in a calm trance now, left the cruiser and walked back, with a blanket a policeman had found in her house and put over her shoulders, to the front steps of her house. The police left.

Lemeilleur followed her up the stairs—a sexless, broken wraith—to find out what had happened to her husband.

Mice's mother draped herself over a chair in the kitchen. She looked like Dali's timepiece in *The Persistence of Memory*. She was drunk and depressed—could barely keep her head up. Oddly the wrinkles around her mouth looked apish. Lemeilleur felt bad for her. How would she get on without her husband? Lemeilleur sighed to himself. Where was Mice? The kitchen was in disarray. The kitchen table had been shoved against a wall, some of the glasses on the table were turned over, one had fallen to the floor and shattered. The leg of a chair was broken off.

On the stove was a breakfast of scrambled eggs smothered in catsup. For some reason Lemeilleur touched them: The eggs were cold. He probably had a heart attack, fell against the table, and broke the chair.

Lemeilleur bent over Mice's mother and asked, "What happened?"

Mice's mother blinked her eyes and cried, "I'mm sa sorry."

"What happened?"

"I dn't know. I called 911," she spat out. "He wss crazy."

"Who was crazy?"

She tried to raise her head to look at Lemeilleur.

"I dn't know what happed. I said sommthin' bout Billy and, and he jist . . . exploded."

She tried to stand up; she was reaching for Lemeilleur.

"I swear. I ddn't know dey'd kill 'im."

"Kill him?"

"I'mm sa sorry I called da police."

She cried. "It wss awful. Jist awful. Dey kneeld on 'im, Lemeilleur."

Numb, Lemeilleur went to look into Mice's bedroom, which was off the kitchen. He was trembling. What had just happened? He remembered Mice's father hated Billy. But why would the police kill her husband?

Over the bureau against a cyanotic blue wallpaper was a portrait Mice had done of himself. An orange, blue, and gold portrait, expressionistic, with white eyes stared at Lemeilleur. Mice looked like a lion in a wind-blown desert at night.

Next to the painting, against the wall where a patch of the murky wallpaper had been torn away above his unmade bed was written "*Parting is all we know of heaven, And all we need of hell.*"

Clothes and books, piles of them, like *Poems from Auschwitz, Giovanni's Room, Le Bateau ivre,* and *Passing* by Nella Larson—strewn all over—books that Mice never mentioned to Lemeilleur, scattered high and low.

Duct tape across the broken pane of glass in the bedroom window sealed the cold out, barely—just a miserable cold mildew-smelling room. He looked in Mice's closet. Mice always looked like an adventurist who had just gotten out of jail—powder-blue jackets and Western-style shirts and dark blue stone bolas. On his Webcor was the last 45 he'd played: "The Wind" by Nolan Strong and The Diablos. Without thinking Lemeilleur took "The Wind" out of the Webcor and stuck it in his jacket pocket. He would tease Mice about its missing later. About to leave, Lemeilleur noticed a trophy on Mice's scuffed bureau. Looking closer he remembered that Mice had come in second in the State Science Contest.

Dazed for a moment, he looked away and noticed an envelope on the floor next to Mice's bed. Lemeilleur picked it up—an application to UMASS/Amherst—but the last page was signed "Mr. Earl."

"What?" Lemeilleur blurted.

He refocused when he heard a noise. He ran out to the

kitchen only to realize that Mice's mother had slipped off the chair and fallen to the floor, like a fucking slinky, one rubber rib at a time. She smelled worse than Tocard's barroom.

Where was Mice?

Lemeilleur stepped over her boneless body and walked into the living room. He found the *Bhagavad Gita*. The book was open to the page with *"Man is made by his belief."*

There was some commotion out on the back porch. Lemeilleur ran to the back door and opened it to see if Mice was coming home.

The people who lived on the third floor trudged by. They were carrying groceries home, and behind them was a pair of eyes swollen with resignation popping out of swollen pouches—sparkless—under a large forehead covered with smooth brown skin—Mice's father.

Lemeilleur's head was a thousand pound wrought iron clapper that tolled:

DEAD.   DEAD.   DEAD.
DEAD. DEAD

Lemeilleur stumbled out of Mice's house, got sick, and threw up.

41

Lemeilleur didn't remember walking home. He sat down on his bed next to a pile of Mice's letters and without thinking picked one to read: "Justice will not be served until those who are unaffected are as outraged as those who are."

"Mice wrote that to ME. I'm supposed to do something," Lemeilleur cried. He rose from his bed to walk around aimlessly. Time had become a crushing weight and breathing more difficult—he was on the edge of panic.

Mice was dead.

42

Lemeilleur's father buried Mice, and he didn't charge the family for his services. Afterwards there was a small memorial service for Mice at the Andrew Johnson Club. Only a few people came, some expected others not. Mice's parents, Lemeilleur's father, Aaliyah, and, at the back of the room, the Nameless One, as well as some people Lemeilleur didn't recognize, who he later found out were friends of Mice's father.

Lemeilleur, also later, found out his father had invited the Nameless One. Lemeilleur couldn't believe she was here—in the same room with Aaliyah. Who told Aaliyah?

Lemeilleur played a cassette of "You Don't Know What Love Is" on the speaker system of the club because years ago Mice, the first time he'd heard Chet Baker, had come running over to Lemeilleur's house to tell him, "You gotta hear this guy, Lemeilleur. I just heard a trumpet cry. Suffering oozes out of every note. But there's something stronger—a sense of . . . of . . . unyielding beauty—as if pain could make music. He's a fucking whacked out genius."

When the music ended Lemeilleur nervously walked over to a podium to recite a poem Mice had written years ago.

Who are the Americans?

Please tell me: Who are the Americans?
Was Franklin Delano Roosevelt really American?

Please tell me: Who are the Americans?
Where are the people who believe?
"Equal justice for all"?

Where are the People in whose blood
Flows: "We, the people . . ."
Was all that wisdom an anomaly?
A freak of history?

Please tell me.

Teach me to believe.

Did an American say:
"I am rich, by God's grace,
Without injury to any man."

Please tell me.

Teach me the truth
of the
Statue of Liberty.

Aaliyah had gained weight and was crying. As she walked away when Lemeilleur approached her, she muttered in his direction, "Nice music," and she left the building.

Aaliyah would later become a lawyer and a distinguished fellow at the Josephine Goldmark Foundation where she worked tirelessly for the working class for thirty years.

At the time of the memorial service, Aaliyah hoped the poster of *Eyes Closed* that she had given Lemeilleur would haunt him for the rest of his life.

The gathering dispersed very quickly after Aaliyah left— nobody had anything to say to anybody. Lemeilleur was last to leave.

On the way out the door, the Nameless One was waiting for Lemeilleur—on the stoop.

"I know you don't want to see me," the Nameless One said.

"I'm sorry," Lemeilleur said, looking directly at the Nameless One. "It just won't work."

"I know you believe that, Lemeilleur. Look, I won't bother you no more. I wrote you this letter," which she pulled out of her pocketbook. "It explains my feelings. Just read it sometime." And handing it to Lemeilleur, she said, "If it means anything to you, call me."

She thrust the letter toward Lemeilleur, and he reached for it the way one takes a poisoned meal from one's enemies while in their custody. The Nameless One turned away, seemingly unaware of Lemeilleur's dread. As Lemeilleur watched her disappear into the shadows, he was annoyed she had selfishly inserted herself into his grief. He stuck the letter into his pocket.

At home that night, Lemeilleur's father asked him if he knew Mice's father had Negro blood?

43

Lemeilleur received a notice to report to his draft board for induction to the military. He—thinking it was easier than running across a parade ground in boot camp naked, yelling "Geronimo!" the way Jack Kerouac had done—went to his draft board and told the officer in charge that he was queer. Lemeilleur was evaluated 4-F (unfit for military service) immediately.

44

A few days later, Lemeilleur got a note from Liza, who had married Tiny. It was a Hallmark *Love You Lots Miss You* card.

Dear Lemayeur,

I pulled the train last week. Got through it thinking of you. Did I ever tell you I love your smile? Thanks for helping me. Were headed for Sturgis now. I hear its real pretty out there.

L

45

His being—whose soul had been siphoned out by Mice's death—refell into a bottomless despondency. Even Marie LaJoie's boundless energy couldn't rouse him. All he could hear was the echo of her French "rrr"s as his spirit tumbled lower, down the rain-rutted cliffside of Crow Hill, into the brambles of hell.

As he mourned Mice's death, Lemeilleur wondered about Rimbaud's proclamation to "change life." What did Mice's death say about that command?

Lemeilleur picked up Rimbaud's *A Season in Hell* and saw the cover for the first time. The red background and the black and peach figures danced in his eyes. He loved this book cover. He'd seen covers like this before—it reminded him how much he loved books. Lustig—he'd seen that name before. He opened the book to a random page and started to read. He wanted to disappear down the rabbit hole of Rimbaud—to the safety of pure fiction—where the real miracle of transubstantiation occurred. And numb and terror-stricken Lemeilleur read aloud, as if in church. *Had I not once*

a youth pleasant, heroic, fabulous enough to write on leaves
of gold; too much luck. Through what crime, what error have
I earned my present weakness? You who maintain that some
animals grieve sorrowfully, that the sick despair, that the dead
have bad dreams, try to tell the story of my downfall and my
slumber. I can't. . . . I no longer know how to speak.

Rimbaud's pedophile, Paul Verlaine, had shot Rimbaud in
the wrist, but Lemeilleur still identified with Rimbaud even if
Georges had only deserted him in a pique of carnal jealousy.
Still, Lemeilleur mourned, it all ended for Rimbaud after
Verlaine shot him. Now Mice was dead. For Lemeilleur the
omens were large and readable: Lemeilleur's life was over!

Rimbaud and Mice, two cannibals, on the *Raft of Medusa*
dead to the world at twenty. Lemeilleur would be twenty in a
year and five months. Only Lemeilleur, and a few billion
people, were left—the filthy flotsam of aspiration.

⅁

A week after the funeral Lemeilleur received a letter from
Mice's mother.

> *Dear Lemeilleur,*
>
> *I can't thank you and your father enough. That was*
> *a beautiful service for my genius son. He knew how*
> *much you loved him. His death has knocked the hair*
> *off the dog that bites me. I haven't been this sober in*
> *years.*
> *As a young gal in Galway, I played Mrs. Gogan in*
> *"The Plough and the Stars." I used to love the theatre.*
> *I ran away to NYC to become an actress, and, oh how*
> *hard I tried. I met Mice's father in a coffee shop near*
> *Times Sq. where I waitressed. He'd moved from*
> *Louisiana and was living in the Bronx. He wanted to*
> *see a play. I was so impressed. We both loved plays.*
> *And he was so handsome, and could he dance, and*

when he spoke Cajun French like "gris gris" (A voodoo curse: do what I say, or I put gris gris on you) my heart melted.

Next thing I knew I was knocked up—talk about gris gris. That was Billy—then Mice came. Mice made it forever—the end of my acting career. We moved to Nouvelle Bouville. My husband had family here. He wanted to write a play, but we needed money to live. He got a job working in the Nouvelle Bouville sewers. He hates that job: he has a morbid fear of rats.

I hated Billy, but I tried not to hold it against the little bugger for separating me from my actress life. Mice wasn't a whiner like Billy. But as I'm sure you know I'm a lot less than perfect. I'm sure you loved Mice more than I did. Please believe me when I say there is much solace in that thought. It makes me feel good he had some love in his life. I wanted to be a good mother—I really did, but I fell into the hands of gris gris early on.

Mice's Mother

Oh, I found this envelope in Mice's room. I was cleaning up. I guess he forgot to mail it to you. I was going to give you Mice's books, but my husband wants to read them. You can borrow them anytime.

P.S. The police department sent me a letter. Their 'internal investigation' of my Mice's 'demise was unfortunate and unavoidable' because Mice's 'behavior presented a threat to the life of the policeman who responded.'

Do you believe that shit. It's real simple, Lemeilleur. We suffer then we die. My son was a dreamer—big, big dreams! Dreams mean nothing.

Lemeilleur stared at Mice's envelope for a long time. He

couldn't bring himself to open it. Finally, he grabbed it, stood up, and put it with the Nameless One's letter in the dead letter department of *Les Fleurs du Mal*, and walked away.

No more pain.

46

Weeks later, still despondent, Lemeilleur craved companionship. As chance would have it, he read in the newspaper that Liberace had won a libel suit in London against a reporter from the *Daily Mirror* who had described Liberace as "fruit-flavoured." And Liberace, after the court case, had responded, "I cried all the way to the bank." Lemeilleur immediately thought of Randy, and quickly found out where Randy was working, now that he had graduated from the Culinary Institute: He was Head Cook at a large restaurant in Massena, NY.

Desperate, Lemeilleur sought a friendly voice, but Randy wasn't friendly. He hated his job. Lemeilleur told Randy he was sorry to hear that. Then Randy told Lemeilleur that Lily, his girlfriend from high school, was living with him, but she had been gang-raped at the 24-hour donut shop where she worked nights. She was still hospitalized. He wasn't sure he'd take her back. Just before Randy hung up, he added, "That friend of yours, Georges, is teaching French at a high school in Nouvelle Bouville."

"Why are you so angry?"

"Liberals are ruining this country, Lemeilleur. It all started with Martin Luther King. Nobody goes to Church anymore. Now they're turning queers loose in a government we don't even need."

The phone went dead. Lemeilleur sighed and said to himself, everything is dying. We die at every stage of life—with some of us our bodies and spirit die, while, for others, only the spirit dies. "I have to get used to death!"

Lemeilleur looked down in his hand at the piece of paper his father had given him with the Nameless One's phone number—he wanted to call her. Her soft mushroom had been comfort, a comfort he needed so badly now. He could get married and own a funeral home!

"Fuck!" he screamed.

All of life was telling him this was his destiny. He'd been considering it for weeks now. He was aching for companionship. Victoria was with a new guy. Was he fucked or what? Marry the Nameless One? What would that solve? He'd only make her more miserable. He couldn't do it. It wasn't right. Marriage. Could he love her? Maybe nobody got married for love. Maybe they all made it up. What was marriage anyway: a license to fuck? Mice, I need you! The only one to gain from his getting married was his father who would spasm into an endless philistine bliss, since marriage preserved the sanctity of the God-ordained urge to propagate that his father so dearly believed in.

⟨D⟩

His thoughts were like a caravan making their way through the desert while dogs barked and barked and barked. He drowned in his waterless depression. One of the barking thoughts he had was about Mr. Wells: *A poem is a group of words that passes through a soul.* Like dogs, his thoughts barked while he choked on the void—his life.

They barked in Rimbaud: *Weak or strong: there you stand, and that is strength. You don't know why or where you're going; enter anyplace, answer everyone.*

What a soul Rimbaud had. Enter anyplace, answer everyone. If only Lemeilleur had Rimbaud's soul.

The more Lemeilleur thought, the more he realized he was nothing but a slave—controlled by the urges in his blood. There is no real life for a slave, no forwarding address. They can only do what enslaves them. They never develop an identity. They have no place to live. They have the sickness unto death—fake freedom—they make believe they are alive.

In a fit of rage, Lemeilleur burned the last bridge he had back to his life—the Nameless One's phone number. "Fuck marriage. Fuck life," he screamed as he watched his ugly, self-serving desires go up in flames. The blast of Mice's death and the bleakness of his isolation had so thoroughly eclipsed the Nameless One's letter, Lemeilleur had forgotten it existed.

Swollen with misery, he picked up Lustig's beautifully designed book to channel Rimbaud, and he read, again in a prayerful moan: *I am lechery's wonder. My vice mounts to heaven, throws me down, beats me up, and drags me on. Now I know: I only sing under torture. I love Satan's moonshine.*

Lemeilleur stared at the ashes of the Nameless One's phone number. He'd steeped himself in sin. His song was Satan's song. *I only have savage words at my disposal to explain my Jug, jug.*

"I will never find the courage, the energy, the hope," he raged, "to write my memoir. Mice is dead—Aaliyah a dream—Liza a tragedy—Simran my greatest illusion—and now the Nameless One, my greatest sin—*mon grand péché radieux* (my great radiant sin)—has gone up in flames. I am as dead as everyone else."

He looked again at Lustig's cover, and then read aloud, *If only books could have replaced all my intoxications, all my regrets,* all my shame . . . something—anything. Please help me find a shred of honesty—I want love.

Lemeilleur was so depressed that even pretending to have Rimbaud's courage could not rouse him. He watched himself sink into an unrousable stage of depression, the ninth circle of hell, where his mother had spent the entirety of her life, shivering in the cold air blown on her by Satan's wings.

47

Mrs. LaJoie got a call from Canada: Her sister had broken her hip and was dying.

"I'm sorrry Lemeilleur, but I have to go."

The day after she left, Lemeilleur made up his mind. It was a beautiful plan: he'd kill himself and destroy the funeral home in one stroke—of a lighter. Fucking brilliant.

He bought an expensive single malt scotch—Oban—and a cigarette lighter—Zippo. He closed all the doors around the kitchen. He threw a mattress on the floor in front of the stove. He blew out the pilot light and turned on all four burners. He could hear the gas hissing into the room—his new song, he rhapsodized. The scotch just sizzled down his throat. He started to like the smell of gas. He was fumigating his soul where the secret odor of tomato plant was rancid.

On the floor next to the mattress, he noticed *Nine Stories* by Salinger, which he had started to read but never finished after Mice accused him of having banana fever with Georges.

As the gas odorizer embraced his broken spirit, he picked up the book to finish it. He found where he had left off and started reading "A Perfect Day for Bananafish." Salinger would be his last paradise before non-existence.

Mice was back in the room with him again—like the old days. Mice and Salinger would guide him out as his ever-vanishing present moved inexorably toward his goodbye to what Rimbaud called "the barbarous sideshow."

As the gas fumes embraced him, Lemeilleur read Salinger's story.

"Why, I've known some bananafish to swim into a banana hole and eat as many as 78 bananas ... Naturally, after that they're so fat they can't get out of the hole again."

When he woke up hours later—the room redolent of odorizer—he was stunned to be alive. How could that be? His head was splitting, his mouth dry—like scratchy dry, and he'd spilled the rest of the scotch. He just sat there, slightly in shock: He wasn't dead.

The smell of gas, which had permeated the room but hadn't

killed his soul, made Lemeilleur think of something Mice had told him: "Chet Baker, man, is a perfume, a perfume of sound—the essence of sadness."

His Mice grief reignited, stabbing him with a pitchfork. He remembered his plan: Light the lighter; sprinkle me with fire. Everything will be expurgated in a cleansing

ball of fire.

He looked around and all he could see were items that belonged to Mrs. LaJoie. He was about to destroy everything she owned. He started to cry. There were voices of the past in his head that were saying things. He had to stop thinking. He wasn't born in a novel or poem. He had to accept he was born in the Loss Column. That was his song: Lo-ser—two notes— not even as beautiful as the Towhee.

He needed a soul, preferably HIS own, to decide. Was he really going to blow everything around him to smithereens? He looked at his lighter. One flick and it was over—the end. He picked up the lighter. New, it shined in his hand. He held THE END.

He then thought of Seymour Glass's suicide in "A Perfect Day for Bananafish." He saw Mice's body bag trundled into the ambulance. Lemeilleur had had banana fever. Time to pay. He raised the lighter to eye level and stared at the sparkwheel—it barely touched the flint. Marie LaJoie's French "rrr"s revved in his brain. He saw her feathery face. How hurt he'd been when Mice died—how crushingly painful it had been. Lemeilleur looked into his spasming memory; Marie LaJoie's owlly face appeared. He didn't want to hurt her—not like he'd been hurt—he could never be that selfish— how could he—she loved him. He could hear her: "We arre memberrs of ze opposition, which iz called LIFE."

Life, he thought, life.

YES—YES—YES—he had to write (RIGHT?) his life— that would be UNSELFISH—finding his spirit—capturing it—and giving it to others with words that came bounding through his soul, like notes in a song, not camels in the desert with dogs barking at them.

Gingerly—a newborn—he put the lighter down, and limp and dazed he rose from his deathbed. His trembling fingers turned off the gas jets. He was ALIVE.

After all the windows were opened, he found some paper and started to write—from the pit of his unraveling—*The Spiritual Hunt for Love*—and he had his first big insights learned from Mice's death: Anger does not cure injustice and betrayal is not necessarily a part of life.

He went to his Webcor and put on a record, the "Rimbaud of jazz", as Mice called Chet Baker.

As the music played he thought he never wanted more to be a part of the world that fosters love because he wanted to give himself and the world one more chance. Where does this insane hope come from? Can he change himself? Would the world accept him? O, Marie LaJoie. He turned the volume on his Webcor to high.

Flirting with this disaster became me
It named me as the fool who only aimed to be

Lemeilleur looked down at the memoir he had started to write and he thought, no, not *The Spiritual Hunt for Love*. He told himself he'd dedicate his memoir to Marie LaJoie and, thinking of Mice, he decided he'd call his memoir *Getting over Banana Fever*.

He was so excited. He sat there on the floor, smiling like an idiot, when he remembered the letter that Mice's mother had sent to him. He jumped up, ran to his bedroom, and, after a twenty-minute search, he remembered where he had put it— in Baudelaire's *Flowers of Evil*.

Dear Speedoo,

You've been talking about love a lot lately. I don't know why I'm like this, but I can't answer you. I wanted it to be different between us. There were many times I wanted to tell you things, but I couldn't. I just let it slide. My soul never opened. I couldn't tell you that I too heard the "seashells at night singing love." I couldn't stop myself from loving you. There I said it. And when you held me on that bed in the furniture store I was crying because I wanted to tell you that they raped me at Shirley, and I wanted to tell you that my brother hated me because we used to have sex in bed at night. Then I asked you to hold me, and you did—no questions asked—it felt so good. I couldn't ruin that moment with truth—the ugly truth. I thought we'd be friends forever—above truth. I thought we would always love one another—above flesh—you were my Beatrice, but you never read Dante.

Then in 1957 something happened. I could feel you slipping away. I didn't understand until the day they pulled you into the police station. Georges! I thought Aaliyah would straighten you out. I tried to hang in, but I couldn't do it. I talked to Aaliyah. I knew you were fucking up. I was so angry with Aaliyah for not saving you!

I joined the military service to forget what I was. That's when they fucked me again. "I was ready to love the whole world, but no one understood me, and I learned to hate." (Mikhail Lermontov, A Hero of Our Time.)

I just found out: Kerouac liked Joe McCarthy! Angelheaded Kerouac—a lying fascist—burning for the ancient heavenly connection—and he had sex with Ginsberg! Kerouac was only words, Lem! I should have told you how I felt!

Passions are merely ideas in their initial stage. Love, Lem, is the last illusion. Our shadow is what is most real about us—you taught me that we can't love all our feelings, that some love is ugly—I'm the Maria in "Clay!" I bet you never read it.

That was it, all Mice's letter, unsigned and unfinished. Lemeilleur was so unnerved by Mice's letter, he swore he'd never open the Nameless One's letter, which stood unopened across from Baudelaire's poem, "La Destruction."

"Mice loved me," Lemeilleur whispered in awe as he put Mice's letter down on his bed.

What misery, he thought looking at the Nameless One's letter, was awaiting him in that envelope? As he sat there a sickening sense of loneliness crept over him. He was totally and utterly alone—not a scintilla of life touched him—the past was gone and the future blank. He looked at Mice's letter again. Whatever compassion Mice may have felt for human suffering had been overwhelmed by the anger he felt for suppressing his love for Lemeilleur.

"I am a prisoner of empty words, words I thought would set me free."

Lemeilleur threw himself on the floor. "Amid all my *Lolita* words, all that gush—I missed Mice's love!"

Devastated, Lemeilleur realized that words were nothing in themselves. Until words rang with truth they are nothing but harlequins out to thwart their master. He had to start over again. Mice had loved him, and Lemeilleur hadn't FELT it!

He slammed the Nameless One's letter shut in his copy of *Les Fleurs du Mal* and marched off to bed. He wanted to know what love means, and his soul squawked like a terrified prehistoric bird. He vowed only to use words that are TRUE— that reflect him—his real feelings.

END OF PART TWO

III

"I care not where my body may take me as long as my soul is embarked on a meaningful journey."

—Dante Alighieri

1

On the third floor in the back hallway of the funeral home, a bare light bulb hung from the ceiling just behind Simran's head. It framed her luxuriant black hair in a Georges de La Tour glow. Lemeilleur just stared at her, as if she were a painting hidden away on a dark wall in an old forgotten monastery. Rabbit-frozen, again, he descended into his timeless fascination of her, this totally unexpected apparition—his genius.

Simran, caught off guard by his speechlessness, saw the stricken look in the creases around his deep, inscrutable brown eyes.

Lemeilleur knew he looked like a horror study deftly sketched for an expressionist painting.

"I'm a dead man," he gruffly mumbled by way of explanation.

"I believe you. You look like shit," she shot back with spirit.

"My best friend just died."

"I'm sorry. God. You want me to go?"

"No."

Lemeilleur couldn't believe he'd said "no"? She couldn't help him now.

"Good. Can I come in?"

Lemeilleur's body passively stepped aside. His genius had come to him. He tried not to cry.

"Nice wickiup. You live here alone?"

Inspired, he said, "I got a ninety-two-year-old girlfriend."

"Where is she now? In an oxygen tent?"

Simran wanted to play.

"Oh, she thinks she lives in Paris. She's at the green grocer's buying lunch. Why are you here?"

"I'm tired of my upper-class trip—it bores me."

"Slumming?"

"I'm sick and tired of the chitchat about the latest article in the *New York Times*, when all that's happening is some Harvard boy is trying to get into my pants. I'm here because I read the short story you gave Agnes."

He'd been right. Giving Agnes his story, "Baseball," had worked. Simran had caught his "Hail Mary" pass. But it was too late. Too depressed to get excited, Lemeilleur whined, "Tell me you hated it—some vague, pathological nonsense."

Hearing a clatter, they both turned to the opening door below them. Up the stairs bounded Mrs. Marie LaJoie, Lemeilleur's roommate.

"Ah, Lemeilleur," Marie LaJoie chimed as she came through the doorway, "you have company—that's good. I found *escargots*—I forget the English."

"Snails," Simran said, as she let Mrs. LaJoie pass by.

"Hi, I'm Marie. He's my boarder. I'm so happy you are here. He needs a friend. He's been so sad for many months now."

"Hi, I'm Simran."

"I have to tell you, you look like someone famous, but I can't remember."

"Oh—Janis Joplin—everybody tells me that."

"Yes, yes—of course—a 'Piece of my Heart.'"

After a delicious meal—*escargots* in homemade pesto, with a baguette, followed by *steak frites* (steak and French fries) with *haricots verts* (string beans)—Lemeilleur began to relax.

"I'll clean up," Marie said. "You two go talk."

"I have a car," Simran said.

Simran drove around until Lemeilleur thought of going to Crow Hill. He couldn't believe Simran had come to see him. All he could do was brood about the memories that made him who he was—sad, angry memories. Still, sitting next to a quiet Simran, he was smitten all over again. What was connecting them—was this love?

Remembering what Agnes had told him about Simran, he asked, "Are you really studying philosophy at Wellesley?"

"With a minor in poetry."

"Why don't you quit Wellesley, if you hate it so much?"

"I guess Agnes told you that. I'll get through it," she continued, "the degree will help me later on; anyway, my father would never survive if I quit. I don't want his death on my conscience. Wow, this place is ugly. Dante would have loved it here."

Fucking Dante. Lemeilleur didn't say a thing. He still didn't know anything about goddamn Dante. He took a long swig from his bottle of wine. Why does everybody talk about Dante?

"So, what did you think of my "Baseball?"'"

"What happened to you that night?"

"I can't tell you."

"There are hints all over the story about your father's motivation."

"Mr. Wells said that too."

"Mr. Wells. From Classical?"

"Yeah, I took his summer course on creative writing."

"I loved his class. Remember that line of his, which he said in that deep voice: 'A poem is a group of words that passes through a soul?' He got that from Anna Akhmatova."

Lemeilleur had another anxious moment of feeling profoundly stupid, which he shook off with another swig. His whole being wanted this moment to work, but there was Dante, standing as tall as a medieval castle door—and who the hell was Anna Akhmatova?

Dante's wife?

"Look," Simran said, "the baseball image of lying fathers is beautiful but misleading. Your father is terrified about your sexuality."

"My father! The first thing he says to you when you meet him is, 'It was so cold when I was a kid, I had to sleep between my brother Tocard's legs.'"

"What does that have to do with your story?"

All Lemeilleur's slugging of wine had snuck up on him,

and he was about to get sick.

"I'm sorry," and he got out of the car just in time.

Simran came around the car and held him.

"It's okay," she said as Lemeilleur vomited, "I don't know what I am either—and I'm afraid too. I feel so bad for that little girl, Jacqueline."

Lemeilleur started crying and screaming.

"I HATE MY LIFE. I'M DOOMED. I LIVE IN PERDITION."

"Perdition. I love that word."

"You do?"

"That's the way I feel at Wellesley. Tell me. What did your uncle do to you that night?"

Lemeilleur was on the verge of passing out.

"Let's go for a ride. I need some air."

An hour later Lemeilleur stopped sipping his T-bird and told Simran what had happened.

"That's how I got to write 'Baseball.' My father saw this guy, Joe P. kissing me—that's why he put Tocard on me—everybody is terrified I'm queer. Oh, my head hurts."

"I didn't realize," Simran said, "how much you drank. Look, I think your father wanted to reassure himself—he wanted Tocard to tell him you're a man."

"Do you still like me?"

"I'm just getting to know you—so far so good."

"I'm not too fucked up for you?"

"Oh, you're fucked up, but I like your story—your attempt to get beyond yourself. You want to see beauty in a pile of dung. That's Zen shit, man. You want to see how the parts go together—that requires a spiritual effort—an extremely healthy detachment in a strong identity. You got some work to do."

"If I do the work, will I know when I'm done?"

"Hmm. That's an interesting question. Hans Hofmann said a work is finished when all the parts involved communicate **themselves**, so they don't need you. Hey, this could be fun."

Simran started to embrace Lemeilleur. He, not knowing

who Hans Hofmann was, was again, of course, tazed directly into the nerve that hooked him to his insecurity. With enormous psychic strength and as discreetly as possible, he pulled back and, almost pleading, said, "Is your identity strong enough for both of us? I mean, can I trust you?"

"That's a funny question," she said neutrally, but secretly alarmed. She looked at his sad face and regained her self-confidence.

"It took trust and courage for you to tell me that your uncle made you have sex with his bartender, Emma. I admire that."

Lemeilleur must have looked unconvinced because Simran quickly added, "We'll have to learn to trust each other if you really want to work on yourself."

Was that like jumping into a snake pit to prove you're not afraid of snakes, Lemeilleur thought?

And Simran pulled Lemeilleur into her arms.

A shocked Lemeilleur froze, and then, to his surprise, melted. If only he could have flown up into the sky with those warm, cloud-soft arms wrapped around him. He felt so at home—no clinks, no odor—just two strong, sexless arms wrapped around him.

⬲

"With Nabokov's dazzle," he wrote in his notebook, "Rimbaud's truculence, Dickens's hope, and Simran's reappearance, I drank from Lethe, the soothing waters of make-believe, to forget the past and move on to reincarnation. In Simran's arms I dreamed of Christ in the *Pietà of Villeneuve-lès-Avignon*, a painting I would see in the Louvre in a few years—so simple, so soothing, so . . . so . . . outside the 'barbarous sideshow' of life."

That night Lemeilleur read his *Lolita*, and on page 19 he read that Dante had fallen in love with a nine-year-old girl, Beatrice. He had to learn more about Dante. Was this what Mice was talking about? Life was much more complicated than he had ever imagined.

2

Thus began Lemeilleur's new life—TRUST.

Rain or snow, two or three times a week, with the same rigor that drove him all those mornings to serve mass at St. Anthony's, Lemeilleur hitchhiked to Wellesley where Simran went to college. He'd promised himself he wouldn't steal any cars. Simran was his new holy communion. He didn't want to mess things up. A Catholic at heart, he wanted to commune in a state of grace. His life depended upon it.

The two Nouvelle Bouvillians, arranged by that masterpiece, life, would sit in some lonely alcove in Tower Court West to talk. Then Simran would often go into some kind of trance—a kind of stream-of-consciousness, a sparkling river of opinions—about Sully, her boyfriend, the unjust war in Vietnam, her father, a stockmarket speculator, her classmates, who, by and large, were so straight and wore such ugly clothes and had such bad taste in music, had to be Republicans.

Totally and irrationally Lemeilleur believed Simran would save him—she was his genius. Mice was right. His fate had hit the lottery. One out of 190,000,000. LEMEILLEUR. He had a friend who went to Wellesley College. He rashly believed he was no longer a social solecism.

Simran, at that time, was studying *Zarathustra,* you know: *"Of all that is written, I love only what a person hath written with his blood. Write with blood, and thou wilt find that blood is spirit."* Which Lemeilleur loved:

WRITE WITH BLOOD.

Zarathustra, Lemeilleur figured out, was about the moral evolution of human beings—the transition between apes and the *Ubermensch*. Next to Mice, Nietzsche got Lemeilleur to think about human beings as moral entities that can change—

what an idea—it would influence his life for the rest of his years.

CHANGE.

And Nietzsche was easier to understand than Rimbaud.

"Silence is worse; all truths that are kept silent become poisonous." Zarathustra

That thought frightened Lemeilleur. He had secrets, life-experiences that were truths he kept silent. Like the Nameless One. He still hadn't read her letter. Was that a truth, a poisonous one, which he was silent about—that would destroy him? Then he remembered Mice's letter—it was full of poisonous truths. Secrets can kill us! What would happen to him with THE NAMELESS ONE? Did he have the rest of his life to deal with it?

The massive, hand-carved oak walls in the common rooms of Tower Court West at Wellesley had, to Lemeilleur's surprise, inured him to his expected fear of inferiority. Who knew, as he looked around waiting for Simran to come down from her room, that these boiseries, made to imbue the upper class with privilege, would work for a guy like him?

Sometimes Simran would stare at him, her eyes burning with some kind of green fire that scared the living bejesus out of him. Did she know about the Nameless One? Impossible, he told himself.

Impassively, sitting quietly in the architecture of nobility, Lemeilleur let Simran's river of words flow around him, like rushing water around a rock—HIM A ROCK. He'd never felt that self-confident. He didn't care if he didn't understand what she said. He was simply happy to be there—in the midst of her stream, with brilliance flowing around him—in the cloister of the upper class. What wonders existed in architecture. He didn't know if anyone would understand this, but just being there listening to Simran brought him such solace—he was an island of confidence—free of anxiety. Low I.Q. didn't matter. To him, Simran was a poetry that communicates before it's understood!

Quickly, Lemeilleur remembered his Kant, the definition of sublimity: *attempting to imagine what it cannot, has pain in the failure but pleasure in contemplating the immensity of the attempt.* He was in the middle of the immensity of the attempt.

Now he was learning Nietzsche: *"'I teach you the Ubermensch. Man is something that shall be overcome. What have you done to overcome him?'* That's from *Zarathustra,"* Simran told Lemeilleur. And those words made Lemeilleur think: What did he do to overcome the man in himself—the rank abuser. Simran, he told himself, was pointing to a way— laying out a direction for him—the vile violator.

Back home that night, he would dream about those words. Yes, he wanted to change—to overcome. Yes, he wanted to be a good person, to stop hurting others. But he had no idea how much his ego and soul would have to change, and how hard that would be. Just keeping his resolve would be hard. But none of that mattered at this time—he thought sacred time—with Simran—the peace he felt was so deep—it surpassed understanding.

The next time they met, Simran read to him: *"'You have made your way from worm to man, and much in you is still worm.'* You can grow—it only takes effort. We must shake off the worm in ourselves." Which meant to Lemeilleur: the slime of slummy sexual desires—the misery of self-centered sex.

"'Man is something that shall be overcome.'" She continued, *"'Man is a rope, tied between beast and Ubermensch—a rope over an abyss. What is great in man is that he is a bridge and not an end.'* We are a bridge to something greater, Lemeilleur. Isn't that exciting?"

Each day was new now. There was so much to strive for, that was beyond him. Now there was something for him to become. He was not dead. He felt no shame with Simran. He was in Xanadu—in Simran's stately pleasure-dome, where Alph, the sacred river, ran through caverns measureless to man and around his shameless body of forlorn and savage Need.

⊕

For months while hitchhiking back and forth between Wellesley and Nouvelle Bouville, he asked himself: What is change? He had no idea.

Over time he began to think the question of change was just a pitiful dream of his—a dream Mice had ignited, and Simran was trying to get him to live. In his most euphoric moments, he thought he was growing a star—his soul welled with irrational hope. "Listen to Nietzsche," Simran said solemnly. "*But the worst enemy you can meet will always be yourself; you lie in wait for yourself in caverns and forests. Lonely one, you are going the way to yourself. And your way goes past yourself, and past your seven devils. You will be a heretic to yourself and witch and soothsayer and fool and doubter and unholy one and villain. You must be ready to burn yourself in your own flame: how could you become new, if you had not first become ashes?'*"

Had he not almost died in the ashes of his biggest guilt, the Nameless One? Had he not almost died in the ashes of Mice's death, in the ashes of Mice's love that Lemeilleur never acknowledged? Was the universe giving him another chance to rise from those ashes—to create a new spirit? Lemeilleur was in transport. Was Simran the beginning of his new self?

⊕

Later in his life Lemeilleur would smile to himself when he realized that hope makes you see things that don't exist. He would learn that thinking has to be kindled, as a fire is by a draft, and kept going by some kind of interest, and if that interest were of a grand enough quality, one might escape the torment of existence and make him grow—that interest was Simran.

Never for a second did Lemeilleur think there might be something wrong with Simran—she was his god. Her words, to him, were a sacred/poetic moment—she was a word-dream where substance floated into his soul on the petals of roses, ununderstood by his mind.

Mice was right: He would find his genius. But it wouldn't be under a bedspread of Russian ermine. Lemeilleur was floating on a mystic construction of words he barely understood. He was Ali Baba and Simran was Morgiana. He was stealing booty from the cave of the rich. And when her verbal fugues ended, he'd walked Simran back to the elevator, and she'd turn to him and say: "You've replaced my father, my first love. You've made my life here bearable."

Thrilled to the bone, but not sure how to respond, he'd manage a little smile. But inwardly he was jolted into a tumultuous, wild, radiant joy. And when she'd vanished, soberly, behind the closed doors of the elevator, he, Ali Baba, would stagger out of the Tower Court West drunk on the dream of change.

Lemeilleur kept this new experience—what was it?—all in his heart, and he didn't mind the hours of hitchhiking to get back to his other home with Marie LaJoie. He didn't care if he froze to death waiting for a ride—he would never steal another car or break into a furniture store. Simran and he were lovers of the soul—friends moving over the abyss—he had found his genius. If only Mice could see him now: He was sprinting through the star-world and would cross the bridge of Himself and go onto the Island of Love, and he sang.

> *Because I've read about it*
> *Heard about it*
> *Talked so very much about it*

⏻

One day Lemeilleur went to the library to look up the Meaning of Simran: A Punjabi word derived from the Sanskrit word स्मरण (*smaraṇa*, "the act of remembrance") which leads to the realization of what may be the highest aspect and purpose in one's life.

REMEMBRANCE.

Without the vaguest idea of what that meant, he broke into song:

> *They say, on moonlit nights*
> *When the stars are, oh, so bright*
> *You can hear the seashells at night*
> *Singing love songs*

3

Winter howled on, and one night Simran read the poem *The Waste Land* to Lemeilleur. She explained every word to him. It was like reading *The Annotated Alice*, only Simran was there, in person, answering any questions he might have. She knew everything about the poem—what everything meant. Lemeilleur went home and bought a copy so he could study it—the way he'd studied *Lolita*.

The next time he saw Simran, he—because he wanted to impress her—said: "I will show you fear in a bloody ball of fur."

Her still, green eyes rose from *The Waste Land* and fixed themselves on him. Those glittering green eyes unnerved him. He was trying to sound intellectual and poetic. Near panic now he realized he had no idea why he and Simran were together, and giving in to his panic he told her the story of the dead cat at the A&P without telling her about the girl he'd taken under the lilac bush who was wearing red duck panties. Now Eliot's words bore into him: "breeding/ Lilacs out of the dead land, mixing/ Memory and desire, stirring/ Dull roots . . ."

"Your father—God Lemeilleur! The more I hear about your father, the more I understand."

Whatever she said to him made him feel better, but now he felt guilty that he hadn't told Simran about that little girl. He watched her closely to see if any memory changed her face. He was terrified she might remember. Then, thinking of his Nietzsche lesson, he wondered if he were hiding a poisonous truth? Would this secret poison them? What a dull root was he!

Simran unexpectedly lurched forward and hugged him, crying big wet tears. In shock, he was motionless, but little by little, he became frantic. Her embrace rattled the roots of his long-dormant clinks in his tormented soul. Had she remembered? The dissonance between the past and the present made him want to cry out in despair as he waited for her to tell him how bad a person he'd been.

She pulled away from him for a moment to look into his eyes.

"I don't know how to say this to you."

In that horrible moment of truth, his clinks were rattling as vividly as her red ducks. O, why had he used that fragment from *The Waste Land* to make Simran like him? Ego. She already liked him. He just sat there, remembering that "*Truths that are kept silent become poisonous.*" Why was he so . . . so . . . had he just sabotaged EVERYTHING? What was the link between his clinks and the red ducks? Too late. The die was cast. She was about to talk. He braced himself for her rejection. Her tears had dried up. Bravely he raised his eyes to hers. He was trying to convince himself he could let go of the river of Alph, the music of her dream-talk, and the confidence of her love. But no: All he thought was "Hieronymo's mad againe." Discerning the disquiet in his watery brown eyes, she, thinking it was the pain of his childhood, said, "We will see the stars again; we will emerge from this inferno."

Aghast, Lemeilleur blurted, "What's that?"

"Virgil says that to Dante as they emerge from hell. We are soulmates, Lemeilleur."

Lemeilleur, who still hadn't studied Dante, quickly changed the subject. He was horribly confused. How had they become soulmates? He was missing something. She was his GENIUS! Calm down; play the relationship on the level, he told himself—tell the truth! Don't blow it like you did with Mice. But he failed. He couldn't ask her why she thought they were soulmates. Still terrified, he looked Simran straight in the eyes and said that he knew what her name meant.

She looked down, smiled, and said, "My maternal grandmother grew up in India. She named me. My father always hated it—not American. I'm glad you like it. I love it. Shall we read a little of Pushkin's *The Prisoner of the Caucasus* before you go back to Nouvelle Bouville? I'm dying to see how the prisoner escapes."

4

A week later Simran sent Lemeilleur a poem, *Of Mere Being,* by Wallace Stevens with a note.

Lemeilleur,

Let the fuck-fangled facts of your life dangle down like this bird's feathers on the edge of space. That's your story, man—the one you HAVE TO WRITE— Your Spiritual Hunt. Rewrite what Rimbaud lost. Do it—you will overcome yourself—and you will show us all how to be a bridge. I can't wait to read it. You will become a moral treasure.

In the meantime, you're going to have to fight against the momentum of your history, which is out to destroy you. I don't fully understand you, but I believe in you. Sing your song, a foreign song. You're my Rimbaud. You will rewrite his lost manuscript, The

Spiritual Hunt, that Verlaine's wife, in a jealous rage,
threw into the fireplace and burned.
  I can already hear you: You will sing a song that
nobody hears, like the nightingale in The Waste Land:
"Jug, jug" You will find the Grail. And when the
world hears you, humankind will tremble in awe.

Your new friend, S

  PS. When I first saw you—in that ghastly
undertaker suit—with the seminarian haircut—I was
struck by how innocent you looked—so otherworldly,
like Shelley. Of course, now that I've read "Baseball"
and heard your confession, I'm now more than ever
sure of your redemption.

Redemption.

Kiss me silly. Simran compared me to Eliot's Nightingale.
I had a friend. Me, a moral treasure!
  A happy, liberated Lemeilleur immediately wrote back.
He'd been reading a 1968 essay by Meyer Schapiro—*The Still
Life as a Personal Object—A Note on Heidegger and van
Gogh,* and Lemeilleur had fallen in love with Gauguin's 1925
description of the emotion van Gogh put into a painting of his
boots.

Dear Simran,

  Gauguin, who shared van Gogh's quarters in Arles
in 1888, sensed a personal history behind his friend's
painting of a pair of boots. I'm sending you this
painting because when I write my memoir, I will paint
you the way van Gogh painted his boots. This is the
only way I can thank you—tears block my language.
  Gauguin: "In the studio was a pair of big hob-

nailed boots, all worn and spotted with mud; he made of it a remarkable still life painting. I do not know why I sensed that there was a story behind this old relic, and I ventured one day to ask him if he had some reason for preserving with respect what one ordinarily throws out for the rag-picker's basket.

"'My father,' van Gogh said, 'was a pastor, and at his urging I pursued theological studies in order to prepare for my future vocation. As a young pastor I left for Belgium one fine morning, without telling my family, to preach the gospel in the factories, not as I had been taught but as I understood it myself. These boots, as you see, have bravely endured the fatigue of that trip.'

"Preaching to the miners in the Borinage, Vincent undertook to nurse a victim of a fire in the mine. The man was so badly burned and mutilated that the doctor had no hope for his recovery. Only a miracle, the doctor thought, could save him. Van Gogh tended him forty days with loving care and saved the miner's life."
(Jean de Rotonchamp, Paul Gauguin, 1848-1903, *published by G. Gres, Paris, 1925.)*

Gratefully, Lemeilleur

5

That night, after he'd sent a poster of van Gogh's painting to Simran, he had a dream. He was floating down a river on a 'Drunken Boat.' The roar of a waterfall was growing larger and larger: He was going to die. Then he heard a gold-feathered bird singing in a palm tree, which was bent over the river. He looked up and grabbed the tree by a branch and lifted himself out of the boat. Then he was on a stage with the fire-fangled feathered bird. The bird sings. Its feathers shine. He is entranced by the song. He's asked to explain the bird. He stands up and says to the audience: "The bird's music is from no place here on earth. It comes from the Meaning of the bird's life." That causes a row. People are yelling. Finally, Lemeilleur understands what they are yelling about: Nobody heard the bird sing.

When Lemeilleur woke up, he reread the last line of Schapiro's essay, " . . . Gauguin's story confirms the essential fact that for van Gogh the shoes were a memorable piece of his own life, a sacred relic."

6

Simran's boyfriend, Sully, loved "We've Gotta Get Out of This Place" by the Animals. It became Simran's group's theme song at all their parties. Agnes was dating a really crazy business major, Abie, and boy did they party. Lemeilleur had become a hippie. In fact, he'd gotten so friendly with Simran's circle, he went to his father and said, "I'm ready to go to embalming school." The school was in Boston, and that would allow him to be nearer to Simran.

HE WAS CHANGING.

Marie LaJoie was so happy—she thought she'd brokered the peace of the century, and when she smiled at Lemeilleur, it was as if she'd gotten the Nobel Peace Prize.

Lemeilleur's father agreed immediately, and, shrewd businessman that his father was, an apprenticeship was arranged with a local funeral home in the Boston area. The funeral home would cover all Lemeilleur's living expenses, which included living in an apartment over the funeral home. Mondays through Fridays Lemeilleur would attend classes. From Friday night at seven to Monday morning at seven, he would be on call, meaning if someone died during that time, he'd get the information, call back-up, and go to pick up the body. For each body he would make $25. His father paid for school. His housing was free. In an average weekend he'd make $175—in 1964.

Now he was close enough to Wellesley College to see Simran regularly. Simran was delighted. Every minute at Wellesley was still a torture to her. Now she could escape to Lemeilleur's two-bedroom apartment over the funeral home.

Only on rare occasions did the embalmer have to sleep over. And when the embalmer found out Lemeilleur had a girl sleeping over, he was like, "get it while you can." The embalmer had no idea of how Simran and Lemeilleur related.

The *Übermensch* stuff between Lemeilleur and Simran was beyond the embalmer. Lemeilleur was enthralled by and loved their difference from the rest of the world. They heard a music through his sexless relationship with Simran that no one else heard.

Lemeilleur saved a ton of money. He and Simran made life for each other more tolerable. And Sully became a good friend. They smoked dope, protested the war in Vietnam, and dreamed of a new world order. Lemeilleur was dreaming about love again. He was sure he would find it. He would cross the bridge. He was dreaming again of flying—this time he'd be Horus encrusted with precious gems.

7

One thing happened that year that reminded Lemeilleur of Mice. Lemeilleur had gotten a call—around three o'clock in the afternoon one Saturday. He drove the hearse out to pick up Joey, his backup, who lived in the North End with his Italian mother.

"Where we going, Lemeilleur?" Joey asked after he got into the hearse.

"447 Dudley St."

"Aw man, that's in Roxbury."

"Not everybody in Roxbury is Black. I guess we gotta find out."

When Lemeilleur came back to the hearse, he told Joey, "It's a Black family."

"What the fuck are we gonna do?" Joey moaned.

Lemeilleur felt bad for them. He worked for an Irish funeral home—no Blacks. Joey kept saying, "Come on—drive away. I need this job. I don't want to get fired."

Lemeilleur went back in and told the family that he worked for a funeral home that only served white people, and he gave them the name of a funeral home that served Blacks. He said he was sorry. They were very nice, said they didn't know—had never buried anyone before. That's when they told Lemeilleur it was their son that they wanted to bury—he'd just been killed in Vietnam.

Martin Luther King's spiritual hunt for justice ended that year.

8

Simran was going into summer recess in a few weeks, and she was wild that she was finishing her junior year. She wanted him all to herself—her "summer wind." He had saved a lot of money at the funeral home, and she asked him if he'd take her to Mexico. She had to get out of the country. Lemeilleur agreed. Thich Nu Thanh had set himself ablaze to protest government regime at Dieu De Pagoda in Hue. George Lincoln Rockwell was alive and thriving in Dallas. And Freedom Marchers had just been gassed in Canton, Mississippi. They'd find sanity, she insisted, in Mexico—just the two of them.

To his stunned father he announced he was dropping out of embalming school.

Lemeilleur's friend, Dizzy, the one who hung out of his third-floor bedroom window, pretending he was Killer Kowalski. Well, he owned a used car lot out on Route 9.

In spite of all Lemeilleur's craziness, he always retained a practical side. He needed a car that would get them to Mexico and back, and he didn't want to spend a lot of money. He figured Dizzy could help him. He did. Dizzy found an old Rambler American. What Dizzy said was "the car was in an accident, the drive shaft is slightly off-center, and will last about 20,000 to 25,000 miles before it wears out. I could get $300 if I didn't tell them about the accident, but for old time's sake you can have it for $150. I paid $100. It would cost me $500 to fix. The cost/benefit just isn't there—I'd rather unload it. Hey, you're not against the war, are you? Fuckin' communists."

"Why do you ask that?"

"You're letting your hair grow long."

"I get more girls that way."

"Really?"

Dizzy could never find the "dirty" parts in *Lolita*.

9

It took Simran and Lemeilleur a week or so to get to Hilton Head, South Carolina in their Rambler American. A friend from MIT was playing in a band at a private country club there and had invited Simran to stop by for a few nights. When they got there, Lemeilleur was super excited because he'd never been south of Pawtucket before now. And so, laughing and celebrating, they smuggled dope ONTO the grounds of the country club—by accident of course—they'd forgotten they'd left it in clear sight. Hey, no problem. They just drove through the gate with smiles on their faces and marijuana on the dashboard while the guard, a geeky Republican college kid, who had checked their names off a list, smiled back.

A couple of days later, on the beach of the club, the Rambler got stuck in the sand. A bunch of guys, some wearing confederate flag emblems on their t-shirts, pushed them out. They'd never met Northerners before, and Simran, to be funny, gave each of them a rose hip tab. They looked at the tabs, then at Simran and Lemeilleur. What they were thinking was anyone's guess, but they were all smiles when they walked away—sorry guys, not peyote.

The next day the MIT friend of Simran asked them to leave because one of the guys freaked out, and now the police were looking into a drug violation—the tab of rose hip had been sent to a State lab to see if it was LSD.

⦿

Somewhere between Biloxi and Gulfport they picked up a hitchhiker. He hopped in the back seat and immediately got down on the floor.

"What's going on?" Simran asked.

"Jist wanna protect you nice people."

"What do you mean?"

"People around here don't take kindly to folks pickin' up niggahs. We could get killed."

Every once in a while the hitchhiker would peek out the window to see where he was until he said, "You bettah stop here. No one around. Thank you; God bless."

⦿

Just outside New Orleans they parked behind a garage to sleep only to be awakened by a police officer who held a flashlight and gun on them. "Can't sleep behind the garage. Come on. Get up. Don't they have hotels up North? Darkies catch you all and you be having troubles."

⦿

In Baton Rouge they decided to rent a cheap hotel to take a rest.

"I can't thank you enough, Lemeilleur. This trip is just what the doctor ordered. I was crashing at Wellesley. All that trance shit and stream-of-consciousness ranting—I was going crazy."

"Yeah. You're a lot looser now. I had no idea you were having problems with Sully."

"It's really my problem. I'll tell you some time."

"What's that trance thing all about?"

"Trance? It's a way I've got to protect myself. I get into some fantasy, and I groove with it."

"Is Wellesley that bad?"

"It was a mistake. I should have gone to a small school with a creative writing emphasis. I am not material for diplomatic service—can you imagine me married to the President?"

"What about Ambassador to India?"

"You know, I like Indian food."

And they laughed.

"I'm surprised nobody down here has commented on your skin color."

"You mean my dark lemon."

And they laughed more.

Lemeilleur liked Simran's analytical mind, and he found her explanation of things extremely interesting. In fact, her approach to problems was giving him ideas about how to analyze his own situation.

"You know, Lem. I'm still a virgin."

"Was that an issue with Sully?"

"It annoyed him, but it's not his problem. Let's explore the city tomorrow."

Lemeilleur hesitated. He venerated her way too much to take what she was saying as a hint, and he didn't think Simran meant it as such. If anything, he believed that sex would destroy their *Ubermensch* relationship. He was much too happy just being with Simran. He was so happy, he tried to believe, except for Victoria, Emma, and the Nameless One, that he too was still a virgin. He didn't count the guys for some reason—like they weren't Real. And Georges—HE DIDN'T COUNT THAT! The brain can create an illusion in a nanosecond—we really are the shadows of our imaginations as Nabokov says. Hey, he wanted to be a virgin with Simran.

Simran simply smiled at him when he didn't answer her. They went to sleep early that night, and Lemeilleur thought Simran was fearless and full of adventure. He loved that. What if Baton Rouge scared the shit out of him, and what if he couldn't get into the botanical wonders of the bayou. The whole South was like his old neighborhood, and he rejected the idea that it would be fun exploring the city.

The second day there, on the street—yes he had caved into Simran's demand to explore the city—it was very crowded— some wizened white woman, while walking by Lemeilleur, squeezed his nuts. By the time he turned around, she had merged into the crowd. That, and all the weed they smoked, was making him very paranoid. At that time Lemeilleur didn't know about PTSD flashbacks and all the rest.

All of which (weed, paranoia, and flashbacks) caused their first big fight. Simran wanted to "check out" night life in Baton Rouge, and Lemeilleur was afraid—all his old fears from Nouvelle Bouville rose in his soul like nasty ghosts mocking the "growth" he thought contact with Simran was fostering. The fight had been so bad, he'd left their hotel, got into the Rambler, and drove around. After an hour or so, he felt like an idiot, so he decided to go back and do what Simran wanted. When Lemeilleur got back to the hotel, the guy at the desk said, "She's gone," and wouldn't let him back to their room.

Lemeilleur walked outside. He couldn't believe she was gone. At first he decided to drive to the bus station to see if she was there. But before he did that, he took a seat on a bench across from the hotel. He looked up at the hotel to see the window where their room was and, lo and behold, he noticed some of her clothes draped over the railing. She was still there. He rushed back into the hotel and confronted the guy at the desk, who looked down his perfect nose and said, "Find another hotel. We ain't got no use for long-hair, niggah-loving Northerners travelling with a high yellow."

Lemeilleur pushed past the guy and found Simran sitting

on the bed crying.

"I thought you left me here—had gone back to Nouvelle Bouville."

"Get dressed. We're leaving. The jerk downstairs told me you were gone."

"Please, don't ever do that again. Stop packing. Did you hear what I said?"

"I heard you. I just want to get out of here. Hey, what's this?"

Lemeilleur was holding a tape recorder he'd found as he helped Simran pack.

"That," she said, snatching it from his hand, "is a surprise."

"What kind of surprise?"

Simran put the tape recorder in her suitcase while she archly countered, "Tell you what—I'll tell you about the tape recorder when you tell me why you wake up screaming about clinks."

Lemeilleur frowned. He didn't understand. He'd massively repressed his clink thing.

◫

Hours later they arrived in Lake Charles, found another hotel, roamed around the city, and generally had a good time—in spite of Lemeilleur's ceaseless turmoil of paranoia—he just could not adjust to Spanish moss and Southern hostility, but he hid it well—so much so, Simran very joyfully told him she was happy to be with him.

They never did talk about how he had traumatized her when he'd left her in that hotel room. No need, he guessed. They were happy again, as they had been all those times in Tower Court West, their Xanadu.

◫

Next day Simran got to swim in the Prien Lake—she was a fabulous swimmer.

That night, near the beach, they saw a group of four guys who were very curious, and they seemed too shy to approach Simran and Lemeilleur. They were white and probably in high school. Simran said she and Lemeilleur should talk to them because Simran was running low on grass. Maybe these kids knew a seller.

Lemeilleur was much more relaxed now. Simran's happiness was his honeydew and milk of Paradise. And so, when Simran suggested they approach these boys, Lemeilleur closed his eyes in holy dread and imagined himself working as a manager in the Office for Corporate Safety for the Sinaloa Cartel. He agreed.

They talked about music, laughed about nothing, shared some beers, and watched the sunset. Everything was mellow: pale orange disc setting, wispy clouds scudding, and their Southern friends asked them if they wanted "to party?"

Lemeilleur looked at Simran and she looked at him. He didn't have terror in his eyes. She didn't want to force anything on him. They both knew this might be an ideal way to score. And as they hesitated, one of the guys said, "No problem." They started to leave and Lemeilleur said, "Sure."

Simran smiled and Lemeilleur wondered what Mice would have done. They got into a car, drove around town, and then headed out. Once out of town they started smoking weed, some of which Simran said she'd buy if they were willing to sell.

Lemeilleur's paranoia mounted an unbroken stallion. Simran, on the other hand, loved being the center of attention. Lemeilleur started throwing his beers out of the car half full as his stallion bucked. He wasn't comfortable driving out into the woods. He was trying to keep a clear head. He had a sixth sense about danger—experts had trained his amygdala.

After an hour or so, they stopped at a gas station, and everyone piled out to take a pee. While in the bathroom Lemeilleur noticed one of the guys making gestures with his hands that seemed obscene.

When Lemeilleur got back to the car, he wanted to tell Simran to get out, but she was laughing. He told himself he was being an idiot—hallucinating fear. He was embarrassed. He hung on to his stubborn stallion.

About fifteen miles from the gas station on a dirt road, the guys stopped the car and most of them got out again to take a pee. They were definitely drunk and stoned now. The one who stayed in the car turned to Simran and Lemeilleur and said, "They want her."

Simran looked at Lemeilleur. He took charge. Nothing was going to happen to Simran.

"Get out of the car and start walking. I'll tell them you're going to piss."

Simran hesitated and Lemeilleur's eyes pleaded with her.

Without a word she headed up the road.

Lemeilleur walked back to where the guys were peeing and acted as if he had to pee as well. When Lemeilleur saw they were finishing, he took off and caught up to Simran. He knew with a car the kids would easily catch them. They had to get off the road. He told Simran they had to jump over a barbed wire fence, which she reluctantly did, but she cut her foot.

They ran into dark woods. Simran was hobbling and crying.

Finally, they found a path. Then the path split two ways. Lemeilleur sent Simran down the left one and he ran up the right one, took off his T-shirt, threw it on the trail and doubled back to Simran, who said she couldn't walk any farther. Lemeilleur found a big prickly bush, picked it up, and Simran and he got under. She still had a bottle of beer in her hand. Lemeilleur used it to clean her cut. He told her to take her panties off so he could use them to wrap her foot. Then they just lay there, silent. For some reason Lemeilleur thought about the lilac bush and smiled. He was feeling proud of himself—as if he were undoing the past, but not far from them—probably where Lemeilleur had thrown his T-shirt— they heard gunfire. That went on for about ten or fifteen minutes—then nothing. After an hour or so, Lemeilleur told

Simran that he had to see what was going on.

"You're going to leave me here?"

In spite of the fear he heard in Simran's voice, he crawled out and found the edge of the woods. There he could see the kids camped out by a fire with a rifle leaning against their car.

"We gotta go," he said to Simran when he returned, "they'll be back in the morning. We gotta go now."

Her foot was sore, but they left, walking all night, until they came to a farm. It was early morning, so they waited until the farmer woke up. An hour or two later, he came out. They did their best to explain what had happened. The farmer, a Black guy, was distrustful, but his wife convinced him to help the distressed couple, which he did—he drove them to their car.

⊕

Once in their car, they drove all the way to the Texas border without sleep or food. Simran had remembered she had a relative who lived in Houston. They crossed into Texas and collapsed. Lemeilleur pulled off the road and they fell into a deep sleep. He dreamed a hooded mob was dragging him to the center of town where they proudly kept their lynching tree. Hundreds of people were cheering. They all had Grosz faces.

10

Lemeilleur woke up to the sun beating down on him with hammers, while Pachelbel's "Canon in D Major" flowed through the car like a divine honey. He opened his eyes expecting to see St. Peter with a list of his sins. The music, he figured out, came from that tape recorder Simran had been carrying around all summer. He now looked down, and Simran, who had unbuckled his pants, was pressing her hot lips on his swelling underwear. Aghast, he pushed her away. He was horribly confused. HE LOVED SIMRAN.

Aggrieved, Simran looked up at him—she was crying

now—and said, "I want to love you. I don't want to be like my mother. I want a man like you."

"Me?"

"My father would never put himself in danger to save my mother. He cheats on her—has been most of their married life—and she's too paralyzed to do anything about it. You would never abandon me. Please, Lemeilleur, I'VE WANTED YOU ALL SUMMER. I saved Pachelbel for this moment."

Her cri de coeur sunk into Lemeilleur like a white-hot branding iron searing into his hard, leathery, fucked up soul, right next to the marks of his burned-in clinks. Lemeilleur hung his head in sadness: he couldn't have sex with Simran— that was all wrong.

"So, you're fucked up—so am I." Simran screamed. "WE'RE ALL FUCKED UP."

Lemeilleur, on the verge of tears, pulled up his pants.

Furious, she grabbed the tape recorder and threw it out the window with lovely Pachelbel still playing.

"Why did you save me from those guys? For what? Forget it. Let's go to Houston."

"What's wrong, Simran? What's wrong?"

"Shut up and start driving. I'm very fucked up, Lem, and I don't know why."

They left Pachelbel playing in the sere stubble of a parched ravine.

All Lemeilleur knew was he was terrified that something would change their relationship. He always thought THAT would come AFTER graduation, after Wellesley. Simran would vanish into that larger world of college graduates. Why did she ask Lemeilleur why he saved her? Why was she trying to hurt him? What was wrong with her?

As they drove on, he started to feel numb. Had their pleasure-dome just crashed? Without Simran, he didn't care about anything anymore. He thought he was shedding the slummy slime of sexual desire. He thought what he was doing was for them. Emotion not emission was what was important here. They lived in a poetry beyond the tingle of sex. Why couldn't she see that?

⊕

Just before they got to Houston Simran said, "You're never going to let anyone love you, are you, Lemeilleur?"

He wanted to shout, "I love you deeper, darker, and with more energy than the woods of Louisiana." But he couldn't say it. That made him feel so alone.

Didn't she see they had no future?

Looking out at the highway, he didn't know where he was or who he was. He wanted to belong—but did he have the right? He stayed quiet in respect for **her** future.

"You need Harlow's cloth monkey."

"Who's Harlow?"

"Harlow explained that issues of intimacy developed as a result of the mother not providing "tactile comfort" for her baby."

"Harlow's monkey?"

"CLOTH monkey! You have an attachment problem. You're afraid to love. It's not the milk you want: You don't want to be hurt. You're a coward. Do nothing. That's so easy for you. *Ubermensch*. Try *mensch*. I thought we were going to write our spirit into a book with your blood. No. You're buried up to your eyeballs in your shit."

"What do you mean?"

"You don't bond."

"But I'm here—where we are—and I don't want to be anywhere else."

"Don't confuse me. I HATE CONFUSION. My father confused me."

Lemeilleur was nearly delirious with misery—she was the only woman he'd ever loved—or at least thought he loved—and all he did was make her angry.

"All you do is dream about us. Fuck Xanadu." Simran expostulated.

Lemeilleur burrowed down deeply into himself. They were just an old Greek tragedy, he told himself—condemned to their fates by some perverted god. Two tragic stars fixed in different orbits who had managed to come together for a brief moment—a wonderful moment—a hurtful moment—an unchangeable moment. Fucking is not bonding—fucking is using.

"My father used to call my mother the 'ring,' Simran said in a calmer tone.

"The ring?"

"The marriage ring. His tether to her."

Lemeilleur wanted to scream.

"My mother's such a pushover. She could never stand up for herself. The only thing she ever did for me was save my name. My father hated Simran. It wasn't American. He wanted to call me Elaine. I can't tell you how sad I am. My soul is twisting in some deep trauma—I'm so sorry, Lemeilleur. There's something wrong with me."

Lemeilleur felt sick.

"There's something I didn't tell you. Before we left for this trip, I walked in on my father while he was having phone sex."

Lemeilleur just stared ahead looking at the windshield. Where was this conversation going?

Simran was now driving wildly, and she screamed: "With his stockbroker. She knew my mother."

She raised her fist and screamed, "My father will never love me," and smashed Lemeilleur in the groin, as the car veered crazily into the other lane.

"Watch out."

Simran pulled back into her lane and said evenly, "You're just like my father. He's hung up on vaginas. His bedroom is loaded with pornography. And you're," she screamed, "locked in the hermetic vision of your mother's vagina."

A shudder of horror seized Lemeilleur, and he flashed on his mother's scar—the wound that dumped him here, on this insane planet. While Simran, in a spray of stones and dust, pulled the car off the road and shook.

"I'm sorry, Lemeilleur. Oh. Please. Forgive me."

From that moment on, Lemeilleur, his heart still wobbling from Simran's whipping, knew that life's course would branch out—ad nauseam—in different directions—all unforeseeable and all uncontrollable, and all hurtful.

Rimbaud's 'Drunken Boat' image was holding up. He had not found love. Truth was a harmony his soul could not grasp. All hope in Simran was disintegrating. No song would be coming.

Deeply dismayed, beyond the clinks and the odor of a tomato plant, he wondered what was God's punchline; what was on the other side of Simran's mysterious freakout?

11

Something ended that summer. Now it was official: Lemeilleur needed a cloth monkey—which wasn't a bad thing—to learn love and develop, as he understood it, feelings of attachment so he could feel love. Simran got her foot fixed in Houston. Fourteen people had been killed in Austin by a lone shooter in the tower at the University of Texas. Lemeilleur and Simran decided they had to be with their friends because they had to save the country from the Vietnam War.

Lemeilleur drove back as if in a dream—untouched by the life around him—protected by a misty fog of grey depression—as he floated through dull space in his dirigible of disbelief. So this is the way it ends with Simran! Good, he plotted with himself, he'd drop her off in Nouvelle Bouville, take the three thousand dollars he had left and fly to Paris and write his memoir. Life, after all, is a masterpiece.

When he arrived at the Nouvelle Bouville exit, Simran shouted, "What the hell are you doing?"

"Dropping you off."

"You're crazy. You know that. You're crazy. Keep going. We're going to Cambridge—TOGETHER!"

"What?"

"You and I will never have a romantic relationship—so what!"

"What are you saying?"

"We're staying friends!"

"We are?"

"I've cut your chains; you're free, Lemeilleur."

"I am?"

"I don't know if you're gay or straight, but I'm out. You can find out who you are on your own. I want only to be your friend."

"You want to be my friend?"

"Are you hard of hearing?"

"I'm surprised, I guess. I thought this was it."

"You're such a drama queen."

"I don't think I'm gay."

"Who knows? You'll find out sooner or later."

In Cambridge, Lemeilleur found an apartment. He was alone now for weeks at a time and all Lemeilleur could think about was the 45 record, "The Wind," he'd taken from Mice's room the day Mice died, which Lemeilleur played over and over again. Lemeilleur wrote in one of his notebooks: "My savior was a bigger mystery to me than the size of the universe. We would stay friends without ever having the possibility of becoming lovers. Somehow this satisfied me. I now could go back to my dream of salvation. A real relationship was not something we'd have to deal with. This kind of setup was probably what Mice wanted too."

12

It was Simran's senior year. Lemeilleur's $60/month, four room apartment in East Cambridge became a refuge for

Simran, who rented one room for $10/month for her and her new boyfriend, Chet. And Lemeilleur, who now had parties every weekend, met a number of guys from MIT, where Chet went to school. Lemeilleur was determined to go on with his new life—without romancing his genius—and he wasn't going to ask his father to save him. He got a job working in a warehouse, loading building product on trucks, which allowed him to think back: How many times had he not felt what he loved until it was too late? He promised himself to keep his eyes open. The gods had bothered to wound him for a reason.

13

Simran, to Lemeilleur's amazement, found Lemeilleur a cloth monkey. McCrae Alliot was a senior who had seen Lemeilleur with Simran and had asked Simran about him. Simran showed McCrae the story Lemeilleur wrote about their summer trip. That cinched it—McCrae, a Southerner, wanted to meet him.

Lemeilleur would learn of this later. For the time being, he had only to see if he liked McCrae. Simran, the matchmaker, sent him a letter to say he had to practice love.

And remember, Lem, Simran wrote to Lemeilleur, *you're not marrying her. It's just a date. McCrae is a lovely woman—treat her with respect. I think you're ready. If you get uptight or something goes awry, let me know—I'll help you. McCrae is very direct and sweet. You shouldn't have any problems. Let me know how it goes. S.*

Simran and McCrae chose to reserve Agora, which was a little romantic building on campus, for McCrae's first date with Lemeilleur. He was super nervous—had he learned what he now thought were the lessons of Rimbaud and Nietzsche: Your words are only as good as your soul?

Sincerity.

He wanted McCrae to like him, and he'd been praying for a relationship for a while now—especially since the absurd blow up with Simran. What was Simran up to? All he wanted was to feel love. He had no idea what the flaw was in the masterpiece of their story. Simran was so like Mice. So, he let Simran introduce him to McCrae. In fact, he welcomed her urging him on, believing it would help him grow. McCrae, Lemeilleur accepted, was his Petri dish.

14

Nashville-bred and though not conventionally pretty, McCrae had a fundamentally friendly face and a natural hunger for freedom and beauty. Unlike her father, who was a Federal Judge and having a difficult time accepting the Voting Rights Act, McCrae, an art major, was liberal—she believed in inclusiveness. Her mother had died of cancer when McCrae was in high school.

McCrae stood 5'2", probably weighed 110, but it was her personality and Southern drawl that hooked Lemeilleur. Her laid-back "Hi there, Lemeilleur" hit him like a shot of testosterone. They saw each other twice—and . . . THEY LIKED EACH OTHER—TUTTI-FRUTTI. They went back to Agora to celebrate. The last time Lemeilleur was romantically involved was with Aaliyah—and we know how that went. He wondered where all his demons were hiding. He prayed he'd made some progress. At least he wasn't drinking or raping no-name throwaways. He had many more mountains to climb before his dream of rehabilitation was *fait accompli.*

Simran had helped him enormously with his social self-confidence. He did not feel like a solecism around college people. And though he felt some guilt about Simran, he didn't want to spend the rest of his life without finding out about love. This would be his first emotional/sexual test. He'd figured out that when it was a quickie, Mr. Penis was hot to trot, but when it got serious, Mr. Penis wimped out. Simran, who had no idea how damaged he was, was helping him get over his fear of intimacy. She told him with McCrae, he was between a quickie and a serious thing—which was normal for this stage of development—just relax.

"McCrae has no expectations," Simran told him. "She just wants a fling with a dashing short story writer."

Lemeilleur didn't tell Simran, but secretly he wrote in a notebook, "I had high hopes that McCrae, my Raphael virgin, would nourish me with intoxicating love, rouse whatever creative powers I had, and soften the hardness I'd acquired up to now."

A year later Lemeilleur showed McCrae the above entry in his notebook and she, after she thought about it, took Lemeilleur to the Fogg in Harvard Square to show him Ingres's painting of *Raphael and La Fornarina*.

When they found the painting, she, laughingly, had Lemeilleur read the museum note appended to the wall next to the painting. To wit: "According to the biographer Giorgio Vasari, La Fornarina led the young artist to an early death from an excess of lovemaking."

From then on Lemeilleur teased McCrae with "You'll be the death of me." But we are getting ahead of ourselves.

At Agora McCrae lit a fire in the ornate fireplace and motioned for him to sit by her in front of the sputtering flame. Her cornflower-blue eyes had a tender glow. Lemeilleur's openness to McCrae surprised him—he told himself this was good—not to stop. He wanted to breathe her into his soul. He would make Simran proud. He would overcome himself and become a man—more than a man, a lover—someone who cared. He was very nervous.

"I threw the *I Ching* yesterday and it said somebody I know is going to get lucky today."

Lemeilleur didn't know what the *I Ching* was, so he smiled, and McCrae added, "I guess it's the will of the universe."

She was wearing some kind of perfume (*Bal à Versailles* that her father had brought back from Paris, Lemeilleur later found out) that made him feel both excited and, thank god, calm. She then pulled a joint out from under her bra, handed him matches, and said, in her Southern drawl, "What do you say we love this flame into being."

Lemeilleur probably strained every muscle in his body not to give away the tremble he felt quaking throughout his ever-hopeful yet sin-filled body.

"Grass just takes me away from all the cares of this dear old world—like the people I just wrote about in the *Bridal Couple of the Eiffel Tower*, do you know it?"

"I wish I did."

"Oh good, I have an excuse to tell you all about it. Isn't this grass good?"

"Yeah—I'm floating," his voice trembled.

"That's what Chagall does. His two lovers float through space as if in zero gravity, far from reality, suspended in celestial bliss."

Maybe, he dreamed, he'd find grace with this woman.

"Come on, Lemeilleur, kiss me—this is the Age of Aquarius."

After a moist, burning kiss, he couldn't keep his hands off her. She leaned into his chest, raised her head, and they kissed again—softly—lingeringly—then breathlessly.

Emboldened and engorged, he entered her and grew ten feet taller.

All his senses were moving at the speed of light—oh Christ. Climax dead ahead.

"Whoa. I guess you've been waiting for me for some time. I say there, lover man, let's do this again."

He rolled over on his back, and she brought him back to life. They did it again and again and again—à la Fornarina. And that night Lemeilleur wrote in his journal:

> *She looks into me*
> *The unknowing heart*
> *To see if I love*

Do I?

The next day, when he told Simran how it went, she said, "Lemeilleur, you're taking this way too serious—this is only a spiritual practice. I'm worried now that you're going to get hurt. McCrae has no idea what she's going to do with her life. Be careful, my sweet. She has no money constraints. She's supposed to marry a rich count."

15

A month later McCrae took Lemeilleur to the Clark Art Institute in Williamstown to show him Renoir's *Onions*.

"That's you. You're the everyday that became art—you're the perfect example of how the working class can become healthier, stronger, and freer. I love you, my onion. You are my world-soul."

After that, Lemeilleur, wildly inflated by his success, told himself if ever you write a memoir, you'll have to call it *Renoir's Onions*, now his favorite painting by Renoir. Lemeilleur a world-soul!

What onions.

16

A month or so later, Simran came down with some mysterious

illness: She'd break out in a fever and sit at her desk and stare at the walls. No one noticed at first. Wellesley-stress was always freaking someone out, but most often, after a few hours, the student would come out of it, and people would breathe easily and say: She's okay. This time, just before Thanksgiving, Simran went into a deep trance. It lasted for most of the day. After a while it started driving her dorm crazy: She was playing The Mamas and Papas's "I Saw Her Again" over and over. Finally, Simran's roommate, Carol, tried to talk to her, but Simran started talking gibberish.

" 'You gave me hyacinths first a year ago;
'They called me the hyacinth girl.'
—Yet when we came back, late, from the Hyacinth garden,
Your arms full, and your hair wet, I could not
Speak, and my eyes failed, I was neither
Living nor dead, and I knew nothing,
Looking into the heart of light, the silence.
Od' und leer das Meer."

Carol ran off and got McCrae, who was studying down the hall. Now standing just outside Simran's room and glancing nervously at her, they didn't know what to do. Getting the school's administration involved would not be well received by Simran, and they didn't want to do anything that might jeopardize Simran's graduation. Finally, McCrae ventured into the room and, recognizing Simran's gibberish, asked Simran, "Why are you quoting *The Waste Land*?"

"How can I be alive if I don't feel?"

"What don't you feel, Simran?"

She turned her angry face toward McCrae and spat, "Nothing matters."

McCrae was put off, but she held her ground.

"Everything matters, Simran."

"YOU will never know, will you? Cripples need the words of others to say what they WANT to feel. You don't need words, McCrae; you feel what you know. Go away—you know nothing of death. Get out. The Buddha was wrong. We do not make the world with our thoughts. I want to be alone."

Simran rose and walked toward the bathroom.

"I'm not going to leave you like this."

Before Simran slammed the bathroom door behind her, she screamed, "I'm his hyacinth girl!"

McCrae called Lemeilleur and quickly told him what had happened. He told McCrae to put Simran on the line.

"Thanks, Lemeilleur. She's still in the john."

"Tell her to pick up the phone. Get some rest. It'll be okay. I'll take it from here."

When Simran came out, she picked up the phone.

"I told McCrae to get some rest," Lemeilleur told Simran, and they talked for over an hour until Lemeilleur asked Simran why she thought she was the hyacinth girl.

"It's over, Lem. Thank you. I feel better. You can go now." And she hung up.

Simran never had another break like that again—but she stopped talking to McCrae.

Lemeilleur, for his part, was so involved with his anxiety that he was going to lose Simran **and** McCrae at the end of this school year, he never came close to understanding what Simran was going through—never asked himself what had set her off. He had disappeared into a new fantasy: He was now Cinderella—the glass slipper that Simran had placed on his foot would shatter in a couple of months and he would lose McCrae when she graduated.

17

For the rest of the school year McCrae and he shared an enthusiasm for art, hiking, and cooking, and developed an affection that Lemeilleur started to believe would endure for more than a year.

He felt like chortling.

McCrae was that rare person who wanted to fly off to the

land of miracles and happiness. He was all for it. Everything was so easy with McCrae. They were Chagall's lovers. Flying in a gravity-free universe, in the inexpressible of beauty. Would his life become a song of never-ending love?

⊕

Simran graduated with a C average, but she won a prize for her senior thesis: "Sterility in *The Waste Land.*" It was dedicated to her father.

⊕

Had it not been for McCrae bankrolling Lemeilleur, he would not have gone back to college that year, become a French major, and spent his junior year at the University of Paris while living with a French family in the 16ᵗʰ arrondissement on *la Rue de la Pompe.*

All that happened while McCrae, who now graduated, was working in a museum in Florence, Italy, where they were still restoring art that had been damaged by the rising waters of the Arno in 1966. Simran had gotten a job indexing books for MIT Press.

Sometimes at night when Lemeilleur was alone in Paris, he would think that his real cloth monkey was Simran; but he never mentioned that when he wrote to Simran—she could be very touchy. He didn't think she liked her new job.

As time went by, he felt worse for Simran; he didn't think she was happy with her boyfriend Chet, who was getting his PhD at MIT, but there was nothing Lemeilleur could do. He would reread Verlaine's poem, *Il pleure dans mon coeur* (Tears fall in my heart), but that only made him feel worse. He prayed for Simran to find love.

⊕

When he finished his junior year in Paris, he bought a BSA

441 "Shooting Star"—a big, single thumper—with money McCrae had sent him; he picked her up in Italy, where they bought leather saddlebags and drove to what was then Yugoslavia.

What a summer.

They traveled all over Europe that summer—from Florence across the Adriatic to Zadar; then back across to Venice, on to Salzburg, then Munich, and back to Paris, where he showed McCrae some of the treasures he'd discovered when he was a student.

18

After they arrived back in the USA, McCrae got a job teaching art at a prep school in Cambridge. Lemeilleur finished his senior year, got his degree, and got a job teaching French in a small prep school in Boston. His father never came to his graduation, but he did walk in on McCrae and Lemeilleur one Sunday afternoon while they were making love on the kitchen table.

"Dad."

"Can I watch?"

Lemeilleur jumped off the table, pushed him out of the kitchen, and McCrae pulled her dress down and ran into their bedroom. Lemeilleur locked his father out of the apartment.

"Who was that?" McCrae, disgusted, spat out.

"My father."

"O god, I never came close imagining the horrors of your childhood."

19

As happy as Lemeilleur was with McCrae, what he called his "clinks," which had been stirred up by his father's desire to watch Lemeilleur and McCrae make love, were now working overtime to sabotage him. Damn those dull roots!

Lemeilleur hadn't noticed, but McCrae had—he was drifting away from her—some kind of creepy psychic dysfunction was crawling on all fours into their sexual paradise. For a year now Lemeilleur had not heard his falling "clinks." He believed they had been held in quarantine in his unconscious, cordoned off by McCrae's love, and he thought that cordon would permanently protect him. It did not. McCrae came to him to discuss how alarmed she was.

"I don't want to say this to you. I love you so much."

"What's wrong—tell me."

"You sure you want to talk about this?"

"Of course—what do you mean?"

"Sometimes, when we're making love, I feel like . . . I feel like . . . Maria Schneider in *Last Tango in Paris*. Humiliated and violated—you disappear into your pleasure—like I'm not there. I feel like we're in a movie—a bad movie."

Lemeilleur broke down. He lay in bed for two days. McCrae had heard his "clinks."

Finally, he realized, he had to release the hellish "clinks" from his enslaved soul. Until now—this very moment— Lemeilleur had not believed Georges had broken Lemeilleur's wings. He still wasn't sure where the "clinks" came from, but he'd never talked to McCrae about Georges. He felt he had to come up with some explanation. Until this moment, he'd believed his love for McCrae was a soaring upwards—a total transcendence of the past. Now he thought he would die when he realized that his love of McCrae had only temporarily immuned him from his past. He knew now he had to tell her about Georges, but when?

McCrae held Lemeilleur's head and whispered, "You need help."

"I agree," Lemeilleur whispered back.

The next morning, McCrae made love to Lemeilleur so tenderly, her moans hung in the air like incense, and he thought, looking out the bedroom window of their Cambridge house as she showered, that he could feel the rain clinging to the leaves of their ash tree. That made him think about Simran and Rimbaud—*Il pleure dans mon coeur/ Comme il pleut sur la ville.* (Tears fall in my heart/ As rain falls on the town)

⌭

It was Saturday and McCrae had many papers to correct and grade for her art classes.

Dressed, Lemeilleur brooded over McCrae's insight. He was downstairs, in the library, standing before a bookcase of the art books she had studied in college. He was lost in thought, thoughts that were making him more and more sullen. *Il pleure dans mon coeur.*

"Are you okay?" McCrae called down from her office.

"I'm just thinking. Thanks."

When he looked up, he saw the name, Balthus, printed on the spine of a book. The name should have rung one of those bells in the never-quiet belfry of Lemeilleur's memory that Proust talks about, but the memory never rang. Balthus?

Bedeviled by his blankness of mind and desiring to rid himself of his gloom, he grabbed the book and opened it, certain it had nothing to do with his life. A photo fell out. He picked it up.

McCrae heard the thud.

"Lemeilleur?"

When he didn't respond, she ran downstairs.

Lemeilleur was on the floor. His glasses were broken, and his face was raw from a carpet burn.

"I think I passed out," Lemeilleur said.

Fearing a heart attack, McCrae took him to the hospital. Lemeilleur was admitted.

Many tests and hours later he was released. He'd had a vasovagal syncope, which occurs when you faint because your body overreacts to certain triggers, such as the sight of blood or extreme emotional distress. The vasovagal syncope trigger causes your heart rate and blood pressure to drop suddenly.

When they got home, Lemeilleur showed McCrae the photo he'd been looking at when he fainted. "The Guitar

Lesson" by Balthus. The image of a sexual encounter between a woman and a girl about twelve years old—the age of Lolita and Lemeilleur when they had their moment. And like Lolita and Lemeilleur, the abused child does not appear to look unhappy. Both child and adult seem lost in the ecstasy of passion. The guitar is lying on the floor; the lesson interrupted. The woman has thrown the child across her lap and pulled the child's dress up above her navel, thereby showing us the child's nakedness from navel to knee. With her right hand the woman pulls the victim's hair, while the other hand thrusts into the child's thigh just below the vulva.

"Oh, Lemeilleur. This is worse than I ever imagined. We have to get you help."

"Where did you get this?"

"I'm not supposed to have this photo. A friend took it surreptitiously when she visited the Pierre Matisse Gallery a few years ago. The painting belonged to Pierre's wife. They kept the painting in a back room. Today "The Guitar Lesson" is hidden in the basement of New York's Museum of Modern Art."

"Was Balthus abused?" Lemeilleur asked, surprised.

"He never said. He didn't like questions like that. He said art was about color and lines."

"Wow. Nothing like this has ever happened to me before," Lemeilleur said as he sat down.

"Come on. It's been a long day. Let's go to bed."

Frightened, Lemeilleur slowly began to tell her about Georges. And as McCrae undressed, she heard the pain in Lemeilleur's voice. It was as if his vocal chords dragged a heavy weight. After she climbed into bed, she started to cry.

Lemeilleur, a frail frisson of freedom fluttering in his immensely sad soul, tried to console her.

That made her smile through her tears.

"You know, Lemeilleur, you're a little like Balthus."

"Really?"

"He also conflated his life with characters from fiction."

"Like who?"

"Let's see. He was as big on Heathcliff as you are on Lolita."

"I wanted to be Lolita when I was with Georges."

"By the way, you wouldn't like Balthus. Somewhere I read a friend of Balthus called Lolita 'a stupid little girl.'"

"What did Balthus think of *Lolita*?"

"Balthus? He thought it was funny."

They both laughed, and as Lemeilleur, safe for the moment in McCrae's love, started to fall asleep, she whispered, "Don't worry, Lem, your imagination will sustain you. Good night, Love."

A few minutes later Lemeilleur whispered, "McCrae? Can I tell you something else?"

"Of course."

"A few months before my sixteenth birthday, my father saw this guy, Joe P., kiss me. I knew there'd be some kind of reaction, and I was on guard. But I forgot about it after a few weeks. Then one day my father says, 'Hey, what dya say we celebrate your birthday?'"

"Is that what 'Baseball's' about?"

"You read 'Baseball!'"

"I've been waiting for you to tell me what happened that night. Simran showed it to me, but she never told me the whole story."

"Tocard made Emma get on the table I was drinking at. I was looped. She faced me and spread her legs. 'I never let her wear panties when she works for me,' Tocard brayed, and he came around back of me and pushed my face into her nappy— I still remember all the smells—sweaty, biscuity, toilet-powdered."

"O, Lem."

"'That's beauty, boy; not this dumb book,' the asshole roared. I was reading *Of the Beautiful and the Sublime*. I was struggling to breathe when I heard the book slap onto the floor. Tocard's fist had clenched my hair as he rubbed my face into her, and that's when Emma said, 'Go easy, Tocard.' All I could think of was her smells—they'd been smashed into one odor—a tomato plant."

"Tomatoes. I understand—you never eat them. I'm so sorry, Lem."

"Then Tocard pulled the table away from the booth, pulled down my pants and underwear, and Emma knelt before me. Tocard watched and his fat jowls wobbled as he—"

"—Stop! This is awful, Lemeilleur."

"Please, let me finish. I barely had enough wit to know the only way out of this was to orgasm, but I couldn't feel it—all I could think of was the sickening smell of tomato plant. After what seemed like a long time, Tocard told Emma to get on the table. It was just high enough for me, and somehow she managed to get my, ah . . . semi-turgid . . . into her.

"'He's good,' she gasped in a fake orgasm to end my torture. Tocard thanked her, gave her some money, and she left. I never felt her. That's it, my madeleine, my '*moment bienheureux*', the epiphany of my life; I've tried to keep it from turning me into Miss Havisham's wedding cake, but I see with you I'm failing. You're right: I need help. I once had a woman against her will."

"You mean," McCrae shuddered with a smidgeon of ghastly hope, ". . . like date rape?"

"I'm so sorry," Lemeilleur broke down and cried, "let me explain?"

Haltingly Lemeilleur told McCrae about the Nameless One.

As McCrae cried herself to sleep, Lemeilleur, his arms wrapped around her softly convulsing body, held on, fearful he would lose her.

The next day they found a therapist who specialized in child sexual abuse.

⬤

A year had gone by, and Lemeilleur's therapy had brought his pride of survival and his vaunted resilience to their knees, and as he entered their apartment late that afternoon he seemed distant and preoccupied, which was beginning to bother McCrae.

"Lem, how was therapy?"

Lemeilleur kept walking, which made McCrae angry.

"Did you hear me?"

"I did."

"Why won't you talk to me?"

"What do you want me to say?"

"What did you talk about today?"

"Oh, the usual. How fucked up I am—insecure—grabbing at anything that resembles love."

"Do you mean me?"

"The damage is done. My father controls my soul through some kind of fucked up mystical possession!"

"Lem. Come here."

"Don't touch me!"

"Lem, I love you!"

"Me or Renoir's Onions!"

"I love all the versions of you."

"I'll try to keep my world-spirit open to you."

"Don't do this. Don't use your anger to destroy us. All your trauma—all your abuse over the years—it's all conspiring to destroy the one decent thing in your life—ME!"

"I have to go to my desk."

"You must be terrified that I'm really not here—not real—that I don't really love you."

"What do you REALLY know about my life?"

"You're testing me, Lemeilleur. I know you; I know you want me to love you. You just can't find the strength to believe it."

Lemeilleur sat down next to McCrae and put his arm around her as he cried—ferociously.

⬭

Nine months later McCrae came home from a doctor's appointment and tearfully handed him this note she'd written on her diagnosis: ovarian cancer.

> *Dear Lem,*
>
> *I'm so sorry. All I wanted was a simple relationship, and eventually kids, which I know, because of your genes, you're totally against. I love you so dearly I was willing to give up the kids. I'm so sorry, Lem. I never thought I'd lose myself. I sincerely wish it didn't have to happen this way. I'll always remember you singing to me: You'll never get to heaven if you break my heart. How your kisses had gotten so deep within me. I wish I could be there when you publish your first novel, but the cancer is taking me away from you. I don't want to go.*
>
> *—McCrae*

A few months later Lemeilleur found himself in their bedroom—McCrae wanted to die at home. A terrified-to-the-bone Lemeilleur watched McCrae slip into a coma. A cold, iron fist crushed his heart. Helpless he stared at the morphine drip. A hospice worker sat in a chair in a corner of the room behind him. She kept a record of McCrae's descent—all the insane details: temperature, pulse, breathing, rate of morphine, etc.

All of a sudden McCrae's head rose from her pillow and she emitted a blood-curdling sound. Lemeilleur jumped up and held her hand.

"What's going on?" he shouted to the worker.

"Her body is fighting for her life."

"Is she in pain!"

"No. She's unconscious."

And McCrae's head rose again, and the same horrible sound came out of her as her face grimaced and her whole body shuddered.

"I'm going increase her morphine!"

"You can't."

"Why?"

"Her body is gasping for breath; she has a strong heart."

"I'm giving her more morphine!"

"She can't feel any pain. We count the doses. There are legal limits!"

"Limits! Limits! She's dying! That's the limit!"

And Lemeilleur grabbed the morphine. The worker ran over to stop Lemeilleur.

"I'll lose my job!"

McCrae stopped breathing.

"My love!" and Lemeilleur collapsed to the floor.

He never told his love-sick father that McCrae had left him.

Simran sent Lemeilleur Robert Frost's poem, "Nothing Gold Can Stay."

20

Chagall was right, love—deep love—true love—separates us from the tawdry, the unclean, the vicious. True love and reality don't mix—the laws of gravity don't apply. Love— was sorely missing in his life—how would he survive that? How did Simran find McCrae? Will he ever find another McCrae?—was McCrae all the love he will ever have in this life? Had he actually loved McCrae?

McCrae's death was more painful than Mice's death, but Lemeilleur felt more hopeful this time around. McCrae had given him something—which he clung to in the hypothermic waters of grief, with frozen fingers, like a survivor of the "Titanic." Sure, McCrae would want him to get stronger; he stayed in therapy. He must become **her** Renoir's *Onions*.

21

Two years after McCrae had left him, Lemeilleur decided to

go to a party in Boston that a friend of a friend of a teacher that Lemeilleur was working with was throwing—in other words, Lemeilleur would know no one there, which felt safe to him.

Once there, he remembered that the host of the party, a redhead named Alice, was an artist and professor at Massachusetts College of Art and Design. And sure enough in the living room over the fireplace was most likely a painting of hers.

Lemeilleur studied the painting. Since McCrae had died, he'd begun to read all her art books. It was his way of continuing a conversation with McCrae—art kept her in his heart.

He walked away from the painting, saying hello to this one and that one, adding a comment here and there, until his host, Alice, an incredibly sexy redhead, came over and said, "Come, I want to know more about you—you look so sad."

They sat down, looking up at the painting. Lemeilleur was drinking wine. She had a scotch. Without his saying a word to her, she launched into her history: had grown up on a farm in Vermont, was part Swedish, and loved lonely men.

In response, he told her his McCrae story. Her eyes immediately watered. Was he moved by her instant empathy? He felt like he was in a movie. Her turn of brain, her sentences, her smooth I'm-in-charge manner wreaked artifice, and there was nothing soft about this woman. He'd never been into domination. However, he was tremendously attracted to her. The war between his heart and his body distressed him. Why—he looked around—out of a room of twenty or thirty people had she chosen him? What sign was he wearing? Therapy had made him aware of triggers, but he never thought of himself as a trigger.

His brain kept saying, remember all you learned about yourself in therapy, and his brainless body kept saying, fuck it—figuratively and literally. She, of course, was intensely tuned in to his ambivalence.

"You know," she said, sipping her scotch, "you don't have

to marry me."

If only he were normal, he sighed to himself, as he stared at her lush red mouth.

"So, you're going to break my heart?"

He sighed again and swallowed his spicy, chocolate-flecked wine. How could he feel safe with this woman? Then he thought: Why do I want safe?

"That's interesting: You're thinking. You're more complicated than I thought. Now I really want you."

He looked into her pussy-hollow eyes, her eyelids batting over them like eager labia; then a swarm of her body parts, especially the usable ones, blazed in his wine-saturated blood screaming "fuck." He was in the moment of *rêves malfaisants* (harmful dreams), but achingly he refused to use her wenchily. He wanted to let Alice down softly.

"Stay with me, tonight. I will give you a total orgasm."

Lemeilleur could feel the fires of hell licking his balls.

"Don't you want to die in the very moment of fecundation?"

"What's your painting called?"

"*The Rosy Crucifixion of Sex*—you have read Henry Miller who said, 'That's why we look so goddamned disgusting to one another,'" she snapped. "I made it for people like you."

And his host, with a hot glow emanating from her white desanguinated skin, rose from the couch, bowed brusquely to Lemeilleur, and, all trauma and no pain, stomped off—to find her next fix.

Lemeilleur was upset—even the jammy *vin triste* (sad wine) with hints of vanilla got sour.

On the way home, he remembered his father's story about the lady and the blueberry patch—Lemeilleur screamed, "I'M DIFFERENT. I'm not playing stupid because I'm afraid."

When he got home he took out one of his older bottles of wine and started to drink. He was well on his way to getting drunk when the words, "Mon Semblable. Ma Soeur," (My fellow. My sister) came to mind.

He stumbled into his library and knocked his copy of

Baudelaire's *Les Fleurs du Mal (The Flowers of Evil)* to the floor. An envelope fell out of the book. O God!

He sat down on the floor and picked up the letter. It was from the Nameless One. He pushed it back into the volume of Baudelaire, found another page, stood up and read aloud in a drunken boat roar: *"Comme les mendiants nourrissant leur vermine."* (Like beggars nursing their lice.) *"Nos péchés sont têtus, nos repentirs lâches.* (Our sins are stubborn, our contritions are weak.) *"Je le connais, lecteur, ce monstre délicat.* (I know, dear reader, this exacting monster.) Drunk, he had this insight: All unresolved trauma creates a coffle of damaged people who want to retraumatize the world so they can feel normal. "O, McCrae," he called out, "if only I could put my head once more on your breast. My little cloth monkey. We had our moment to dream in the sun with love and gaiety. My sunny valentine. Are you smiling at me as I bump around in the dark? Am I too damaged to be around other people? I'm trying hard NOT to believe you were only a crazy man's fantasy."

He sank back flat onto the floor and cried. Love—it was so simple—what he had with McCrae—and it felt so natural. He banged the floor with his fists. He couldn't believe it—he'd felt love. In tears, clutching McCrae's picture, he drifted off into sleep as the TV reported snow in the Sahara Desert.

He dreamed that lascivious adjectives were pursuing virginal nouns. That language corrupted the feeling the soul turned into a sound. Then the adjectives found and raped one of his nouns. Now they prowled for more. All his nouns were hiding—trembling.

When he woke up, he brushed himself off, put McCrae's picture back on the bookcase, and as he put his Baudelaire away, her letter fell out again. The Nameless One. She was insisting. His head was pounding. This was not the time to read it. Would he ever read it?

Quietly, respectfully he put the letter back. As his headache raged on, he thought he'd gone beyond the grief of losing McCrae, his brain throbbed with guilt. He knew he was slipping back, losing it: Thinking he was a weak character in a poem, a bad poem, written by a soulless pedophile, who had destroyed a little boy's soul. He had to get back to the real Lemeilleur, the ambitious 106 I.Q. plugger. Then he realized he hadn't talked to Simran for over a year. He stood up and screamed, "Baby, we were born to run." His hope was short-lived. The dust of the floor floated up and surrounded him like a bad dream. He told himself he had to start going to AA meetings. He didn't want to die and rot, unfound, like a potato in Mice's bin.

Determined, he walked over to his library. The books of his life, the books that would lead him to paradise, were arrayed, a phalanx of what? He pressed his fingers to the spines of his soldiers and read titles. He stopped at James Joyce's *Dubliners*. He remembered what Mice had said about Joyce's short story "Clay." Would Lemeilleur end up like Mice: paralyzed in a fear so great love was forever locked out?

His books, Lemeilleur realized, had been his Marble Halls—where his search for beauty and desire for love started—and, now he realized, where his life was going to end as well—in the Marble Halls of dreams.

I'M TRAPPED between MY CLINKS and LITERARY CHARACTERS!

"Rage," he screamed, "can push you into dimensions of existence undreamed of by the mildly traumatized. I have to tear down these walls of quotes; my Marble Halls are my prison."

END OF PART THREE

IV

"And your own soul will tell you that however false and foul our forms and systems are now, still, through the many centuries since Egypt, we have been living and struggling forwards along some road that is no road, and yet is a great life development."

—D.H. Lawrence

1

Agnes called Lemeilleur to say that Simran had rented a huge house on six acres of land on the Neponset River surrounded by six hundred acres of town forest. And that Simran had found a new lover, Bernie, who was from Brooklyn and had studied at the University of Chicago, and they were starting a commune. As Agnes put it: "We should do this while we get ourselves together for the next thing in our life. Who knows what will come out of it. Everything is negotiable, right?" Lemeilleur wondered what was negotiable.

"Oh, I forgot to tell you, Lemeilleur. They have a motto for the commune. It's in French. I'll try to say it: *Là, tout n'est qu'ordre—*"

"—It's from *Les Fleurs du Mal*, Agnes."

"What's it mean?"

"There, all is order and beauty, opulence, calm, and harmony. Baudelaire's definition of paradise."

Lemeilleur decided it would be nice to be around people again, especially Simran. He'd flourished in her energy once; maybe now that she was happy with her new boyfriend, things would be better between them. Also, the commune thing intrigued him. Mice would have liked that—a home with no yelling and lots of left-leaning anarchists.

So, he decided: From each according to ability—to each according to need. No longer paralyzed by grief, Lemeilleur thought, by living there, on the railroad-line to Boston, he could also keep his job teaching French; he said yes.

2

"The magic carpet waits for you."
—Jimi Hendrix

To get to the property, you had to drive down a curvy dirt road, maybe two hundred yards long, cross a white wooden bridge, which spanned the Neponset, and you were home. And to further isolate them from the corrupt capitalist society that was bombing Vietnam was a town forest of six hundred acres that surrounded their communist six.

The house itself was two hundred and fifty years old, had six bedrooms and a dormitory that slept twelve more. They also had an office, living room, dining room, large kitchen, and a second living room with large open-hearth fireplace, where, in the autumn, they would boil down gallons of sap to make maple syrup.

Long live the unfinished American Revolution.

Since Lemeilleur was working, he got a desk in the office. He also got a nice corner bedroom on the second floor. It didn't have heat, but none of the bedrooms had heat. The kitchen only had a slop sink, but it had a beautiful wood stove, a refrigerator, table, some chairs, some cupboards, and a piano.

They all had separate bedrooms, though Bernie and Simran slept together.

Gladstone, an old MIT friend, worked but didn't want an office. A photographer, he wanted a darkroom—one was created in the dormitory. Agnes's bedroom was across from Lemeilleur's.

They pooled their money, helped each other with problems, and looked forward to the future. They were modeled on The Hog Farm. They even had a dog: Calvin, in memory of human corruption.

The thing the sixties did was to show us the possibilities and the responsibility that we all had. It wasn't the answer. It just gave us a glimpse of the possibility.
                                                        —John Lennon

3

Their first community crisis came when Chet, Simran's last boyfriend, returned from Vietnam. The war was just about over, but people were still very upset. It was, like all wars, based on lies.

Unbeknown to Agnes, Gladstone, and himself, Simran and Bernie had decided Chet would simply be a little love addition to their relationship. And to further complicate things, nobody had told Chet that Bernie existed, never mind was sleeping with his girlfriend.

Chet showed up two days later in uniform.

"Hey, Chet, welcome home," Lemeilleur said as he embraced him.

Lemeilleur had written to Chet four or five times while he was in Vietnam.

"I'm sorry about McCrae, Lemeilleur."

"Thanks, Chet."

"Hey Gladstone."

Chet and Gladstone had been roommates at MIT.

"Hi, Chet," Agnes said.

He only nodded to her. And then Simran came forth.

"I begged you not to go to Vietnam, didn't I?"

Chet nodded to her too. But he was putting two and two together as he looked over at Bernie.

"I told you if you went, I wouldn't wait for you, didn't I tell you that?"

"Are you asking me to leave?" Chet finally said.

"No." Simran nearly shrieked.

"Hi, I'm Bernie, good to meet you. Simran and I want you to stay with us. We're gonna defeat collectivism not through protests or dynamite but through philosophy, art and literature."

That night Lemeilleur asked Chet how he was feeling, and with typical understatement he said, "It took a war and Simran to make me grow up. It would have been nice if you had warned me."

And that's how it started. Each night Simran would sleep in a different bedroom, Chet got odd nights, Bernie even.

At first the tension was subtle, but as time progressed, the competition between Chet and Bernie intensified. And it positively burst out into the open one day while they were gathering firewood for the winter. It happened on the two-man saw, which is also called, appropriately, the misery whip. Bernie and Chet were alternating pulls to cut through a huge oak that had fallen in the forest. They were both sweating and breathing hard, but neither would let the other know he was too tired to go on.

Chet's face was flushed red and Bernie's hands were visibly vibrating on the handle. The saw was moving so fast there was smoke rising from the cut. One of the ends of the metal broke off from the wooden handle and lashed out. Bernie felt the metal burn against his ribs.

That night Bernie decided to call it quits. Simran was devastated.

During that same night Simran, who was sleeping alone in her own bedroom, started to scream. Neither Bernie nor Chet could calm her down—in fact, she wanted both of them out of her room—IMMEDIATELY. When they left, she called for Lemeilleur. He walked in. She was still crying. Lemeilleur stood by the door wondering what he would say.

"I need you, Lemeilleur."

"Okay."

"Come over here."

He did.

"Get in bed with me, Silly," she sniffled. "I want you to hold me."

That was a strange night for Lemeilleur. With Simran having two lovers, he had become afraid of her. He didn't know why. Her sexuality and his were worlds apart.

That night he thought about Georges as he held Simran. He was thinking about all the therapy he'd had, and how he had undervalued the power of sex—what misery it could inflict, directly and indirectly, through the twisting of one's emotions into a Gordian knot. Somehow Simran was tied into that knot. All that therapy and he was still confused.

In the morning, she said she was fine, but that Lemeilleur was still feral.

"Why feral?"

"Nothing changes, does it, Lem?"

"Why are you saying that? I changed."

"I have the same problem with Bernie that I had with Chet."

"What problem?"

"Why would I tell you!"

"You know what your problem is!"

"You're feral because you're alone—always alone. How can you stand it?"

"I changed with McCrae. I'm not alone—McCrae is in me!"

"We're both feral, Lemeilleur—that's why we're friends," and she stomped off.

That afternoon Gladstone got a good picture of Simran and Chet sitting on the tailgate of Bernie's yellow pick-up truck: She, in her sorrow, wore a green woolen cape and had the hood over her head, looking like Catherine of *Wuthering Heights,* and Chet, to mock what he believed were her romantic pretensions, played an understated Heathcliff. Then Bernie left, disgusted.

⟊

As Simran mourned the loss of Bernie, she and Chet fought about everything. The damage that had been done between her and Chet was irreparable. Lemeilleur felt incredibly sad for her: Simran had never had a McCrae—a simple uncomplicated love.

But Simran, a trooper, continued on her journey, now trying to get Agnes to sleep with Chet—in fact she tried so hard, Agnes decided to move out. Simran was ever the mystery to Lemeilleur—especially because even he knew Chet had no interest in Agnes. But life went on—a slight shift, with Chet's energy: things went from Hog Farm to Brook Farm.

4

The commune always had many visitors—you know political friends of political friends—East Coast/West Coast—who came by and stayed a day or two—that was the best part of the commune—it was a wayside for all sorts of people and ideas—Lemeilleur loved that. On the other hand, house chores and the distribution of work responsibilities were boring, and with two fewer comrades, it got more boring.

That's when Jackson—from an old aristocratic family of Atlanta—and Kaarina—a pugnacious Russian from Arkhangelsk—showed up—both were going to school at Berkeley in California, and they brought good dope, and they wanted to move in for the summer.

During their first meal Jackson told them how he hated his father, "Dad's a doctor who wouldn't see Blacks. And, get this, his ancestors gleefully rounded up Cherokees for the Trail of Tears." And that prompted Kaarina to say, "My father's a high-level apparatchik in the Communist Party and he sent me here to get a capitalist education. Communism means you love everyone. Whereas capitalism means you only love winners. I love communism. By the way, I have to tell you the Civil War never ended in this country. There is no sound over all waters."

"What?" Lemeilleur exclaimed.

"I'm majoring in American literature," Kaarina said by way of explanation.

Simran absolutely wanted them to live in the commune.

The community went along with her, and so did Lemeilleur, a bit in awe, because he had never met a real communist before. That night he dreamt about Mice—"equality for all," Mice had shouted from a distant horizon on an ice floe.

The first week of their stay went amazingly well. Jackson was very energetic and easily covered Bernie's responsibilities and he knew Ray Mungo. Kaarina, who had spent a week with the Nearings, not only did more around the house than Agnes, but she was also willing to sleep with Chet. And Chet liked Kaarina. Jackson was cool with all of it. All of which would keep Simran's dream of the commune alive— at least through the summer.

Lemeilleur liked the idea of communism but found the reality boring when not scary. As he looked back at that time, he realized they were just kids, and some of them were looking for a family—friends being the family you chose.

For me, the lame part of the Sixties was the political part, the social part. The real part was the spiritual part.

—Jerry Garcia

5

Lemeilleur was bored teaching French, and as that masterpiece, life, would have it, at the end of his fifth year, the Headmaster, a Republican, began sleeping—indiscreetly (THE WHOLE SCHOOL KNEW)—with his secretary. And to offset the mounting opposition to his administration, the Headmaster had discovered a pile of new federal money for prep schools—everyone would get a raise—all they had to do was accept Black students. The world was a-changin'—or was it?

And so, without a word to faculty, i.e. zero academic preparation for what was about to happen—the school, that since the 1920's had served only white middle and upper middle income students—that school's fearless leader wrote an application and received a huge federal grant that doubled the size of the student body the next school year.

It was a disaster and Lemeilleur was sick to his stomach by the racism that exploded. He resigned in protest. The school collapsed two years later. Leave it to a Republican to prove big government was the problem. Things were not much better at the commune.

After Agnes moved out, there was a shift in the dynamic of the house—mainly Simran disappeared into her new thing with Kaarina, who, by the way, believed so deeply in communism that she thought it was outrageous that Lemeilleur wasn't sleeping with anyone—like he didn't have the individual right not to share himself.

A freaked-out Lemeilleur asked himself: Where did he belong? That this communal contretemps occurred around sex—well, of course, that started, irrevocably, his separation from the commune. Sex was still a minefield for Lemeilleur.

Lemeilleur was also freaked out by Simran's sexual interest in Kaarina, which in Lemeilleur's mind empowered Kaarina.

To protect himself from Kaarina's charge of selfishness, Lemeilleur decided to have a relationship with the apostate, Agnes, who, lonely now, had an apartment back in Cambridge. This only pissed Simran off, which allowed Lemeilleur to deepen his resolve to stay away, and forced Simran to confront him for not supporting commune values.

Annus mirabilis, for the first time in his life, Lemeilleur exploded in fury—he was sick and tired of Simran's quest for the perfect life or whatever it was that drove her. Simran waved Shulamith Firestone's *The Dialectic of Sex* in Lemeilleur's face; she was furious that he was abandoning her. "You're a parasite," she screamed, "feeding on the emotional strength of women without reciprocity. I play well into your preconceived fantasies. But we will crack the structure of society. You'll be back. Your trauma has a built-in destructive urge. You'll be back!"

Lemeilleur was very sad, but he walked away. Somehow

he'd found the strength to say no to abuse!

Lemeilleur, as he thought about his rupture with Simran, believed McCrae had changed him, and he refused to let Simran's words scare him. Hippiedom was ending. Communism's brief appearance, in this country, was faltering. The straights were winning—again. Jerry Rubin had invested in Apple computer and was on his way to becoming a multi-millionaire. But all that kind of political change didn't matter to Lemeilleur. His relationship with Simran, which he believed had saved his life, never seemed to work out. It made Lemeilleur think: Simran had said she knew what her problem was. If that's true, and if that problem is the source of their discord, he would be colossally pissed off she never told him.

6

Lemeilleur moved out. He had to write *Renoir's Onions*. Only Chet said goodbye: "Live YOUR life, Lem. You're an original—be original."

"Original?"

"Yeah. You're like Julien Sorel—you know *The Red and the Black* by Stendhal."

"I'll have to read it."

"Between you and me: You have no idea how fucked up Simran is—it's a charming part of you. Look, we all think you're an artist—prove us right. Good luck."

Strong Chet, he never told Lemeilleur what was wrong with Simran. Though Chet knew what drove Simran, and though he didn't love her anymore, he watched over her for many years—until he went to Paris for a mathematics conference and found the love of his life.

⟨D⟩

Lemeilleur and Agnes had to stop sleeping together—they were boring each other to tears—boring sex, there is no greater torture. Lemeilleur had done it to get away; Agnes to hurt Simran. But Agnes, who wanted to come out on top, morally, ended the relationship by saying she had to stop Lemeilleur from "using her to masturbate."

Hurt at first by Agnes's lithographic transfer of her pain to Lemeilleur's heart and not sure of the truth of her claim, Lemeilleur decided to whistle his goodbye to Agnes to himself. He and Agnes, he told himself, had only been *"copulating clichés,"* which, of course, tickled his *Lolita*-loving funny bone, but deeper down, he worried about what he was sexually. Had McCrae been an aberration?

Weeks later, overcome by his break with Simran, he experienced a profound need for McCrae. He threw himself on his knees to thank his lucky stars that McCrae had rescued him from the banality of clichés. He had experienced love. Later that day, trying to believe he'd been rescued, he attempted to write a poem.

To McCrae

I still burn in your love;
The touch of your lips
Haunts me holy.
My heart glows
Where all the clichés are ashes
In a flame we loved into being
Where the spark of your love
Burned beyond my need
And now dies
Before I could love you back.
O memory.

The Sixties are most generously described as a time when people took part - when they stepped out of themselves and acted in public, as people who didn't know what would happen next, but who were sure that acts of true risk and fear would produce something different from what they had been raised to take for granted.

—Greil Marcus

7

A week after Lemeilleur and Agnes broke up, Lemeilleur, hung over, got a call—his mother was dying of pancreatic cancer. He couldn't believe it. He had no idea she had any kind of cancer. He hadn't talked to his parents in over a year. She was in palliative care at UMASS Medical School, a social worker told him.

As Lemeilleur drove from Cambridge to Nouvelle Bouville, he tried to remember his mother. She'd been a ghost for most of his life. Her depressions had been crippling, leading, usually, to hospitalization. As a result, she was exceedingly self-effacing because she didn't want to expose herself to any reality that gave her those dark, dark thoughts.

Then out of nowhere a memory came to him—he must have been six or seven—she was on their back porch trying to climb over the bannister and he was clinging to her, begging her not to jump. She kept pushing him aside, but somehow he managed to hang on. Eventually his father heard them and came to pull her back onto the porch.

"What the hell's wrong with you?"

"I asked Dr. Plomber to help me."

"Goddamn it. I told Pointeur that the rhythm method is for the birds."

Lemeilleur then remembered wondering, even in his exhausted state on the porch, what was the rhythm method?

"I told him we couldn't afford another baby."

"He wouldn't help, huh?"

"He said as a Catholic he'd rather see me go on welfare."
She never had the baby—it was a stillbirth.

⬤

At the hospital, Lemeilleur held his mother's hand, and she opened her dry pussy willow eyes. He was shocked by how her appearance had changed. She looked like a wounded animal—with eyes full of fear and truculence. Choking down tears, Lemeilleur bent over to kiss her forehead—he couldn't remember ever touching her—and as he leaned into her, her face turned fierce, her nostrils gaped, her skin stretched taut, and her mouth amazingly vivid, like a shaman's, seemed painted for visions. Her whole face had a kind of steely rapture, and she started to whisper. He put his ear next to her crusty chapped lips. He could barely make out what she was saying.

Here's what he heard: "Get priest. (inaudible) father (inaudible) touched (inaudible) drunk."

Lemeilleur ran out to get a priest. What was his mother trying to tell him?

When he got back she had slipped into her final coma. All Lemeilleur could see now were two small tears in the corners of her closed eyes. Her lips were slightly parted, parched and thirsty—they'd never tasted the nectar. Now her lips would turn cold, forever, as her shriveled, yellow husk died slowly on a morphine drip. He leaned over and kissed her face which had become a palimpsest of all the disappointments that had accreted since she dropped her infant sister.

All his life Lemeilleur had believed his mother didn't love him—ever since she beat him for taking Simran under the lilac bush. All her energy had been consumed by her depression: When she wasn't fighting with her husband, she was a blank space behind two wild eyes.

As the undertakers wheeled his mother out of her hospital room, Lemeilleur puzzled over her last words and let the sadness of her life sink in. Existence for her had been scary and unforgiving.

At the door of her room, one of the undertakers came back to tell Lemeilleur not to worry, that his father had called from Florida, and all the arrangements for the funeral were taken care of.

Lemeilleur left the hospital wondering. What was her confession about? Was she trying to get it right with God? Did she want to go to heaven? Is that what we all want? There's no heaven—so why do we want one? The imagination is always willing to set up rewards for us—create Meaning where there is none. He wandered off: Imagination—the playground for politicians.

⟨Φ⟩

Lemeilleur didn't cry at his mother's funeral. And when his father's surrogate put a rose on her casket, the signal to lower the casket, Lemeilleur watched his mother's embalmed life-without-consolation body descend into the *bouche d'ombre* (dark mouth) of the grave and he thought he heard a sigh: "A peasant I was born, a peasant I will die."

He remembered her at the hospital, her face with its little tears, and out of nowhere it dawned on him: His mother—not for a fraction of a second—felt—and this took his breath away—love.

⟨Φ⟩

A month later Lemeilleur got a postcard from his father who was still vacationing in Florida.

Dear Lemeilleur,

Your life will work out . . . whatever it may be . . . you will be genuinely happy. Be patient and always keep your spirits high. Your mother got screwed. I hate eating out. Did I tell you I found someone who likes to cook?

Love, Dad

8

After a year of AA, Lemeilleur thought he was strong enough to deal with his father in therapy. Lemeilleur had showed his therapist his "Baseball" story and told her the story behind it. For months they'd discussed Lemeilleur's father, which helped Lemeilleur see more clearly the situation he'd grown up in.

With more therapy, his repertoire of emotions had expanded from shame and guilt to rage and terror. Now, Lemeilleur wanted his father to know how he felt after that incident with Tocard.

The first shock came when Lemeilleur's father said he'd come to therapy. He'd remarried six weeks after Lemeilleur's mother died. Maybe he was happier, felt more self-confident—Lemeilleur didn't know.

The second shock happened when right from the beginning of the session, his father so dominated the meeting with his riff about how he had risen from relative obscurity to the third busiest funeral home in Nouvelle Bouville—an amazingly comfortable spot he had now attained—and how he had never cheated on his wife—even though he could have had Femme any time he wanted because she laughed harder at his dirty jokes than she did at her husband's, etc, etc.

Lemeilleur was furious, but his father went on—about his new wife—"his virgin-bride"—how his family had been so poor he had to sleep between his brother's legs at night—and now he was at the pinnacle of his success—for forty-five minutes.

Lemeilleur's therapist—drop-jawed—never interrupted him, never refocused the discussion on Lemeilleur's feelings.

Lemeilleur was pissed; he was done with her.

Outside her office, he told his father what Tocard had done, and how angry and humiliated he'd felt.

"I wanted to kill you."

His father listened quietly as Lemeilleur raged on about his problems with women. But his father's calm unnerved Lemeilleur. He stopped talking.

"It's not a big deal," his father said. "I used to suck Tocard. Don't worry about it: Family is sacred. I'm okay. It'll all work out with you too. I saw you with McCrae. I know you like girls. America was built on desire, Lem—remember, your father said that. Let's have lunch."

His father never asked about McCrae.

When Lemeilleur got home he threw up—he couldn't stop. He had dry heaves, was crying uncontrollably, and mumbling the words "All I ever wanted was for you to love me." He was terrified he'd bust some part of his body—his retching was straight out of *The Exorcist*. What hurt the most was, in his father's terms, his father loved him. That what Lemeilleur had waited for all his life could never come out of his father, at least not in any form different than it had just come out of him now. All Lemeilleur's life he'd heard "FAMILY IS SACRED."

Was that possible—that the values of two human beings can be so different that love between them becomes impossible because the values are so different?

IS THIS WHAT'S WRONG WITH THE WORLD?

Lemeilleur's body twisted into a coil, and he collapsed—paralytic in the realization that his reach for beauty was outside his father's notion of existence. Memories swirled in his head, like a school of crazed fish. Besides Dolores dying, her black eyes screaming for help, his father, a bottom-feeding catfish, now swam up in the glaucous blur of memory. His father had come home, roaring drunk.

"Hey, Lem, come here."

His father fell into his black leather rocking chair.

"Come here, Lem. I wanta tell ya somethin'."

Lemeilleur stood next to the rocking chair. He must have been seven or eight.

"When I was in Brazil, cinque cruiserros, five cents, that's all a girl costs."

And his father laughed.

"Da fathers down deir put deir little fingah inta da little girl's vagina ta break deir cherry so it don't hurt when dey sell dem to da American sailors BECAUSE THEY CARED! Poverty is a terrible thing." Then his lips quivered as if disturbed by the acridity of the spat out poisonous potion that glistened on those angry lips.

"You don't like fathahs." Alcide exploded. "You don't believe dere are good fathahs, do ya? I'm a good fathah. And you're jist like me. I read *David Copperfield*. In high school—yeah, I learned English in Canada. I'm not as sstupid as ya think—that book was about my life. Why can't ya see how far I came?"

He fell asleep, his neck bent like a doll's, as his venomous slobber dripped from his mouth.

⊕

A week later Lemeilleur got another letter from his father.

Dear Lemeilleur

    Your presence is always wholesome and refreshing and a delite to be with. When I graduated from High School my Mother would tell anyone "il a gradue du grand ecole" and when I worked for the government in 1943 she would tell others "il travaille pour la government." She was so very proud. And yet I was embarrassed. I knew how insignificant both were. So, I pray you are not embarrassed. I could never articulate my feelings of love until recently. I'm a late bloomer.

Love, Dad

Lemeilleur's lips quivered: All he wanted was the love of his father.

9

Marie LaJoie was one hundred and nine when she ran out of energy and came to a floating feather finish. Lemeilleur would go to her funeral. It was a grand affair—the who's who of Canadian royalty. A bishop, a police commissioner, a union organizer, and hundreds of others jammed the chapel where she was waked.

Then there was the graveside service. Ordinarily his father gave the eulogy, but Marie had left specific directions: Lemeilleur's father would read the eulogy she wrote without any changes. And so, at the burial of Marie LaJoie his father intoned:

> *My husband and I wrote a book about the oppression of French-Canadians by the maudit (cursed) English. After the death of Montcalm in 1759, the English—for over a hundred years—cut off all communication with France. They passed laws to "denaturalize" us of our Frenchness, to limit our ability to participate in Law, Medicine, and Business. In short the English did everything in their POWER to make us English.*
>
> *Now—over 200 years later—there is a secessionist movement in Québec. English Fools.*
>
> *The same French-Canadians came to the USA, and guess what? They are not secessionist here. No. Here, in the United States, these same people became Americans, as did the Irish, the Germans, the Italians, the Chinese, the Japanese, as will others who come here, like Russians, Cambodians, and Muslims—Why? Freedom works. Freedom unites.*

As Lemeilleur's father read, his voice became less steady. It seemed to Lemeilleur that his father was less than comfortable with Marie's message.

America knows how to assimilate. Democracy is inherently liberal.

Alcide smiled sheepishly and ploughed on.

Accept, keep accepting, America. We must measure success by how many people we liberate. Democracy allows the energy of the people to flow. Freedom is profitable.

A small applause rippled politely across the mourners. His father was confused. He just stood there, stunned. Lemeilleur felt the tension in his father and acted. He took the rose from his father's paralyzed hand and laid it on Marie's casket. Many wept aloud; some clapped as the casket began its mournful descent. His father tried to smile as he looked out over the 700+ people who had come to mourn. Finally, Marie LaJoie's casket reached the bottom, where her dust would sleep until resurrection morning. Lemeilleur, with a tear in his eye, said a prayer for McCrae. He then bowed his head and resumed his last goodbye to Marie.

A group of mourners began to sing. *«Gens du pays, c'est votre tour/ De nous laisser parler d'amour.»* (Folks of the land, it's your turn to let you speak of love.)

Lemeilleur was crying. Grief had brought up Dolores's big black eyes from the prison house of his memory. She stared at him, a female kabuki mask with a tear hanging from one of her black *battus* (beaten) eyes. Her gaze penetrated Lemeilleur's heart like a rapier, and the face of death whispered, "It was your turn to let yourself be lovingly spoken to. I liked you."

As Lemeilleur walked across the cemetery, a dark, angry thundercloud appeared. He wondered if his father's attitude about love had made him idealize Simran into an unreal and unattainable dimension? The cloud, militant now, scowled down at the mourners who, disassembled, scattered to their cars. Was his search for grace, his salvation, nothing but a smokescreen to disguise his descent into a swirl of self-destruction? Lemeilleur studied the sky and remembered something Marie had said to him: "Know life, Lemeilleur, and love it!"

END OF PART FOUR

V

"Your willingness to wrestle with your demons will cause your angels to sing."

—August Wilson

With Simran and his mother tucked deeply away within the folds of Lemeilleur's hippocampus, you could say his sad and disillusioned adult life began the same year, 1986, that Reagan's veto of the Comprehensive Anti-Apartheid Act was overturned by Congress. Lemeilleur, still stoking hope, was now, temporarily, a teacher's aide in a Cambridge school for mentally disabled juvenile delinquents. His plan, ever ambitious, was to work in Cambridge for two years while he got a Master's in psychology at night school at UMASS Boston.

The head of the school in Cambridge was named Layla.

Michael, one of his students, was a fourteen-year-old terror. He had a nice smile, white even teeth, a big Afro halo, thin legs, and a motor mouth of pre-cast sarcasm made from the molten pig iron of poverty. He checked his switchblade with Lemeilleur every morning. After which Lemeilleur would take him aside to an empty classroom to teach him how to read.

Michael had the usual teach-me-to-read-you-fuckface attitude, so Lemeilleur threw away the Dick and Jane books the school had given him. Instead Lemeilleur read to him from *Last Exit to Brooklyn*. The kid, however, wasn't sure it wasn't a trick. After Lemeilleur finished Selby, Jr's book, he said to Michael, "Now you're going to write a book."

"Shiiit," Michael smiled, "I can't even read."

"I want you to tell me what you did last night."

"Fuck me, man, I stole me some Eldorado hubcaps. What the fuck's that to you?"

Lemeilleur was ready. He wrote Michael's words in a notebook.

"How did you do it? What are you going to do with the hubcaps?"

Michael told Lemeilleur the whole story, and Lemeilleur wrote as fast as he could to get it down accurately. Then

Lemeilleur went home and typed Michael's words just as he told them. Next day Lemeilleur showed him the transcript.

"What's this shit, man?"

"Here let me read it to you."

"Hey, fuck, that's my story. Let me see that."

He looked at it for several minutes.

"Shiiit, how you'd do that?"

"See that word?"

"Is that what 'fuck' looks like?"

"Bet your ass."

"Show me 'motherfucker'."

"You already know fuck, see if you can find it?"

He did.

"Goddamn. You're a genius."

It took several months, and he had to learn how to sound words out. He was actually quite bright—in fact he was probably smarter than anyone else in the school. By the end of the school year Layla, the principal, had decided to give Michael the most improved student award. Lemeilleur would present it.

When Michael was told he was going to get an award, he got very diffident.

"I don't know, man; if my boys hear some dumbass school is giving me an award. I don't know, man."

"Think about it. The one thing I know is you deserve it."

⊕

At the beginning of the school year Layla had been ordered to get all of her ten-year-olds tested for I.Q. before the school year ended. Quite fortuitously one of the courses Lemeilleur had selected for his second semester in night school was I.Q. tests—the WISC—because he was curious about the test Georges had given him. In fact, he had to practice.

By the first week of May, Layla realized that her I.Q. schedule was off—too many kids and not enough school psychologists. When Lemeilleur found out about her predicament, he offered to help the few psychologists she had. She thought about it, talked to her school psychologists, and they agreed if Lemeilleur administered fifteen tests, which would take about an hour for each one, they could score them and analyze them before the end of the school year.

In the meantime, Michael was getting extremely nervous about Awards Night, which was scheduled the day before graduation. Lemeilleur did everything he could to keep Michael's courage up, including losing to him in a one-on-one basketball game.

The I.Q. testing was going pretty well too. Lemeilleur had all his kits, had studied them, and had a good stopwatch. He'd record as accurately as possible the kids' responses in a neat and legible way and passed everything on to the psychologists. They made sure they understood what had transpired between Lemeilleur and the kids.

The day before Awards Night Lemeilleur was to meet the last ten-year-old boy to test. When Lemeilleur went to get him, however, he was asleep in class. Lemeilleur woke him up and they headed to the testing room. On the way, Lemeilleur asked him a couple of questions.

"I see you're a little tired today?"

"Ya, man, I'm beat."

"You know this is an important test I'm going to give you?"

He yawned. When they got into the room, he immediately put his head down on the desk.

"Did you sleep okay last night?"

"No."

"Why not?"

"The police come."

"Last night? To your house?"

"Yup. My father beat my mother, so I call 911—that's what my mother says to do. The motherfucker's crazy."

"What happened?"

"The Man shoot him dead."

"Your father?"

"Yes, sir. Six bullets."

Lemeilleur couldn't bring himself to test the kid under these circumstances. The test results would stay with him for the rest of his life. Lemeilleur took him back to class. He had probably saved his mother's life.

When Lemeilleur told the school psychologists what he had done, they hit the roof.

"You have no authority to make that decision. You go back there and test that kid."

"I'm not."

"We'll just see about that."

Lemeilleur walked back to the testing room and waited. As expected, Layla showed up. She closed the door behind her.

"I'm sorry, Layla, but I'm not going to test that kid."

"You're such a purist—we're almost home—one more kid—what the hell is wrong with you?"

"I don't know that kid from a hole in the wall, but that score is going to stay with him until—"

"—He goes to jail. Grow up."

"That kid's a hero."

"You don't test that kid, you can kiss this job goodbye."

"Fine. I'm still giving Michael his award tomorrow night."

⊕

The next day, a few hours before Awards Night, Lemeilleur's phone rang.

"Mr. Lemeilleur?" the voice whispered.

It was Michael.

"Gotta talk, man."

"What's happening?"

"Gotta talk, man."

"You want me to come to your house?"

The phone went dead.

When Lemeilleur got there three police cars and a mob of mostly women were in the parking lot across from Michael's apartment in Cambridge's Angel's Court.

Shit. They were going to be late for Awards Night.

Lemeilleur knocked on Michael's door. Gingerly Michael cracked the door open. His afro stood proud, like a black allium from an exotic garden. But he was wearing a denim shirt—not dressed for Awards Night. The shirt was unbuttoned and on his light brown hairless chest was a silver cross.

"One more outburst from you and I'm gonna run you in under protective custody," a policeman barked at Michael's mother, Flo, from the living room.

"Why don't you arrest them—those lunatics out in the parking lot?" Flo yelled back.

From Lemeilleur's angle he could see she was pointing frantically out the window, and from the kitchen, as Lemeilleur walked in, he saw through that window the angry women that Flo pointed to.

Flo was drunk and every time the police said they were going to arrest her, Michael's little sister would scream, "Don't, Ma. Don't, Ma."

Flo then broke away from one of the police, tripped over a non-spinning fan, cursed it, did not fall, put her head out the window, and called somebody a slut, a dirty liar.

The police grabbed Flo and pinned her down on the couch. Michael was playing with his silver cross.

"Arrest them," Flo screamed again.

Michael's little sister put her hands over her ears and walked around in circles.

"We're going out there and talk to them as soon as you settle down," one of the officers said.

"Talk to them—outside. For chrissake, arrest them," Flo shouted. "They're the lunatics, you gutless badge."

"Look, Flo, button up. You know we're in the middle of this thing. We're not taking sides."

"For the love of god, they're turning my kids against me. And all you're gonna do is TALK to them."

Michael asked Lemeilleur if he wanted a beer.

"Ah, no thanks."

One of the policemen, as he dried the inner band of his hat, took Lemeilleur aside to ask, "Is there anything you can do? If she keeps this up, we're gonna have to take her in."

Lemeilleur sat next to Flo on the couch searching for words. Finally, he said, "The police can't arrest them; they haven't broken the law."

Michael's mother was exhausted. Faintly she grumbled, "They're murderers." Then she sighed and said, "I know who you are. You taught my boy how to read."

Then she turned to the perspiring policeman and said, "He's the best teacher Michael ever had." Then turning back to Lemeilleur, "Ya know, Mr. Teacher, if they was arrested, we'd be burnt out in a week. That's life here. The cops know that too."

"Why don't you take a shower, and we'll all go to Awards Night and see Michael get his gift," Lemeilleur urged her.

"Please, Mommy," the little girl said.

"Hey," she yelled to the police, "if I go, will ya watch my windows. I don't want them all broken when I get home."

"You take a shower; we'll do the rest."

Flo disappeared into her bedroom and came back in her bathrobe and shouted, "Those witches had no right to talk about my Joey that way. He's not a murderer. It was an accident. It said so in the paper. His appeal is coming up soon. My Joey is a good boy. They got no goddamn right."

"The shower, Flo," said one of the officers.

"I'll take a shower, Mr. Teacher, but will you go out there and listen to what they say? I don't trust cops."

Outside the women called Flo a liar, scum. The police stayed between Lemeilleur and them.

Another woman separated herself from the group and came up to Lemeilleur to say, "We got feelings too. Yeah, we called the cops. That Michael's a good kid. She ain't got no right treating him that way."

"What way?" Lemeilleur asked.

"All she had to say was I can't afford it and that's the end of it."

"Can't afford what?"

"You know Michael learned to read this year. Michael wanted a suit to wear to the school party. Look at his back: She beat him with a broomstick—that's why the cops is here."

Lemeilleur got everybody to Awards Night. He made his little speech and Michael came up and got his award, a copy of *Moby Dick*.

2

Two years later Michael called Lemeilleur.

"Hey, man, I finished."

"That's good, but what did you finish?"

"Moby Dick."

"That's great. So, how you doing?"

"Got into Community College. My mother can't believe it. I just wanted to thank you."

"Good to hear, Michael."

"Hey, I know this happened years ago, but I gotta ask you something. Since I got to college, I been thinking about politics. You dig? What was your thought about that Reagan guy? I'm writing a paper."

"Good for you, Michael. Reagan? Ah, you wouldn't be thinking about his 'welfare queen' comment and his attitude about Black people?"

"Goddamn, man. You always knew what I was thinking."

"The difference between conservatives and liberals is how much you believe in people. Conservatives can only imagine others as they see themselves—self-serving opportunists. That's why they don't believe in evolution—too scary—where's it going?—no control."

"Can I tell you a story about Reagan?" Michael asked. "Before I went to college I worked all summer parking cars in a lot in Boston. My mother was so proud of me she told her counselor at Social Security. They found out how much I made and deducted $5 per month from my mother's monthly check. When we asked why, they told us I had made too much—our family was over the limit. We got a lawyer from an anti-poverty nonprofit to ask Social Security to waive the penalty. The Social Security guy was embarrassed and told us that if it had been the other guy, Jimmy Carter, they would have looked the other way. But with the new guy they can't."

"Change is the beginning of beauty for some and a curse for others."

"It only took my mother three years to pay the bastards back. So, tell me, Lemeilleur. Why'd you believe in me?"

"You strengthened my belief in people exactly when I needed a jolt."

"I helped you?"

Lemeilleur didn't have the heart to tell him that Reagan's rhetoric had pushed middle-class white Americans to vote against "undeserving minorities" to punish them for receiving too much public assistance, and that at that time Lemeilleur was deeply depressed by his lovelessness. Though Lemeilleur was touched by Michael's interest in politics, he knew the kid had a long road ahead of him. So, he simply said, "Reagan said government was the problem. He was a cowboy at heart—rugged individualism—pull yourself up by the bootstraps and—"

"—But that's what I did."

"I know, Michael."

"Now listen, Lemeilleur, when I was reading *Moby Dick* I said to myself, if it hadn't been for you, I could have become a Captain Ahab—you know: a lunatic hell bent on ruining his life by getting all fucked up about trying to find and destroy the demon that was going to make me what I was sure to become."

"You evolved, Michael. I'm so happy for you."

"Lemeilleur? You know when I started trusting you—I mean really trust you?"

"No—when?"

"The night of that award—do you know why? My mother was so proud of me she wanted to sleep with you."

"You saw that?"

"Yup. And you handled her with respect and let her down so nice."

"Thanks. I didn't want to ruin a good night."

"You didn't use us, Lemeilleur."

"I'm gonna have to get a reference from you."

3

One day, not long after his conversation with Michael, Simran informed Lemeilleur she'd met THE ONE—a professor whom she met two years ago in an ashram in San Francisco. This Emily Dickinson poem was engraved on the trysting invitation of Simran and Demi.

> *"Hope" is the thing with feathers—*
> *That perches in the soul—*
> *And sings the tune without the words—*
> *And never stops—at all—*

Mazel tov! Demi had taught social work at a major university in the Boston area, and now she and Simran owned their own business, a speakers' bureau for presenters of topics in human services.

Oh, there was a PS on Lemeilleur's invitation: *Still waiting for you to show your feathers. Write your memoir. Love, S.*

Lemeilleur was so happy Simran had finally found love in her life, and he was deeply relieved Simran had written to him. He had put her on a pedestal, right up there with McCrae. Now he considered these two women the foundation of his healthier and stronger personality. He couldn't wait to meet Demi.

Simran's good news renewed his interest in writing his memoir. He told himself he would label his folders and sort his notes into some kind of order as soon as he found a stable job.

4

Lemeilleur had his Master's in Psychology.

He was walking around Central Square in Cambridge where he had been living. And just as he turned off Mass Avenue to walk down Brookline toward the river, all this commotion started, people were running, an ambulance was tearing a hole in the night, and police cars were screeching to a halt and officers were running into an alley.

Lemeilleur edged closer to see what was going on. Michael was sobbing hysterically, and Lemeilleur rushed over and knelt down beside him. It took a moment to get Michael's focus. Behind Lemeilleur, EMTs trundled a body out of the alley.

"He's gone," Michael said looking up at Lemeilleur. Then looking down again, Michael shook.

"Who?" Lemeilleur asked.

"My brother, Joey," he said looking up again. "My mother was worried. She called me at home and told me to follow him. He owed some people money. My girlfriend didn't want me to go."

Michael started to cry again.

"Joey met them. They pulled him into the alley. I ran in. He was screaming he'd get the money, but they stabbed him. I couldn't stop them."

Lemeilleur grabbed Michael and hugged him. His brother died that night. Lemeilleur went to Joey's funeral. Flo was drunk, happy to see Lemeilleur, and came on to him. Lemeilleur let Flo down softly, and Michael, in front of Sarah, his girlfriend, promised Lemeilleur he'd stay straight, and Michael raised his right hand and said, "By hot blooded sea-born Moby Dick, hunted by monomaniacs, I will remain true to myself and family." They all laughed.

①

Michael kept his promise. He became the manager of a boutique grocery store in Harvard Square and has a family. He calls Lemeilleur every once in a while, which always cheers Lemeilleur up. Michael probably doesn't see himself as a direct affront to Reaganism, but Lemeilleur thinks so. Lemeilleur has to smile when he thinks of Michael helping Harvard professors' wives find truffle-flavored butter and unfiltered virgin olive oil, and wonders where fate will take him next.

5

A few weeks later, Lemeilleur got a letter from Demi. Simran had been hospitalized. She was catatonically depressed. This was Simran's sixth hospitalization and Demi had had it: She was leaving Simran.

He had no idea what was going on with Demi and Simran, and terribly upset, he called Demi to find out what hospital to visit, and then he asked Demi what had happened to Simran.

"This time. It was Anita Hill."

"Anita Hill?"

"I was upset too—watching those unconscious males hammer away at her. Even the good guys had no clue about structural sexism. But I don't lose my mind and make life miserable for everyone around me. I'm sorry, Lemeilleur, but I can't take it anymore. She's not getting better."

Before Lemeilleur could ask Demi what was wrong with Simran, she had hung up.

⟐

When Lemeilleur got to the Boston hospital, he happened into Demi, who was leaving. At first she waved Lemeilleur off, but she relented when she saw the hurt in his eyes.

"What's wrong, Demi? Why is Simran so upset?"

"It's been years, Lemeilleur. I'm sorry. I just burned out. I can't tell you how I've tried. She's a very damaged person. How I missed that when we met? Doesn't matter. We all have problems. Life screws everybody up."

"I can understand that. My best friend had serious mental problems, and I had no idea."

"It's really true—love is a wonderful blindness—sometimes. I'm exhausted, Lemeilleur. I tried to help Simran—we even did couples' therapy. But I'm not the problem. I'm incidental. Anything can set her off. She has demons in her blood."

Lemeilleur froze. How many times did he believe he had demons in his blood?

"Goodbye, Lemeilleur. I have to go home and get some sleep. I'm so tired."

"Please tell me what happened?"

"You don't know, do you? She was watching Anita Hill get hammered on TV and she lost it. But she can't identify what's wrong with her. All she can do is lock herself up in a trance."

Lemeilleur just stood there, his mouth probably hanging open. Finally, he responded. "What about Anita Hill?"

"You don't know what's wrong, do you? I thought you were her friend. She's totally repressed. She can't orgasm."

Demi tore herself away with tears in her eyes.

Lemeilleur watched her walk unsteadily down the corridor. He was in some kind of shock. Eventually thought returned to his bombed-out brain, and all he could remember was Simran's love moans when they lived in the commune. He'd always thought Simran was thoroughly liberated and enjoyed sex. He must have misheard Demi.

When they let him in to see Simran, she was ice-block catatonic. He sat next to her for an hour or two. It was hard to tell if she knew he was there. Eventually he rose and bent over to kiss her on the forehead. She was motionless. He stood up and sadly patted her hand. Not a lash moved. Slowly as he backed out of her room, he noticed a book next to her bed, *Down Below* by Leonora Carrington. All he could think was this person, Simran, locked in a profound anger, was one of the women who had saved his life.

6

Lemeilleur, after six years with Alcoholics Anonymous, was finishing with his amends. He'd found Aaliyah's address. She was working in Waltham at the Josephine Goldmark Foundation, a pro-democracy think tank that said in their mission statement "only genuine democracy can create the evolutionary conditions for humankind to save itself."

He wrote her a long letter explaining what happened to him as a kid and asked for her forgiveness. He also wrote to Victoria, Donald, Agnes, and Liza. Liza's letter came back: "Address Unknown." Gayle of "Polishland" must have married and changed her name—he couldn't find anything about her.

Then there was the Nameless One—and he remembered he still hadn't read her letter. He was starting to believe he had the courage to read it. He decided to wait for Aaliyah's response.

⬤

A few months later Aaliyah wrote back. She was happily married and loved her job. Her kids were in college and doing well. Aaliyah's big worry was the Republican Party wanted to take the country back to the "Golden Years" of the fifties "when rape, child abuse, and abortion didn't exist."

> *All the while school committees around the country have banned* The Catcher in the Rye *from school libraries and the memoir of a pedophile moaning over the loss of his Lolita has made $55 million for the author. If society gets any more stupid, I fear for our evolution.*
>
> *Republicans just don't want the middle-class to*

grow. I can't believe how fearful they are of Black people. As E. Goldman said over a hundred years ago, "Our culture—or what little we have of such a thing— is" (still) "clogged by masses of dead people who have no conscious inner life."

*Speaking of weird—remember, Lemeilleur, in 1974, a book came out—*Comprehensive Textbook of Psychiatry, *edited by A.M. Freedman and H.I. Kaplan? Look under 'Incest' by D.J. Henderson, and I quote:* **'Such incestuous activity diminishes the subject's chance of psychosis and allows for a better adjustment to the external world . . . The vast majority of them [incest victims] were none the worse for the experience.'**

I now understand why you wanted me to study Lolita. *Thank you for your apology. I forgive you Lemeilleur. God knows how little we know about how sexual trauma changes brain chemistry.*

Look, Lem, no one who begins by hating himself can love. You're a lot like Rimbaud. You dragged yourself through stinking alleys and you offered yourself to the god of fire, but your soul, alas, remained incurably dark. For years I hated you; I wanted to obliterate you with Mice—my bad. Today you have all my sympathy.

A week before Mice hurt me, I found out a professor of mine had written a book about Rimbaud. It was published in France under the title Rimbaud Par Lui-Même (Rimbaud by Himself*). I'd ordered it for you, but it arrived after our breakup. I'll send it to you. True poetry is born in the very presence of death. It's your resistance to death that I admire today.*

I wish you the best, Aaliyah

Donald, the paper boy whom Lemeilleur had unjustly thrown to the ground, had worked in a hardware store all his life. He thanked Lemeilleur for writing.

The letters made Lemeilleur feel better. He was relieved that Aaliyah had done so well.

That Victoria didn't write back was no surprise. Lemeilleur remembered seeing her picture in a magazine and, after some digging through piles, found her in a *Yankee Magazine* article about the Bishop's attempt to close and sell St. Joe's Church. She looked matronly—no make-up, and her hair in the picture was lilac gray. She was wearing a rose-dust sweater, the color of sunset, and a dash of white strangely caressed the nape of her neck as she milled around with the other rebellious Catholics who were getting ready to bed down for their vigil to keep the church open.

It wasn't hard for Lemeilleur to see in Victoria's face a soul that sadly was now dedicating all her energy to the service of an eternal cause to lift herself off that endless treadmill that had never arrived at fulfillment. For the first time in his life he saw Victoria as a human being who suffered just like he did. To Lemeilleur, Victoria looked like a picture in one of McCrae's art books that Lemeilleur had been studying that week. A Piero della Francesca's head of Saint Mary Magdalen, who grimaced in grief and terror as Victoria readied for her overnight. Lemeilleur believed he had been part of that grief and terror. How could he apologize for treating her as his personal animated merkin—he had been so shallow, so abusive.

He continued to stare at the pictures in *Yankee Magazine*. Suddenly he remembered that Victoria had, by her bed, when he used to visit her during those times of craven need, a sacramental French-Canadian *clochette* (bell), that her mother had given her, to ward off the evil spirits. It amazed him, as he now meditated on this picture, that she had never rung her *clochette* when he came by. She, a fortress of emptiness, had trusted him. How could he have been so unreal? We have to do better, he raged to himself; we have to change life.

He put the magazine down and grieved about who he'd been, what he had done. Slowly it came to him: Why wasn't he there in that photo? He realized he had plucked himself out of that picture by a savage hope. He had gone on—but to what? He was just like them—looking for grace.

As for Liza, he knew he'd never find her. He hoped she had survived. And Gayle, well, she had a 50/50 chance. He wanted to believe she was happily married. He got a short note from Agnes thanking him for remembering her. She, unmarried, was living with her sister's family in Chestnut Harbor, CA.

And that brought him to The Nameless One—what had happened to her? How would he ever atone for that? Then he remembered her letter. He should read her letter. He promised himself he would read it. He was strong enough now. Yes, he was ready.

Lemeilleur then drifted off into a reverie where he was in a dark room, holding a candle that sputtered in a cold breeze. The de La Tour radiance of the candle pulsed against dark walls as he, driven by a demonic force, searched and searched for the unfindable—the cause of evil.

When he woke up he realized he should have read the Nameless One's letter years ago—when she gave it to him. What would reading it now mean? He had protected himself—there is no good or evil, Lemeilleur thought—only human beings, like himself, insecure and susceptible to whatever gives them a feeling of belonging—be it a religious community, the Nazi party, or a lonely girl found in the gutter on a dark night.

What Changes Life?

7

Around that time, he got a letter from Simran, whom he hadn't heard from since her hospitalization. In her letter Simran told him she'd been in treatment for many years. He'd never thought much about what held Simran and him together, though she always seemed to appear whenever he needed her. This letter, however, made him feel completely different. He sighed and continued to read. She'd discovered in therapy that her behavior showed severe symptoms of sexual abuse. He felt creepy. Instantly he thought of that moment, when he was six years old, under the lilac bush with her, the landlord's daughter, and her red duck panties.

Frantically he scanned the letter, but there was no mention of that.

Simran, in fact, couldn't imagine who it could have been. Still, Lemeilleur was plunged into a deeper and scary awareness of the bond that held them together—and he got sick thinking that they shared some miserable chemical similarity—their brains were altered by a similar ugliness— was that the mystery of their attraction for each other?—was that the love potion *à la Tristan and Isolde* they'd drunk?— from the same cup of sexual abuse?

He put the letter down.

If it was true, he knew what Simran was up against. He lived the struggle to become human. O Simran. Your abuser betrayed you. Betrayal—that's a hard one—betrayal is such a violent rejection. He immediately sent Simran a poem, "The Journey" by Mary Oliver, with the intention of following it up with a phone call, but the phone call didn't go well.

"I'm sorry, Lem, but I can't trust you. I don't trust anyone. I don't know where you fit into my nightmare. It all started when I was a kid. Isn't that what bonds us?"

She hung up.

There is a shock that comes with sudden trauma—a

blinding realization that you are not feeling this unbelievable wound that is happening to you—as you, for instance, watch a buzzsaw cut off your hand. Lemeilleur was watching his severed hand fall to the ground when Simran hung up. He threw himself down on the floor.

"Did I touch her?"

That night Lemeilleur had the strangest dream. McCrae was holding a painting by Dorothea Tanning, *Birthday*, for Lemeilleur to see. At first he locked eyes with the bare-chested woman. He could not pull away. In his peripheral vision he saw motion—writhing. Was that a dress that shimmered?

Upon closer inspection he saw a writhing face, his mother's. Upset, he searched the writhing mess and Simran's face, then Dolores's face appeared! Fear was mounting in his lungs. He looked back at the bare-chested woman's eyes, then at the open doors, and a voice said, "I am the Nameless One!" In full panic, Lemeilleur could not move. He was going to die. He struggled for air. The voice went on, "Today you have been born, out of abysmal sorrow and knowledge. Sex is a cruel, laughing force extravagantly beyond all notions, and, above all, indifferent to existence. But you left the door of the imagination open. Today I marry you to the future," and the writhing face of the Nameless One smiled.

8

Lemeilleur was now in his forties and still living in Cambridge. After that dream of *Birthday*, he'd given up trying to write his memoir. He attempted to calm down as he tried to acknowledge all his misdeeds. He took long walks and refused to hate himself.

A week or so later he wasn't as propelled by guilt as he had been after that dream. His trunk of memories, he tried to convince himself, was nothing but a colorful mass of disguises. He would never write his memoir. He could not organize his past. His notes, with all the changes, additions, and revisions, he now hoped, would take on the chemistry of a cellared wine. What he couldn't do consciously he hoped would happen by a miraculous chemistry. As the days passed, he dreamed of young bold notions of fresh fruit gradually becoming more subdued, reminiscent of dried fruit, and other flavors, previously hidden by those bold notions—all coming to the fore, like honey, herbal spices, hay, mushroom, stone, and earth. Lemeilleur wanted to believe his evolution had created a well-structured wine and his long fermentation had produced a soul steeped in an ambrosia of grace, the unmerited divine assistance given for regeneration. That beneath his ever-developing awareness, he had become a healthy human being—had made all the necessary changes to his soul. He wanted to believe that the *Birthday* dream had announced his salvation. But his faith in this image of his "spiritual fermentation" was only a hope, not an actuality. He never soared; his soul never sang; no beauty had ever assaulted him and knocked him into timeless ecstasy. Still, he wanted to believe in the *Birthday* dream.

As his hopes ebbed away, like spilt wine, he remembered the Nameless One's letter—wasn't it only a long-sequestered jury that had decided his fate a long time ago? Maybe, if he had read her letter, he could have changed things? He didn't believe that because to think about what he could have changed was too overwhelming. Instead, he picked up the book he was reading, *Confessions* by St. Augustine. He had found a section that he had to copy into his notebook.

Forgiveness is the remission of sins. For it is by this that what has been lost, and was found, is saved from being lost again.

⊕

One morning Lemeilleur woke up to find that something had changed in him overnight.

He was still alive psychically.

In a new dream he remembered waking up during the night to the sound of metallic clinks. His mother had rushed into his room. She bent over picking up the pennies. She was crying. His father was in the kitchen yelling at her. He looks up at his parents, and the dream tells him that before the pennies fell to the floor—they'd been put on his blanket around the edge of his bed. The dream then connects his mother's dying words: "father—touched—drunk" to produce an explanation. His father was in the kitchen for only one reason: To hide after knocking the pennies to the floor. Therefore, it had been his mother who put the pennies on his blanket to protect Lemeilleur from his father who, drunk, would come into that sad room to touch him.

"My father started me on my life of sexual dysfunction."

Lemeilleur's thoughts now rose from his fevered brain like billowing incense from a swinging thurible in a religious service he didn't understand or want to be part of. His father, Lemeilleur's brain galloped on, unconsciously hated him because he semi-consciously desired him. How often does that happen?

"My father touched me: Did I always know that? I hated him all my life—I still hate him. He's the last void in my soul—a cobweb of the ugly past. I was wounded before I had memories. Does knowing that change me?"

Lemeilleur's thoughts now cantered on: Poor mother, she'd spent the rest of her life in a depression—her parents and her husband had never loved her. His father's sexual abuse by his brother had wrapped his father in an impenetrable narcissism—the fate of so many sexually abused. No wonder Lemeilleur wanted to see between Simran's legs.

"I'd been stimulated BEFORE I knew what desire was."

All these thoughts were making Lemeilleur's clinks clank louder. He was discouraged. All he wanted to do now was think about Simran. He wanted to help Simran. He didn't even know what happened to Simran. She still wasn't returning his calls. "There is a justice in things—a cruel justice." He was terrified she was going to accuse him of sexually abusing her—he was his father. Isn't that how it goes?

As he sat there devastated by guilt, a cauldron of burning, illicit loves bubbling in his soul, he decided to return to Nouvelle Bouville to prove to himself he was better than his father.

⊕

Driving in, he worried he was too eager to uncork his uncertain, still fermenting wine?

As he drove around Nouvelle Bouville he noticed all the hospitals. Healthcare had replaced most of the manufacturing that had made the city a destination for immigrants. "Was this a metaphor for progress?" Nouvelle Bouville had produced most of the barbed wire that settled the West. Valentine cards had been invented here, as well as candlepin bowling and the monkey wrench—to say nothing of the iconic yellow smiley face.

Lemeilleur decided to confront his father, whom he hadn't seen in many years. When he arrived at the funeral home, his father didn't recognize him. All Lemeilleur wanted to do was ask his father if he'd touched him when he was a kid. But when his father shouted: "Hi. I'm extraordinarily rich. Who are you?" Lemeilleur shelved his question. Instead, he spoke to the female caretaker.

"Your father is not doing well."

"I can see his dementia."

"It's more than that. His prostate cancer metastasized three years ago. It's in his lungs now."

Lemeilleur also found out that his father's marriage—to that woman he'd met years ago at the hospital where Lemeilleur's mother had died—a candy striper—the one who liked to cook—had ended abruptly ten years after he'd married her. She'd taken half his money and run off with one of his funeral workers—a flower car driver who was two years **older** than his father.

As the caretaker talked, Lemeilleur could see how this older man, the flower car driver, had been a catastrophic slight to his father's *amour-propre* (self-esteem). Live by the ego, die by the ego.

"Since," his father's caretaker went on, "he sits in an armchair all day watching TV. His funeral business is deteriorating—though he has help to manage it. He refuses to sell."

Lemeilleur watched his father wheeze as he clutched his inhaler and watched a TV game show.

"About the only thing that changes in his life," the caretaker went on, "is his Depends. Well, that's not exactly true. He gets very excited when Newt Gingrich comes on TV."

9

Feeling little sympathy for his father, Lemeilleur shook off his annoyance with the futility of the meeting. He left and drove away in his rental car. He wanted to satisfy a long-time urge to see the marble replica of the statue of "The Dying Gaul" that stands in the foyer of the *La Maison Française* building at the college, where Georges had gotten all his degrees.

On the way over to the college, he remembered an owner of *The Telegram and Gazette* had been one of the founders of the John Birch Society, a fact from which his father had derived much pride. It's weird he thought to himself—what possibly could his father and John Birch have in common?

Fear? Everything about his father was FEAR—fear of poverty, fear of gay, fear of Black people, fear, fear, fear— fear of any change. Like Mice, his father's fear had obliterated love. Then he remembered his father wanted to go to Boston to picket *Exodus* when it was showing at the Saxon. But his father couldn't go because someone had died and required his services.

His father had really believed in America and had found all he wanted out of life here. Now standing before "The Dying Gaul," it dawned on Lemeilleur that he was saying goodbye to his father and the life he had led in Nouvelle Bouville. "Goodbye clinks: I know where you came from." That made him feel better.

After Lemeilleur paid his respects to the statue, and while he was on campus, he decided to go to the college bookstore where they had a diverse collection of Franco-American history, including Marie LaJoie's book, *The Evolution of French Canada.*

After browsing for an hour or so, he bought a few books, and as he checked out, a chunky woman in a blue corduroy vest with orange roses appliqué that hung over her tubular torso took his credit card and recognized him.

"Lemeilleur. You don't remember me, but I remember you."

"Hi," Lemeilleur said uncertainly.

And she blurted, "I can't tell you how much I admired you. You were always running away, and when you came back, you always had a great story to tell. I used to sit on the top step in front of the house on Hamilton Street and listen to you. All the kids from the neighborhood were there. It was like a stage with all of us sitting there under the streetlight. You scared the daylights out of us, but you made us happy too. You were like . . . larger than life."

"I'm sorry I don't remember you."

"I'm Jean. You were so free. I could have listened to you all day. Then one day you disappeared. You don't know how sad we were. We talked about you for years. Then we heard all sorts of stories about you."

"Like what?"

"Somebody said you were gay, but we didn't believe that because Boris told us you were in love with a Syrian girl. We thought that was far out too. Now my husband hates people like you."

"He does? Who is he? Do I know him?"

"My husband did three tours in Vietnam. That ruined him. You went to college? He never got over the friends who were killed in Vietnam while you college kids protested. He still doesn't believe all that killing was for nothing. Now he doesn't trust anyone—especially the government. Everybody lies."

Lemeilleur just stared at her. He couldn't "get" where she was coming from.

"What are you doing now?"

"Writing a book."

"So did you marry her?"

"Who?"

"The Syrian girl."

"Ah, no—I didn't marry her. Does your husband really hate me?"

"People like you—he never met you. He's been working two jobs for the last ten years. All you people care about is Black people, gay people, Indians, Chinese, and now the Muslims. It's not fair what's happening in this country. When do we get a break? I'm glad we never had kids. You want another world war, keep running up the debt."

"That's not true—I care about all people."

"My husband says he's not poor enough for the likes of you. Don't worry about it. Some things never change. I get it. We're the bad people."

Lemeilleur started to walk out. He was on the verge of disgust.

"Hey, before you go. I have to ask you one question. Did you know my sister, Lorraine?"

"Lorraine? I don't think so. I don't remember any Lorraine."

"Yeah, that's what I thought. I shoulda known better. She was a junkie and a drunk—had cirrhosis—died of an overdose years ago."

"I don't understand."

"Whenever Lorraine brought you up, her boyfriend would start yelling, 'You're hallucinating again—Stop it.'"

"You sure Lorraine meant me?"

"Oh, when she got good and drunk, she'd start talking about how you were the father of her child. She wanted to marry you. We called you the delirium tremens boyfriend."

"Child?"

"She had a little girl—smart as a whip—but totally out of control."

"What happened to her?"

Jean's cell phone rang.

"Sorry, it's my husband. Hello? What's up? What? No, don't go over there. Just mind your own business. You don't know if he's illegal. No. Don't call ICE."

She hung up and stared at Lemeilleur who refocused her.

"Her daughter, you—"

"—Oh yeah. After her mother died, her boyfriend died."

"Her daughter's boyfriend?"

"No, her father. He was a good-for-nothing junkie too. But I'll say this for him, he put up with my sister—stayed with her—right to the end, and then some—was still holding her hand when Lorraine died—a shot directly into her heart."

"Who was he?"

"Johnny."

"Johnny?"

"That's what I said," Jean almost shouted at Lemeilleur. "Look I have to call my husband back. He's not thinking straight."

"What's her daughter doing now?"

"No idea. She doesn't talk to me. She was an argry wise ass—she's probably a bra-burning feminist Nazi now. Split when her father died. I think she moved to Boston to go to college. I dunno. She has nothing to do with us. No Christmas card—nothing. We're not good enough."

"You have no idea where she is?"

She looked at him and said: "Look, I heard she changed her name. She calls herself Vivian Darkbloom. It's her professional name. She writes books. We don't want to know any more about her. Goodbye."

As she handed Lemeilleur his books, she turned away to call her husband.

He picked up his bag of books, but he couldn't move.

Jean hung up and stared at a paralyzed Lemeilleur.

"Darkbloom@lolita.com," she shouted at him, "she's a college professor."

"What's her real name?"

"Beatrice."

10

After driving around for hours, Lemeilleur ended up sitting in front of 46 Houghton St. He was trying to remember what happened the day he took little Simran, the landlord's daughter, under the lilac bush. What the fuck did he do to Simran? How many times had he gone over this?

He tried to call Simran. No answer. He just sat there in his car crying. What the hell was he going to do? His soul was full of . . . what? He was struggling to find some hope.

He drove off in a daze and, after wandering around French Hill, ended up in "Polishland" on Dorchester Street looking at Dolores's old house, where she'd lived a million years ago with the two ex-nuns. What was he doing here? His memory of Dolores waded deeper into the swamp of decaying guilt— the putrid pillage of time. All of a sudden he remembered, "Don't, Lemeilleur, don't leave me like this."

It was Dolores's voice.

He'd tied Dolores to a pole in the cellar of that house—she was naked—was trying to get him to fuck her—and he left her there—for the ex-nuns to find.

"What a fucked-up bastard I was," he screamed. "I did that. I was one of the bastards that pushed her that much closer to the bottle of iodine."

When the ex-nuns found her later that day in the cellar NAKED, that must have been when they decided to send Dolores to the convent in Marlboro, where she killed herself.

"I fucking killed her."

Everything he had worked for was evaporating—years of consciousness-raising were going up in smoke. What brazen ego made him think he was healed? He'd done that to Dolores to punish her because he was too afraid to fuck her.

"She liked me," he screamed as he banged the steering wheel.

Fuck: Faulkner was right: The past is never dead; time merely rubs a wound raw, keeping it suppurating. Pain keeps history alive. This can't be—life has to be more than a series of Meaningless experiences that certify your guilt. Why can't I believe Kafka was right?

His cell phone rang. It was his father's caretaker.

"I'm sorry, Lemeilleur," she said, "but your father passed away this afternoon. We found him with the clicker in his hand. The police are here with the coroner. They say no foul play. He died watching *The Price is Right*."

Lemeilleur hung up and started to laugh—a wild convulsive laugh—"He's dead. Was watching *The Price is Right*." Lemeilleur couldn't believe it. He never resolved anything with his father. The last thing his father said was "Who are you?"

"He died the way he lived—untouched by truth," marveled Lemeilleur in a brief moment of calm lucidity. "Death of a dignity-desiring Dad."

Lemeilleur resumed sobbing as he remembered how he had fit into Simran's arms so long ago—when she came to Marie LaJoie's to talk to him about "Baseball." And he remembered how much at that time he had wanted her not to let go—how he had wanted her to hold him forever—the lilac girl.

And then he thought about McCrae—how much she had loved him. Her love gave him strength—that wasn't a Meaningless experience.

He stopped crying. He wasn't going to let the ghosts that danced around rattle him. He wasn't going to let thirty years of struggle slip through his fingers. He wasn't going to die like his father, in the chalice of lost souls—to use Rimbaud's image—only to be drunk by a blood-thirsty god with no complaint.

How long had he believed the void in his heart was gone? That his insane needs were no more? That he, like the snake sheds its skin, had shed his past over and over again?

"Am I a human being? Do I want to love? Am I done destroying?"

Memories continued to swirl in his head. His father snarled in Lemeilleur's memory.

"You don't like fathahs," Alcide exploded. "You don't believe dere are good fathahs, do ya. I'm a good fathah. And you're jist like me. I read *David Copperfield*. In high school— yeah, I learned English in Canada. I'm not as sstupid as ya think—that book was about my life. Why can't ya see how far I came?"

ⵙ

Sick to his stomach, Lemeilleur drove back to Cambridge, as more grinning, sharp-toothed memories, shimmering like a shiver of sharks in a blue/green sea, thrusting their tails to escape the Jurassic Park swamp of his unconscious.

ⵙ

That night Lemeilleur played Chet Baker, got drunk on *Pommard*, and thought about Mice.

"I will die like you and Rimbaud—alone, abused, and unchanged."

He stood up and screamed, "I WAS ALMOST ME."

Lemeilleur walked unsteadily across his living room. He'd broken his pledge not to drink. A massive depression was mushrooming in his heart. He wanted to go to bed and forget he'd ever been born.

Approaching the hallway to his bedroom, he bumped into

his bookcase. *Les Fleurs du Mal* tumbled to the floor and the envelope from the Nameless One popped out. He stared at it. He was terrified. The letter grimaced disgust. He couldn't face the jury.

Looking away, Lemeilleur noticed his landline had a message. Relieved, he shuffled over to the table, pressed the button, and listened.

"Lem. I know who it was. Who touched me. My father. Call me. I'm sorry I didn't trust you. I've been listening to Ruth Young and Chet Baker sing "Autumn Leaves." It's us, Lemeilleur—two cripples crooning about loss—our innocence. Call me."

Lemeilleur played her message again and again as little tears dripped down his face. He hadn't touched Simran. Under the lilac bush had been a ceremony of innocence. Lilacs, the lullaby of love.

Greatly encouraged by Simran's message, Lemeilleur leaned forward and picked up the Nameless One's letter. He stumbled into his bedroom, threw himself onto his bed.

Was he ready to read it?

He tore it open.

Dear Lemeilleur,

Please give me a chance. I have dreams too. Your father told me you read a lot. I do too. I'm even reading a book of poetry. I bought it at the drugstore after you saved my life. I want you to take me serious. Johnny and me don't do much sex. We just like hanging around together. I pretty much remember everything that happened that night you saved me.

Johnny didn't want me to throw up in his car. God only knows what would have happened to me if you didn't come along. I know about bad people. I only tickled your balls because I thought you were Johnny. It was a mistake. I was thanking Johnny for coming back for me. It always made him happy when I did that.

I shoulda opened my eyes.

    Please believe me. But I'm happy you are attracted to me. Look, I can change my ways. Please don't be prejudice. I have dreams too.

    I really like the book of poetry I bought. I put together my own poem from different lines I found in the poems. I put them together myself. It's a poem about us. I hope you like it.

    I think a higher power put us together that night. I'm kinda sure now that we belong together because I missed my last two periods. Please don't get mad. I want you to see me and feel me and love me because I know I have a good soul. Here's my number again. I'll wait for you to call. Here's my poem.

Maybe love, Lorraine

Passing stranger. You do not know
How longingly I look upon you,
You must be he I was seeking.

Within your shadow I am bound.

Your questioning eyes are sad
They seek to know my meaning
   . . .

It is as near to you as your life,
But you can never wholly know it.

Here begins a new life—(A baby, she added)

You and I will be together
Till the universe dissolves.

I love you as certain dark things are to be loved,

in secret, between the shadow and the soul.

I might be driven to sell your love for money
Or trade the memory of that night for drugs
It well may be. I do not think I would.

How can I keep my soul in me,
so that it doesn't touch your soul?
. . . .

Yet everything that touches us, me and you,
takes us together like a violin's bow,
which draws one voice out
of two separate strings.

That voice is our child—her name will be
Beatrice.

When will we feel the moonlight dry our tears?

what you were
will not happen again.
the tigers have found me
and I do not care.

"Lorraine," Lemeilleur wondered aloud as he put the poem
down. He'd never felt lonelier.

He called Simran.

"Hi, Lem. I just heard your father died."

"He was watching *The Price is Right*."

"Perfect. I had no idea that the carnage of my life was
nothing but a perfumed lie that my father loved me. Light only
penetrated where I was wounded. There's no truth—only a
narrative!"

"You don't sound right."

"I have a terrible migraine today. When I read 'Baseball' I

knew somehow we were destined to be friends. After our failed trip to Mexico, I tried to end my dependence on you. I was so crazy. I'm sorry. I was messed up about sex. My head is killing me today."

"Have you seen a doctor?"

"O Lem! Rimbaud had his mother, and we had our fathers! We always knew each other's pain."

"Yeah, I know."

"Think we'll ever recover?"

"I used to hope so."

"Until you I was like the guy who worked in the dead letter section of the Post Office—Ah Simran! Ah humanity!—stubbornly resisting the absurdity of my existence. I lived in paralysis! I had no idea my father raped me. We got nothing! Our lives were empty."

"I have a daughter."

"What?"

"I have a daughter. Her name is Beatrice. Simran? Are you still there? Simran? Did I say something wrong?"

The phone had gone dead. Lemeilleur didn't call back. His thing with Simran never worked out. He was frustrated.

⨀

That night Lemeilleur had a dream. He was in a schoolhouse, and, as he pulled Lolita's *"inky, chalky, red-knuckled hand"* (Book II, chapter 11, last paragraph of *Lolita*) under the desk, Lorraine's voice began to scream at him: "I won't let you get away with this. Take your daughter's hand AWAY from you—you pervert!"

He woke up in a sweaty shudder, more miserable than ever. He could not live another moment with this kind of dream. He couldn't be another Humbert Humbert—an aesthetic lie. Nietzsche was right: Reality is ugly. We have art lest we perish from ugliness. What was the truth of *Lolita*? That art can make a feasting maggot look O so graceful as the lifeless cadaver is consumed.

He had a daughter. He smiled to himself. He was understanding. He still loved life. He'd never felt more peaceful: He had a daughter.

Later that day Demi called. Simran had died of a brain aneurysm. Lemeilleur was sickened with grief.

"I'm so sorry, Demi. Simran never had a chance, did she?"

"We had some good times, Lemeilleur. She was a fighter." Demi was crying.

"I never got to thank Simran," Lemeilleur choked up, "for saving my life."

"We talked about that, Lemeilleur," Demi sniffled. "Simran respected you. She always thought that someday you'd give yourself the credit you deserve."

Demi paused, then resumed. "Simran did think of herself as your Virgil, and like Virgil, was blind to her salvation."

Demi paused again. "You know, Lem, she really wanted to be your Beatrice."

Though Lemeilleur was blindsided by the allusion to Beatrice, he managed to say, "I've been lucky all my life, and she was my best stroke, coming in, as she did, at my absolute bottom," Lemeilleur said holding back his tears.

"You were a good friend to her, but I can't talk right now. I'm too upset."

"I'm so sorry, Demi. I'm upset too. Let's talk in a couple of days."

Lemeilleur hung up. He had wanted to tell Demi about his daughter, but he felt it wasn't right at that time. He still didn't know how his daughter felt about him.

⊕

Simran's sudden death had motivated him. She had never emerged from hell, as she had promised Lemeilleur so many years ago. Terrorized by Simran's fate, that night in a totally irrational leap of faith, Lemeilleur gathered all his writings, his letters, and any notes he'd kept about his life, and put everything in a box, which he closed with tape after he'd put a letter in that he had written all aglow with hope.

Dear Beatrice,

Please accept these notes of my life, and please imagine we live in a well-kept secret of fate's generosity. Please extend the shadows of my life beyond the skyline of your soul. Show us the blue of tomorrow's mist. I want to believe life is a masterpiece.

Your very sorry father
Lemeilleur Ducrotte

He found her address, and with a thick black magic marker addressed the box.

Next day he took the box to the post office and mailed it.

When he got home, he talked to Mice: I found my genius; I have a daughter, and, get this, Mice, she teaches college! Then, throwing himself on his back, on his couch, he, dreaming of McCrae, blubbered merrily, "O my love, pray that this is the way it happens in books."

END

Acknowledgements

To my wife, Lisa Kaplan
who,
High on a mountain,
Heard a nightingale sing
Faintly far below

To Arthur Goldhammer
who,
over lunch,
many years ago,
the day my father died,
suggested I choose freedom

Gene Bell-Villada
whose observations and editing improved my manuscript
and whose book, *On Nabokov, Ayn Rand and the Libertarian
Mind,* was seminal for me

Karen Cusano, Heidi Leugers, Sandy Lewis, and
Andrew Dixon
for undying enthusiasm

My sister Celeste Morin
for love never in doubt

Tom Holbrook
editor par excellence,
who pruned and shaped this book from a
deep sense of structure

Made in the USA
Middletown, DE
03 August 2023

36135420R00163